M000022191

The Tzaraath Chronicles:
The Turn
Book 1

By
Ric Lee and Linda
Steinert

The Tzaraath Chronicles: The Turn (Book 1) by Ric Lee & Linda Steinert
Copyright © 2020. All rights reserved.

ALL RIGHTS RESERVED: No part of this book may be reproduced, stored, or transmitted, in any form, without the express and prior permission in writing of Pen It! Publications. This book may not be circulated in any form of binding or cover other than that in which it is currently published.

This book is licensed for your personal enjoyment only. All rights are reserved. Pen It! Publications does not grant you rights to resell or distribute this book without prior written consent of both Pen It! Publications and the copyright owner of this book. This book must not be copied, transferred, sold, or distributed in any way.

Disclaimer: Neither Pen It! Publications, or our authors will be responsible for repercussions to anyone who utilizes the subject of this book for illegal, immoral, or unethical use.

This is a work of fiction. The views expressed herein do not necessarily reflect that of the publisher.

This book or part thereof may not be reproduced in any form, stored in a retrieval system, or transmitted in any form by any means-electronic, mechanical, photocopy, recording or otherwise-without prior written consent of the publisher, except as provided by United States of America copyright law.

Published by Pen It! Publications, LLC
812-371-4128 www.penitpublications.com

ISBN: 978-1-952894-06-0
Edited by Dina Husseini
Cover Design by Donna Cook

Table of Contents

Chapter 1...4
Chapter 2...12
Chapter 3...16
Chapter 4...20
Chapter 5...24
Chapter 6...28
Chapter 7...32
Chapter 8...38
Chapter 9...42
Chapter 10...46
Chapter 11...48
Chapter 12...56
Chapter 13...62
Chapter 14...66
Chapter 15...72
Chapter 16...78
Chapter 17...80
Chapter 18...84
Chapter 19...86
Chapter 20...90
Chapter 21...94
Chapter 22...100
Chapter 23...108
Chapter 24...120
Chapter 25...126
Chapter 26...132
Chapter 27...138
Chapter 28...148
Chapter 29...156
Chapter 30...162
Chapter 31...170
Chapter 32...174
Chapter 33...180

Chapter 34.. 190
Chapter 35.. 192
Chapter 36.. 198
Chapter 37.. 202
Chapter 38.. 204
Chapter 39.. 212
Chapter 40.. 214
Chapter 41.. 218
Chapter 42.. 222
Chapter 43.. 230
Chapter 44.. 238
Chapter 45.. 242
Chapter 46.. 248
Chapter 47.. 252
Chapter 48.. 260
Chapter 49.. 272
Chapter 50.. 282
Definitions 288

Acknowledgements

God our Lord Jesus Christ

We would like to thank all of **Pen It! Publications, LLC** for taking a chance on us and making a dream come true with the publication of this book.

> **Debi Stanton**

> **Dina Husseini**

Sarah Steinert, for always willing to destroy our work with a red pen.

The ones that read and helped with our book:

> **Christine Cornejo**

> **Andrea Likins**

> **Joshua Hemsley**

> **Connie Pauley**

Tracy Wainwright, one of our first editors

Mrs. Kelly Hoffman-Cutcher - For the class assignment to set up a government on an island. That inspired the start of this series.

And to all the Beta readers, that were willing to read a stranger's rough draft and give feedback.

Dedication

To: Eldora Jane Blanchard for always encouraging our writings and listening to our story's. We love and miss you. Wish you were here to see this dream happen.

Chapter 1

The sounds of chirping birds and children's laughter filled his ears. A soft breeze carried the smell of spring flowers. Rocco's parents' car sat a few blocks ahead of him in front of the park. He could see their heads through the rear window, as they waited for him. His stomach growled in anticipation. He cocked his head as a man strode towards the car, he had something in his hand. A salesman maybe? Rocco squinted to see that it was the barrel of the pistol flashed out at him. His chest tightened, and he stopped for only a moment before he took off running. He tried to yell, but a loud pop rang through the air, drowning out his warning.

Time slowed. His feet refused to push faster. "Dad," he yelled.

What did this man want? There was another loud bang followed by shattering glass. No! Why couldn't he move faster? Why couldn't he have left two minutes earlier? His brain struggled to make sense of the scene before him. The sound of his mother's screams.

The gunman darted to the other side of the car, he threw open the passenger door, and another shot rang through the air.

"No!" Rocco yelled, desperation tearing through his lungs. "Leave them alone! Please, leave them alone." His mother's body hit the pavement with a thud.

He'd almost reached them when the wailing from his little brother pierced his ears. Somewhere deep inside, he finally found the strength to push his feet even faster. He had to save Kyle. He had to get to his little brother. He was just a kid.

Almost as if in slow motion. The man turned and fired again. Kyle's terrifying cries became silent and his body was torn from the car, landing on the hot pavement. His dad's body was the final one to fall as the killer climbed into the drivers' seat and drove away.

Rocco finally reached the scene, skidding to a halt over his family. He sank to the ground at the sight of his little brother, pulling his limp body onto his lap and cradling it in his arms.

He didn't need to check for a pulse, he could see he was dead. The tears finally came, but they couldn't wash away the blood or reality of what had just happened.

The shouts of witnesses reached his ears. A crowd began to form around him, but he didn't look up. Somebody knelt by his mother, checking for signs of life, but nobody else approached. They wouldn't risk it. He knew it was hopeless. All he could think about was the monster that did this. He could sit there and feel sorry for himself or he could go after the monster.

The fear which once consumed him left, replaced by a fire in his belly. He narrowed his eyes and gently set Kyle's body on the ground. With one last look at his family for strength, he took off after the car.

Rocco knew he would never catch him on foot. Out of the corner of his eye, he spotted a man on a motorcycle at a stop sign. He didn't hesitate shoving the man from his bike, jumping onto it before the rider could retaliate. *Wait, was the man on the motorcycle a monster?* Rocco could have sworn half his face was missing. No, it couldn't be. There were no real monsters here. They were only on the news. He shook his head bringing himself back to reality. It didn't matter who's bike he was on he would never see that man again.

He had to do this to avenge his family's murder. No matter what, this man would pay for what he did, and he would pay with his life. Kyle was just a kid, and this monster had killed him, for what? It couldn't be for the little gas in the car, could it? The rage which filled his heart was uncontrollable, filling every pore of his being. There was no putting out this flame. Even if he could, he didn't want to.

It didn't take long for him to find his parent's car. He followed it for only a few miles before the gunman pulled into a driveway. Rocco parked the bike a few driveways down. He needed a weapon. Only a fool would go after a man unarmed. He crept to his family's car and looked in. Blood covered the seat where his father had once sat. A glance at the blood-soaked seat on his mom's side was all he could handle before turning away. He couldn't think of his mom. He would never be able to hug her or say he loved her again.

Something inside him drew him to the back seat. Even though he didn't want to, his eyes raced there against his will.

There was no time for this, no time for sorrow or tears. He closed his eyes sweeping away the memories which were crashing down around him. He reached through the shattered window and touched the blood on the seat, his baby brother's blood. A pistol lay on the floor, it was the one the creature used to kill his family. It's justice he sought, and providence had provided him with the tool with which to carry it out. With a deep breath, Rocco grabbed the gun and pulled himself up from the ground.

"This is for you Kyle." He checked the chamber. Five bullets. "I hope this is enough." It would have to be. "I love you guys," he whispered as he silently shut the car door. He turned and walked to the front steps of the house.

He glanced at the house the monster entered. It looked the same on the outside as the one he parked the bike at. The neighborhood was one of the wealthier ones in town. How could someone from this place be a killer? Why did he target Rocco's family?

He turned his focus again to the gunman's house. What would he find on the inside? With trembling hands, he reached for the doorknob and slowly twisted it open. He crept through the door. With narrowed eyes, Rocco scanned the room in search of the man who had taken away his family. His heart pounded and sweat beaded on his hands and forehead. The burning filled his lungs and seeped into his bones. Everything within him needed this.

A rustling came from his left someone was coming. Rocco crouched hugging the wall waiting for the kill. Something leaped at him from around the corner. It wasn't human, but as it hit his chest his hand reacted. One-shot was all it took, and the dog sunk lifeless to the floor. Four bullets left.

"Black?" a shout came from upstairs.

Rocco smiled. Good, now he had taken something precious from the man who'd taken almost everyone he valued. He wanted him to suffer before he died.

A surge of energy shot through Rocco's body. He turned and crept upstairs toward the voice, stopping to listen at the landing. The man was here, but where. He stood motionless waiting and listening. He heard it, the man who was struggling to hold his breath, gasped for air. That gasp would cost him his life.

Rocco stepped toward the door where the sound came from. His body pressed flat against the wall so he could peer into the room. The killer was hunched over pacing back and forth in a small circle. His face told his story. He wasn't a man; he was a monster. His hair was thin and lay in patches on his scalp. Pus oozed from open sores covering his head. The flesh on his face was peeling away leaving the bone and muscles exposed. The skin he had left was pale and his red eyes sunk into his skull. He hadn't been holding his breath after all. His breathing was raspy like a dog's growl. This man was diseased. Rocco had never seen one; he didn't believe they were real until that very moment.

It looked Rocco in the eyes, starting to smile as he lifted his shotgun. But Rocco put a bullet in his skull before the thing even lay a finger on its trigger. The next bullet sank into the monster's neck. Two more times.

Bang. Bang.

Closing his eyes, he took a deep breath. He had accomplished the task he had come there to do.

"I killed him," he said aloud. "I killed him for you, Mom, Dad, and Kyle. I got the justice you deserved."

Seeing this monster lifeless at his feet didn't calm the rage pulsing through his veins. It only added fuel to the fire. The black hole in his soul grew.

It was time to go back to his family. He kicked the corpse on his way out. It didn't help. He paused at the family car; the keys were in the ignition. It was his car, but no, he couldn't sit in it. This was the place his family breathed their last breath. Taking the motorcycle, he returned to the park. He needed to get to his family's bodies before the clean-up started.

"No," he yelled. "Why did you take them? I wasn't gone long." There was a small trace of blood left where his family had laid. He slumped to the ground and set his hand in the blood where his brother had been. "Kyle, I'm sorry I didn't save you."

He didn't stop his tears this time, but instead, let them flow. With the increase in crime and bodies lately, it was common practice, for people to collect dead bodies and burn them. This was to prevent them from turning into monsters. There was no proof that a dead person would change but people were scared. Couldn't whoever had taken his family see they had been murdered and were not infected? Yes, it was cheaper than a funeral but a proper burial was what he wanted for his family. They deserved nothing less.

The next time he opened his eyes, it was dark. The surrounding shadows pressed against him, any number of creatures hiding inside. He pulled himself off the ground and started to run home. With every step, he thought he saw movement. Was it a monster, or just the wind? Was he being stalked, chased, or was he seeing things? Not wanting to be their next victim, he sprinted to his house and stumbled through the front door struggling to catch his breath.

Hearing the commotion, David was at the door in seconds.

"What's wrong?" he asked. His eyes scanned Rocco from head to toe and back again, probably assessing him for injuries, taking in the blood and tears. "Rocco, what happened."

Rocco stared at David, unsure of how to put anything into words. He pushed back his dark blood-stained auburn hair and rubbed at his face. Tears he could no longer feel dripped onto his bloody palms.

"What happened." David shook him more urgently. His eyes wide and watery. "Rocco, you need to tell me what happened. You are starting to scare me." Rocco could tell he was fearing the worst.

The images of his family replayed in his head over and over again. David had already lost his biological family how could he tell them their parents and brother were dead. How could he put it into words?

"He killed them." Rocco blurted out, and pounded his hands against the wall. His chest grew heavier as he spoke. "He killed them all."

"Who killed who?"

"First, the monsters come and now God leaves us." Rocco threw his fist up in the air. "Why didn't you save him? How could you let a kid die that way? So much for guardian angels. Where were they? They didn't help Kyle. The monster killed him, no, he killed all of them. Where were you, God?" Rocco dropped to his knees. "Where were you?"

David grabbed Rocco's hand and pulled his gaze to him. "Rocco, what happened?"

"Monsters are real. It is just like they said on the news. They are real and they are here. None of us are safe anymore."

"They killed Kyle?"

"Mom and Dad too."

"This can't happen again," David stumbled back an sank onto the couch. He buried his head in his hands. "Not again. I can't lose another family. When my parents died in that wreck... No." He lifted his head, his eyes met Rocco's. "I don't think I can go through this again. Why is this happening?"

"It was a picnic." Rocco wanted to comfort David but didn't know what he could say. "I don't know why he killed them." Rocco cursed as he sat on the couch next to David. "I didn't even get to say I love you. Why didn't I say I love you?" They sat on the couch the radio played softly in the background.

"Breaking news." The radio announcer interrupted the music. "The terrorist organization is known as 'The Aeyden Group' has been sighted in the state capital this week."

Rocco stood and listened.

9

"This has been the first sighting in the state. Approach strangers with caution. Attacks appear to be random and untargeted. Any suspicious behavior should be reported to your local police department immediately." There was a rustling of papers then the announcer continued. "This disease causes decomposing skin, tearing it away from their bones. Be careful this group can think and feel, yet they are full of rage..."

Rocco could remember how the monster who killed his family looked and smelled of death, yet he was very much alive. Rage filled Rocco again as he ripped the radio plug out of the wall sending the radio tumbling to the ground.

"I watched them die. I was close enough to see it all, but I was too far to do anything about it. It will haunt me until the day I die." He paused. "Three bullets took everything from us. I want them back. I want my little brother back. I want more time with them. I want to say I love you." He walked over to the punching bag hanging in the doorway. "Kyle was a kid." He punched the bag. "Who shoots a kid? He had his entire life ahead of him." Rocco's fists continued to fly. "Kyle was twelve. He had his whole life ahead of him. I would give anything to take his place." He stopped, letting the bag swing in silence, and turned back to the sofa. "I took things into my own hands. I did it my way. I killed the monster, David."

Today, he had killed his first creature and hadn't felt any remorse. He turned back and continued to punch and kick the bag until he had no energy left. Dropping to the floor, he closed his eyes and tried not to let his visions take over, the smell of the monsters rotting flesh filled Rocco's nose. He used to think terrible things were only happening in other places in the world, now they were happening in his town. He should have seen this coming as the price of gasoline and food had skyrocketed in the last year. People were being killed for a gallon of gas or a loaf of bread.

Vigilante had become the norm of law enforcement. The world was changing, and leaving two types of people in its wake, the diseased and the un-diseased. Rocco had become part of the vigilante. He had done what he'd needed to do today. He served as judge, juror, and executioner, to his family's murderer.

The more he thought about it, the darker his heart turned. That final shot firing through his mind again and again. It was the shot that had killed his little brother, and also the one that had turned Rocco's soul to stone.

"I'll kill every monster I see until I rid the world of them all."

"God said vengeance was his." David's voice was soft.

"I didn't see God helping when the monster killed our family. You weren't there. You didn't see what I saw. There is only one way to stop them. I'll take it from here. I won't rest until they're dead, every last one of them."

Chapter 2

Lena tossed and turned most of the night. Something felt off, but she didn't know what. A thundering boom echoed through the house and her feet hit the floor before she had time to think. Smoke poured in underneath her bedroom door. She grabbed a scarf out of the closet, tied it around her mouth and nose, and crept into the hallway staying close to the ground.

"Lena," her dad yelled. "Where are you?"

She found him at the top of the stairs. "I'm right here."

"We need to get out."

He grabbed Lena and her mom and shot down the stairs, aiming for the back door. As they approached the kitchen a group of diseased men stepped in front of them. Lena froze. She had heard horror stories about them. Nightmare tales about women's skin being used to cover the sores of the diseased.

"I'll fight them off. You two run." Dad threw a punch at a monster. Lena watched in horror as a flap of skin dislodged from the monster's face as his fist made contact.

Lena felt her mom grabbing her arm and pushing her past the sink towards the back door. A monster grabbed her leg. He was too big for her to push off. She couldn't move. Kicking and punching did nothing to him. She was trapped. When she woke up, she thought she was going to die in a house fire, now she wished she would have. These monsters terrified her.

"I'm the one you want, come and get me." Lena's mom pushed past the diseased and darted out the door.

"Dad, help her." Lena fought back the lump in her throat. The monster threw her to the ground and gave chase. "Don't let them hurt mom."

She stood at the door and watched as her dad killed one of the monsters with his bare hands. Fighting his way to his wife. She needed to help. There had to be something she could do. Lena started toward her mom.

"No Lena." Her dad pushed her toward the shed. "I can't help mom until I know you're safe. Run to the cellar, climb in, and shut and lock the door. Don't open it for anyone. I have the key I'll unlock it when it's safe"

"No, dad. I can't."

The sounds of her mom's screams echoed in the night.

"Now." He pushed her a little harder. "Run, Lena. Run to the cellar."

The desperation in her dad's eyes was all she needed to see. She sprinted to the cellar as fast as her feet would carry her. At the cellar door she stopped and looked back, she froze. Maybe she could help them.

Her mother's screams filled her ears again and tears filled her eyes. Her father's yell told her it was too late.

"I love you," she whispered.

Lena dove in the cellar and locked the door. It was dark and the smell of rotten meat and mold filled the air. Is this what death smells like? "Please stop this. Help us." The darkness was closing in around her. She hated it there. Nothing she did could drown out the fighting going on outside of the cellar. She attempted to swallow the lump in her throat, and listen for her parents.

Remember the good times, she told herself. Mom and dad love her more than their own lives and were giving up their lives for her to live.

She closed her eyes. All she could see was her mother's face. What would those monsters do to her? The horror stories of the things they did to pretty women rushed to her mind.

"God," she cried out. "Please save them." She hushed her cries. What if the monsters heard her? She couldn't let them know where she was. Her parents risked everything

13

Help them, she said silently. Don't let the monsters hurt them. Her tears covered her face. Don't think about what is going on outside. Think of happy times. It was no use. The fighting raged on. The cries of her neighbors joined her parents. "Please make it stop," she whispered.

The rain started. Heavy drops pounded on the cellar door. The lightning flashed and Lena jumped. The voice of her dad was getting closer. She would soon be safe. He would take care of her. She reached for the handle to open the door.

But the words of her father raced through her mind. She couldn't disobey him. Her hands dropped to her side. His screams filled her ears. What were they doing to him? He needed her help. She reached for the handle again but couldn't open it. He said not to unlock it for any reason. He had a key and would unlock the cellar when it was safe.

Was he safe? Could she help him? Where was her mom?

Silence filled the air. Lena counted to a thousand. No more thunder. She listened for any noise.

"I'll kill you," her dad growled. The fighting started again. It was closer to the hatch this time. Lena hoped her dad was winning, but in her heart, she knew he wasn't. A loud thump hit the top of the hatch. Lena jumped.

"I love you." This was the first time Lena heard him cry. His voice was soft. "I'm sorry I won't be here for you. I didn't want you to worry. I'll make sure you're safe."

"Don't talk like that. We will always be together." She pressed her face against the door to feel close to him, and so he could feel close to her. She needed to be strong but didn't know-how. She never had to be strong before. Her parents were always there to take care of her.

"Listen to me, Lena." Her dad's voice grew weaker and his breathing slowed and gurgling sounds came from his throat between every breath. "Do not leave the cellar until morning. Before you open this door, listen for any noise. Make sure you are alone and all of the monsters are gone."

"I won't leave." She struggled to hold back her tears.

14

"What do we do with this one?" A gruff voice grumbled.

Lena sat as still as she could barely breath. One of the monsters was right above her standing over her dad. She couldn't let them find her.

"Leave him. He will die before we can get him back to camp. He is of no use to us. Is the woman still breathing?"

"She is for now; it won't be long before Aeyden kills her. I can't wait to see what he does to her pretty face before then."

Lena clasped her hands over her mouth to choke back a sob. The monster's laughter filled her ears. Her mom was alive, and there wasn't a thing she could do to help her.

She sat in silence. The monsters had gone, but her dad didn't say it was safe yet. A few drops like water dripped through the cracks in the hatch. Her eyes closed tight. She knew it wasn't water but her father's blood. "Daddy," she whispered. "Daddy, stay with me. I'm scared."

"Don't be afraid princess; I'll always be with you." There was another long silence before he spoke again. "I want you to remember your mother and I, love you."

"I love you both." Lena listened to his breathing as it slowed and eventually stopped. She curled in a ball and wept. Her life had ended when his breathing stopped. She sat cold and alone. How was she going to make it without her parents? They were all she had. She was alone in a world filled with monsters.

Chapter 3

15 years later...

Heavy darkness covered the night's sky as David crept through the woods. He turned the tactical flashlight on, making his rifle his eyes. His index finger hovered over the trigger, ready to kill anything, which moved. He glanced back to see if Rocco was still following, he wasn't there. Fear imprisoned him. Where had he gone? They agreed to stay together. Had something happened to him and David hadn't noticed?

David's instincts kicked in knowing he could be gone next, with no forewarning or noise. He didn't know what or who to look for. They had never encountered this enemy before. His heartbeat quickened, body tensed, and his muscles twitched, as he looked left and right surrounded by both physical and emotional darkness.

His eyes scanned for monsters. He had become the hunter, striving for survival. With every step, his head throbbed, and eyes watered. He was going crazy seeing things, which weren't there. Headlights from a car sped towards him. David threw his hands in the air covering his face and braced himself for impact, and the blinding pain to follow. But there was nothing.

Wait... what?

What was the sound? He glanced around. The car was gone. He needed to focus on Rocco.

Something tickled his arm. He brushed it away.

"Stop it," he yelled swatting his arms and his legs. He inspected his torso. There wasn't anything there. "Rocco where are you?' he yelled.

Something rustled behind him. He turned with his rifle aiming at the possible threat. Instead of an enemy, his mother stood in front of him. His heart sank. It couldn't be her. She was dead. He'd seen life drain from her body as she bled out on the pavement in front of him.

He'd held her hand as she took her last breath. Her death was real, but now she stood in front of him, watching him. Almost close enough for him to reach out and touch her. He inched forward, looking to the left and the right. Where was Rocco?

"Honey, I miss you," she whimpered. "You didn't save me?"

David tried to approach her, to comfort her, but she started to shriek. "It hurts. Son, help me." Her cries continued as she turned and ran.

"Mom, I tried. I'm sorry," David screamed, running after her, knowing she wasn't real, yet praying she was. "Don't leave me." He reached out for her, but couldn't touch her. She stopped, turned toward him, and fell to the ground.

She was gone. No, she was never there. Confusion clouded his mind. He crouched, body shaking, his heart beating against his ribs. Laughter filled his ears. He looked up as something dark towered over him. The eyes of this creature loomed with hatred that pierced into David's core, draining him of all hope and coating his heart with fear. This monster had to be a demon. Its mouth spewed out vomit filling David's nostrils with a stench, which could only come from hell.

Pulling out his gun, he closed his eyes and took a deep breath. He turned off the light, hoping to hide in the darkness. He couldn't hide. The demon grabbed him, digging its claws deep into his flesh separating it from his bones. He could see the Demon smirk, enjoying his agonizing methods. Screams from tortured souls filled David's ears.

Darkness consumed what little light shone from the moon allowing only the piercing eyes of the demon to glow through it. He had to get away but how?

"Keep it together," he told himself. "This can't be real."

He tore at his senses, desperate to keep his wits about him. This wasn't real. It couldn't be. His mother was dead. Demons don't exist.

A fire filled him from within. He kicked the demon away and jumped to his feet, taking the two pistols from their holsters. His hearing heightened and his vision cleared. He was facing his fear, overcoming his fear. The fog was less dense. He took in slow, deep breaths, filling his lungs with air. There was movement in the trees behind him. He jerked to the right. Both guns aimed in front of him. He peered through the trees searching for the sound, letting a little more air slip through his lips. The demon was in front of him.

He prayed and shot three times. The darkness faded and the sun casted a hopeful glow over the earth as he walked toward the figure. He could see the body wasn't a demon but the body of a man.

"Oh God no, please no." David howled, looking at Rocco.

Blood poured from the bullet holes and formed a small pool around his body. It had not been a demon but Rocco. He had murdered him out of fear.

The demon's voice pulsed through his mind again, an evil chuckle that threatened to draw the darkness back in.

"I will take you like it took them. You can't stop me. I was in the driver's seat the day I took your family. I took Rocco's family and I will not stop until I have you."

David's eyes shot open, and he jumped out of bed. Sweat dripped from his chin and trickled down his back. He searched under the bed finding nothing but dust bunnies. His eyes landed on the closet, dread gripping him from all angles. Standing with his back against the wall he flung open the door. All he found were clothes hanging on the bars. He took a deep shuddering breath.

It was a nightmare. Yes, only a nightmare.

Chapter 4

It felt real, but it was a dream. Rocco could still be alive. He whispered a quick prayer, darted into the hall, and cracked open the door to Rocco's bedroom. A wave a relief washed over him as he saw his best friend safe, asleep in his bed. His mind eased. He padded over to the bathroom working out the kinks in his neck. He put his hands under the water and splashed it on his face. In the mirror, he caught his reflection. There, a man stood, where there once was a boy. He had long hair because he didn't trust Rocco to cut it. His face was full of lines he hadn't noticed before. David thought he was much too young to look this old.

He remembered his dream. "I miss you, mom," he said watching his tears fall. "God help me. I can't make it without your strength. Jesus help me."

David shuffled to the kitchen to make breakfast. Cooking fell under his side of the labor division. Rocco hunted and took care of most of the household repairs. David had the brains and Rocco the brawn. They were a perfect team. Their system and the way they did things worked well for them.

"Rocco," David leaned against the back of the sofa and rested his hands on his full belly. "Do you remember when gas prices started to rise?" He needed to think of anything other than his dream. Talking to Rocco would help.

"Yeah."

"It's just..." He glanced at the newspaper dated ten or fifteen years ago sitting beside him.

"It's just what," Rocco groaned in the middle of another pull-up his muscles straining through his t-shirt. "Why are you reading those? What do you think you can learn from old tabloids?"

"I was reading about the advances in technology. Looking back, it's all a joke. I never dreamed gas would run out, I was sure I'd be dead before it did. In high school, I remember thinking about the future. I pictured flying cars, people living on the moon, and robots doing the housework. We would have a cure for AIDS and cancer, cars would drive themselves and trains would go 600 miles per hour." David stared out the window lost in the memories. "I thought people would live forever. It's almost as if we've restarted the human race, but this time with monsters."

"Yes," Rocco met David's gaze. "Do you think all the gas in the world is gone?"

"Huh?" David mumbled, lost in a new train of thought.

"What's your point? I know technology didn't advance much after the war. We don't have can openers who can talk or dryers folding and putting your clothes away. We have no cure for anything. We're all dying, so what's your point?" Rocco dropped from the bar, grabbed his water bottle from the table and took a big gulp.

"I don't know," David confessed. "I don't know if I have a point. Maybe the world changed so fast I didn't have time to think about what was happening. I never thought I would see a world war, yet I've lived through one. It was a different kind of war. Humans fighting monsters, not themselves." He set the paper on the table which was stacked with old newspapers and magazines. "Here we are at your parent's house. They've been gone 15 years, and we're living off what we grow and kill. This was how they lived in the 1800s. This wasn't how I thought our lives would be."

"Why do you care? This is our life now. I know what we've had to do and what we've lived through." Rocco scowled. "I know how hard it was for you to get power to the house with the solar panels. I know we have to carry guns and weapons at all times. I know now and then; we have to go out into the world and kill the diseased. I know. I know. I also know we're lucky we're not infected, or dead." He tossed his water bottle to the side, dropped to the floor, and started to do pushups. "We've done things I never thought we would. We've seen things I try every day to forget. Life isn't fair David, but this is all we have," he sat back, his hands dropping to his side. "The sad thing is I don't feel a sense of remorse." Rocco punched the bag until his knuckles bled and fell to the couch. "Why do you have to dwell on the past?"

David regretted saying anything. He should have known it would put Rocco in a mood. He couldn't help it, he needed something else to focus on getting this nightmare off his mind.

Rocco sat and looked at David. His eyes burned with sadness.

"I miss them too." David stood and strode toward the kitchen. "I lost my family for the second time."

"I know. We lost everything at the park." Rocco met David in the kitchen.

"We haven't lost everything; we still have each other. Look at the sky." David said, standing next to his brother. The sun was rising, coloring the sky with pink and fiery yellow light, as the first of its rays peeked over the trees. "In all this chaos and horror, there is still beauty." David wished he hadn't said anything about the past, and decided to change the subject. "God hasn't left us."

"I hate when you talk about God, even more than I hate talking about the past. God left me the day mom, dad, and Kyle died."

"I know." David turned away from Rocco. "I'm sorry."

"If there were a God, he would have saved Kyle." Rocco stopped his rant there and started to work on their daily chores.

Monsters attacking at the house wasn't an issue for them. They had killed all of them in the neighborhood. Rocco took care of them. Being the militaristic one, he scouted while David, the brains, kept the power going to the house. He used the sun and wind, and a lot of hard work, to keep the house running.

He knew he'd said too much this morning. Instead of dredging up the past, he should have told Rocco about his dream, but he didn't. It was only a dream. He submerged himself in his work to take his mind off the past. Dwelling on how things were or what they could have been clouded their judgment and would get one of them killed.

Neither one of them interacted with the other all day. "We better lock the doors," Rocco said as night crept over the horizon. "We have all day tomorrow to work."

"We have the rest of our lives," David joked. Their jobs were either being at the house or out gathering supplies. They didn't know any other humans, and they couldn't take any chances wandering away from home. The disease was out of control. No matter what the doctors and scientists did, they found no cure. At first, the government put anyone with the diseased in prison hospitals. It didn't take long before people got scared. The infected started killing everyone they met. No one was safe. War broke out between the non-infected and the infected.

The diseased won and took over the world.

Chapter 5

David was the only other non-diseased person Rocco had seen in years. He often wondered if they were the only two left in the world. He had dreams of getting married to a beautiful woman and starting a family. He knew it wouldn't happen now, but he couldn't stop his mind from thinking about how things could have been. Where had the days gone when all he had to worry about was who he was going to hang out with on a Friday night? He missed those days.

It was as if they had lived in two different times. David was right; it felt like the 1800s had crash-landed into their century. They have to hunt and grow their food, yet they have electricity and running water. He wondered if any other humans had electricity like they did. The more he thought about it the more thankful he was for David's brains.

Their fathers had been hunters and gun collectors, so they had a vast selection of weapons used to hunt and protect themselves. It was because of their fathers; that they knew to collect empty shotgun shells from the streets, reload them and add them to their inventory.

Shaking off the haze of memories, Rocco did a mental check of the things he needed to do before calling it a night.

"Did you remember the front door?" He asked as he lifted a metal bar and placed it across the back door.

"Yes," David called from the kitchen. He was cleaning tomatoes in the sink and placing them next to peeled potatoes.

After securing the house, Rocco went to the kitchen to help David cook dinner. He couldn't remember a time in his life when David wasn't in it. They started out as friends before they could even walk. There were even pictures of them as newborns sleeping in the same crib. Now they were brothers. Rocco would give his life for David.

"Jesus, thank you for this day…" David started to pray when they sat to eat.

Rocco shook his head, lifted his fork, and took a bite. In his mind when Jesus left the disciples, he never came back. Jesus came to earth, saved people, then ditched everybody. There was a time in Rocco's life when he believed every word in the Bible. Now his faith, tainted with anger, was gone. He believed in himself. God left when he took his family and left Rocco to trudge through this world without them.

"Bless this food to our bodies, Amen." David finished praying and opened his eyes. "Would it kill you just once, to wait for me to finish praying for our food before you started eating it?"

"Would it kill you to stop praying for my food and let me eat?"

After a few minutes of silence, Rocco changed the subject. "Did you finish making toothpaste?"

"It's done, but it is too strong, so I wouldn't swallow it. It'll whiten your teeth just fine. I put it in the bathroom." David said.

"Do you think our parents knew the world would end like this?"

"How could they?"

"I don't know, but they taught us everything we would need to know to survive," Rocco said. "Our dads taught us everything we would need to know about hunting, trapping, guns, and ammo."

"And I never thought I would live to say it but, I am thankful my mom made us work at her all-natural beauty shop."

"Yeah, her hippy shop." Rocco laughed. "I remember we hated learning how to make that stuff. I guess they did a good job making sure we were self-sufficient."

"I made soap, with the fat of the fish you caught. It's also in the bathroom. David stood and took his dish to the sink. "Look, bro, we also have dish soap. Maybe you could try using it." He liked to harass Rocco about doing the dishes; it's one job Rocco hated. David didn't mind doing them but enjoyed pestering him.

"I'll do them tonight," Rocco grumbled.

Someone should invent a self-emptying dishwasher. You're smart enough, David. I think you could come up with one."

"You give me way too much credit," David chuckled.

After the dishes, were done Rocco went to his room. Nothing he did got the images of his family out of his head. Why couldn't he stop thinking about them? Why had David mentioned them? Time was supposed to heal all wounds. He kicked off his shoes, which had holes in the toes, hung his slacks on a hanger along with his shirt and lay on his bed, staring at the ceiling.

His room was nothing impressive. It had a few action figures from when he was younger and a few posters of old football stars. Rocco reached to his nightstand drawer and pulled out a pistol. He slipped it under his pillow and set the magazine on top of the nightstand. One bullet was in the chamber, it was enough. With one hand under his pillow on his gun, he said goodnight to the photo of Kyle looking back at him and drifted off to sleep.

Chapter 6

David lay in his bed reading his bible by candlelight until his eyes were too heavy to keep open. He blew out the candle and rolled on his side.

A sweet aroma woke him, his stomach gurgled. The smell triggered a memory. He sat on the edge of his bed, his feet not quite touching the floor. He was younger, about nine years old. The room changed before his eyes. The colors of the wall went from a dull, gray to a bright white trimmed in dark blue. He walked to the door and turned the knob, also new. He followed the aroma, filling his nose, to a hallway filled with family photos. Music filtered through the hall from another room. It was a peaceful melody, which relaxed him. The sweet, buttery smell grew stronger. His stomach longed for the food and growled again in anticipation. His mother stood at the door cooking chocolate chip banana nut pancakes. They were his all-time favorite and she knew it.

"Honey, have a seat, the pancakes are almost done." His mother said, turning over the pancake on the griddle. She looked at him and smiled.

Her approval melted David's heart. He missed her tender expressions. He loved her. His dad walked into the room and kissed his mother's cheek. "Got to go to work, I love you beautiful," Then he walked over to David and kissed his head, "I love you too buddy."

When the door shut, David's eyes popped open. He still sat on his bed. The walls were back to the dull, gray, yet the smell of chocolate chip pancakes still hung in the air. He pushed off the bed, got to his feet, and headed toward the door. Looking at the rusting broken doorknob in his hand. He longed to be with them, safe in his parent's arms having no care in the world.

28

Walking through the hall, he scanned for the pictures, only to find an empty hallway with barren walls. Faint marks of where frames had once decorated the space. No music played. He walked into the kitchen knowing his mom wouldn't be there, yet somewhere in his mind hoping she would be.

Rocco stood at the stove turning over a pancake. David's heart sank. He longed to see his mother, but all he got was his friend and chocolate chip banana pancakes. "They're almost done. Can you get the drinks?"

There was no choice. David forced a smile, grateful to have Rocco. After pouring two glasses of water, he glanced at the hallway hoping to see his dad standing there. He saw nothing but a fly buzzing along until a newspaper hit it and it fell to the floor.

"Huh, I got him. He's been getting on my nerves all morning." Rocco tossed the paper to the floor. He set the plate of pancakes on the table and sat across from David.

"Rocco, do you remember when you used to stay the night and my mom made these for us?" David drizzled syrup on his pancakes.

"Those were good times. She's the one who taught me how to make them. There's nothing better than breakfast for dinner when you're a kid."

"No there isn't." David agreed.

Rocco lifted his fork, steaming pancake skewered onto it, and toasted David's mom.

"I dreamt about them last night," Rocco said, taking his first bite. "I was back at your house and your mom was teaching me how to cook. It was the day she told me she tried to teach you, but you told her…"

"Cooking for girls. If you want to teach someone, teach my wife," David finished the sentence for Rocco. They laughed.

"I wish I'd listened. I'd let her teach me how to cook anything in the world if I could have her back. It's funny how you think you have all the time in the world with people. You put off spending time with them because you have more 'important' things to do, then, they are gone. They leave you longing for more time and dreaming of the things you would do differently."

"Yes," Rocco stared at his plate.

Without another word, they finished eating and started their daily routine. They could do it without thinking. First, they removed the bars from the doors and windows to let light in. Then they went outside, each toting a gun.

The wooden garden fence, in the back yard, stood tall. The weathered paint was chipping and peeling.

Rocco unlocked the gate to get into the garden and stopped. "You've got to be kidding me."

"What?" David ran to the gate afraid of what he would see.

The plots were a mess, tomatoes scattered across the path, cabbages torn to shreds and soil leading a trail to a small hole in the back of the gate.

"I'm sure it was a raccoon." David sauntered through the gate and began gathering whatever vegetables he could salvage.

Chapter 7

"Now we're going to have to go find some food. Great! Is anything ever going to work out right for us?" Rocco ranted.

He stomped back into the house to get a rifle from his room, he didn't feel his pistol was the right weapon for the job. He lifted the floorboard took out a gun case and laid it on his bed. There was a cleaned rifle and two polished desert eagles with gold plates on the handles. They read:

1st place

Gunslingers

Rocco Menn Lee

Taking out the pistols, he set them on the bed along with the rifle, then slid the case back under the bed. He put the holster over his shoulder with the pistols in it, grabbed the rifle and headed back outside, ready to kill whatever was destroying their garden, no, he was ready to kill anything that crossed his path.

The weeds and grass had taken over the roads. Abandoned cars lined the sides of the streets and fields.

"It's a big empty world we live in," Rocco said as he walked through the backyard.

He wanted human contact, female to be exact. His world consisted of him and David. They lived in their parent's old house, in northern California. It was a beachfront property that backed onto a redwood forest. It was a dream house for people who liked to fish and hunt, and also a great place for post-apocalyptic living. One could live off the land still and have plenty of trees for building purposes and protection. The only thing missing was normal human beings; his friends, and neighbors. They were all gone. Nothing but a jungle left.

Rocco told David he was leaving. They needed food, and it was his job to hunt for it. David stayed back to watch the house and salvage the rest of the vegetables with instructions that if Rocco wasn't back by dark not to go out looking for him unless he set off a flare. This meant danger come ready to fight.

Rocco trudged his way through the tall grass to a path he made. The feed bags of corn hung in the middle of the field. He climbed into the treehouse; they had built when he was a kid and waited. No one could see it unless they knew where it was. All he had to do was wait for an animal to take the bait and he'd shoot it for dinner.

He watched the horizon where the wind blew the grass back and forth swaying to the music of nature. The sun's rays began to dim and the sky was turning pink. His eyes grew heavy. He was on the verge of dosing when a rustling in the bushes startled him. He lifted his hat and looked at the feed bag through the scope of his rifle. One spot caught Rocco's eye. It moved in the opposite direction of the wind. He watched the moving grass, waiting to take his shot. Everything went still and he lost sight of whatever was out there.

Frustrated, he contemplated heading back home. He couldn't take the chance of staying out after dark and running into a monster. Looking through his scope one last time, he almost dropped it when he saw a buck staring back at him. Rocco flipped the safety off, set the cross arrow over its heart, took a deep breath, and pulled the trigger.
Click.

Nothing happened. The buck turned at the noise and took off.

Rocco cursed. He'd dozed off and forgotten to load a bullet into the chamber. How could he be so stupid? He had to work fast. He grabbed the magazine, put it in, and loaded a bullet into the chamber, caught the deer in his sights, then whistled, a trick his dad taught him. The deer stopped at the sound and he pulled the trigger. The deer disappeared under the tall grass with a dull thud.
Yes!

Rocco jumped to the ground and ran toward where it had fallen. But something was wrong. He felt eyes staring at him before he saw them. Grabbing the two guns from their hostlers, he ducked in the grass, deathly quiet. With the sun almost gone, he needed to find the buck and get back to the house.

He couldn't see them, but he readied himself for whatever was out there. If they were looking for a fight, he would give it to them. His pulse raced, pounding through his head in the silence. Sweat beads dripped into his eyes. He looked to the left, then to the right willing for something to move so he could work out where they were, he hoped a diseased person would be so stupid.

Someone was out there watching him, but why hadn't they attacked him yet? He clocked light breathing not far away and bent closer to the ground. His mind raced wondering whether it could be an animal trying to take his kill, or could it be a monster?

"I think he knows we're here." a voice whispered.

"Shh," another commanded.

A smirk lifted the corners of Rocco's lips. Without a sound, he crept around them from behind. He grabbed a rock and threw it across the field. The rock hit the ground and skipped into the grass in front of his attackers. They turned and Rocco was behind them with two desert eagles to their heads. His buck was right next to him on the ground.

"Don't turn around or I'll shoot," Rocco growled.

"Please don't," one of them said in a hoarse voice.

"Please, we're hungry. We have not had food in days," the other said. "We mean you know harm. We were merely looking for food."

"I don't care if you starve," Rocco didn't have time for this. He needed to gut his kill and get it back home. "You're of no use to me."

"We can help you," one pled.

"No! We can't," the other screeched out trying to talk over his friend. Rocco turned the butt of the gun and hit him with it, knocking him to the ground.

"How can you help me?" Rocco pointed both guns at the stranger left standing. He wasn't sure why he hadn't killed them already. He needed to stay focused or they might kill him.

"I, um" the monster stuttered.

34

There was another thud as Rocco's gun came down on his skull. Without a second thought, he grabbed a sheet to drag the buck back home. There was a time when he thought the infected had hope. He thought they might find a cure for the disease but now wasn't the time. Monsters were dangerous killers and needed to be ended.

The buck was heavier than he thought. He struggled as his muscles cried out in pain, slowing his pace. The moon and stars gave little light through the clouds. Rocco had a flashlight, but he didn't want to use it, fearing it would lead his enemy to him. He shouldn't be outside this late.

For a second time, the sense someone was watching him overwhelmed Rocco, stopping him in his tracks. Two guns out, he crouched lower to the ground.

Something jumped on his back trying to sink its teeth into his neck

He couldn't let one of those monsters bite him. Throwing his head back he caught his attacker in the face then swung his pistol around to hit it in the ribs, freeing himself. The second monster kicked Rocco in his side. He lost his balance and fell. His weapon flew out of his hands, leaving him defenseless.

The monster lunged forward and Rocco threw his fist into the infected man's face, smiling as blood dripped from its nose. He rolled to his belly and reached for his gun. A foot crashed on his hand and he fought the urge to cry not wanting to give them the satisfaction of knowing they hurt him. Fighting through his pain, he again stretched for his guns. He had to reach at least one of them or he would never get back to David.

"I should have killed you when I had the chance," Rocco hissed.

He struggled to get to his feet, but the monster kicked, landing a foot in Rocco's mouth. The other monster jumped on his back, pinning him down. He grabbed Rocco's hair slamming his face into the ground repeatedly.

"Not if you become one of us," the monster whispered in his ear.

This was how his life was going to end. Blood oozed down his face into his mouth, leaving a metallic taste. How could he have lived through so much in his life, to die at the hands of these two? Two monsters he should have killed, but let go. "Why was I so stupid? I should have shot them when I had the chance," he mumbled to himself.

"Don't kill him," one of the monsters said. "I want him to live and suffer like we do. I want him to feel the pain of the disease eating the flesh off his face. I want him to suffer this Hell on Earth, the same way we suffer."

The monster shifted his weight, taking the pressure off Rocco's hand. Rocco seized his opportunity took hold of his gun tightened his finger around it rolled to his back, and lifted the gun to the man's throat. In a second it was over, the monster fell limp. He threw him aside and turned to the next one.

"Don't shoot." The second monster threw his hands up in surrender.

"I made the mistake once. You should have thought harder about attacking someone who spared your life. Have fun in Hell."

Lifting his gun to the monster's forehead, he squeezed his index finger and let his bullet do the rest. Grabbing the deer by its two front legs, he threw it on his back. He needed to get home the fastest way he knew. Knowing the diseased were still out there, didn't stop him. He knew he shouldn't go home he should hide out until morning. But being too tired, he didn't stop.

As he crept through the night, he had two things on his mind: getting the meat home and not dying.

Chapter 8

"What have you gotten yourself into Rocco? Why aren't you home?" David watched out the window for a flare in the sky. Total darkness looked back at him.

What if they got Rocco and he came back diseased, or worse, what if he didn't come back at all? David tried shutting off his mind, not being able to bear the thought Rocco might be dead. But despite all his efforts, the thoughts kept flooding back in. Nothing he did made them go away. He sang to himself, and when singing didn't work, he tried reading. Nothing seemed to take his mind off Rocco. He needed to keep busy.

"I might as well do something productive." He muttered walking towards the kitchen sink.

"God, look after Rocco," he prayed. "Bring him home safe."

Glancing out the window, every few moments, he hoped to see Rocco or a flare piercing through the night sky. He saw nothing and went back to dicing carrots. His stomach reminded him he hadn't eaten. He tossed some of the veggies into a pot of broth to make stew. Rocco would bring home the meat, then they would eat.

Turning the burner to low, he let the vegetables simmer, as he continued to wait. He walked to the living room and sat in his usual chair. Grabbing a sports magazine. The cover picture was a football player who announced his retirement. This player had played for eighteen years and the magazine was dated 2008. He had read the article at least a hundred times already. Most of it he knew from memory.

His mind slipped back to Rocco again. What could have happened? "Oh God, he better not be dead. What if they took him?" He shook his head. "Shut up," he told himself. "He's fine, and there's nothing to worry about."

He tossed the magazine on the top of the pile of old papers on the table. Running out of things to do, he reached for his bible and flipped it to Luke chapter twelve When he had gotten to verse twenty-two, he gave a little laugh.

Then Jesus said to his disciples. Therefore, I tell you, do not worry about your life, what you will eat or about your body, what you will wear. Life is more than food, and the body more than clothes. Consider the ravens: They do not sow or reap; they have no storeroom or barn. Yet God feeds them and how much more valuable you're than birds! Who of you by worrying can add a single hour to his life? Since you cannot do this very little thing, why do you worry about the rest?

"Thank God." David set the bible back on the stand. "It's settled. I'm done worrying. God, you have this under control." He rose and strode to the kitchen to check on the veggies. A loud bang made him jump.

"Let me in," Rocco yelled, pounding on the door again. "David, open the door now."

David ran to the door, removed the bar, and grabbed two legs of the deer.

"It looks like the deer got the best of you, but I'm glad to see you won." David examined Rocco's puffy eyes and the blood dripping from his nose.

They attacked me, but they won't be attacking anyone else. I can assure you," Rocco kicked the door shut and put the bar in place.

"What happened out there? I thought you were dead. I didn't see a flare. Man am I glad you're back. I would say in one piece, but it looks like they got you pretty bad."

Rocco told David about the two monsters attacking him as they took the deer to the garage. They needed to get it in the freezer as soon as possible. David opened a door letting a cool breeze into the garage. After dressing and cutting the deer Rocco wrapped it in freezer paper, placed it inside then shut the door.

Rocco's stomach growled as he entered the house again. "Smells good," he sat at the table. David was in the kitchen frying some of the venison.

"I'm sorry if the veggies are overcooked." David sat the bowl in front of Rocco. "You see I sent my brother out to get meat and he forgot to come home," David smiled.

"What a lame brother you have." Rocco shoveled a mouthful of food into his mouth.

"I would have to agree with you there. I think he was out on a hot date and didn't want me to know."

"Maybe next time he'll bring her home to meet the family." They laughed. Rocco was glad he was home.

"I'll grab the first aid kit," David said rinsing his bowl in the sink. "You finish eating and I'll get you taken care of. You look beat."

"Thanks." Rocco continued to inhale his meal. His stomach thanked him with silence.

******

The sound of glass shattering woke Rocco. Still thinking he might be dreaming, he didn't move. He heard more banging and pounding. This time, the noise came from outside.

"What's going on? If it was a fight they want, I'll give it to them." He grabbed the gun from underneath his pillow, placed the magazine in it and got to his feet.

Chapter 9

The shattered glass from the broken window covered the living room floor. They were in trouble. He reached the entryway and the front door shook. Someone or something was trying to get in. Within seconds, Rocco's smoking gun had left two bullet holes in the door. One at the top where an eye would be and another about a foot below it. The pounding stopped.

Confident he had killed whatever was behind the door; he removed the bar and tried to push it open. Something was blocking it, keeping it from budging. Pushing with all his might, he found himself staring at the body of one of the monsters. Amusement flickered in his soul, as he looked at the rotting flesh on the monster's face with a bullet hole in the right eye and another in the middle of its chest.

The pride swelling in his chest was short-lived however, as the sound of gravel crunching underfoot meant trouble. There was a small group of diseased running toward him cursing and swinging sticks. In a panic, Rocco fired off five poorly aimed shots. He cringed realizing he had hit nothing but the scenery behind his targets.

And now he was out of ammo.

Running back into the house his thoughts raced to David. Why was he not here helping him fight? Rocco hurried to get to his room to get more bullets and in his haste, he forgot to shut the front door.

Heating the commotion, Rocco raced to the living room. There he found David with a bloody knife hanging at his side. He frowned, not because David had killed a monster, no, he wished he could have seen the action. David didn't kill, it just wasn't who he was. He couldn't believe he'd missed it.

"Duck," Rocco yelled, and in an instant, David was on his knees. Rocco stood at the end of the smoking barrel with a smirk on his face.

"Looks like I just saved your life." He nodded his head toward the monster slumped over the sofa with a bullet in his brain.

"Is that so?" David nodded at the pile of bodies in the kitchen. "I think I did my fair share." Rocco chuckled noticing the glint in David's eyes.

Rocco and David stood silent in the hall listening for any sign of more monsters coming. No sound emerged for some time. Everyone must either be dead or gone. He dipped his head toward the door and David nodded in agreement.

Outside they scanned for any more threats. It was clear. No monsters were in sight. They headed back in the house. Rocco grabbed the ankles of one of the monsters, dragging him out of the house. David followed suit with the second body.

"What happened here? Better yet, how did it happen?" David snarled, peering at Rocco. "Did you forget to tell me something about your hunting trip?"

"I don't know," Rocco said looking at the ground. "Maybe someone might have followed me." He screwed up and he knew it. "Look on the bright side," he joked. "We took care of the problem."

"I hope so." They went back inside and locked the door behind them. "I hate seeing them but not as much as I hate killing them. I don't think it's right. It could just as easily be us. I know you think I'm weak, but right now, I don't care. I hate killing and tonight I've done a lot of it."

They'd had this conversation a million times before. Rocco believed the second you became diseased you were no longer human, and had no problem killing them, he had made the mistake once of letting them live, it wouldn't happen again. The monsters were not in control of their actions, the disease was. He saw it as doing them a favor when he killed them. David wasn't weak, but nothing he said would make David feel any less guilty, so he said nothing.

Silently, the two bleached the walls and floors. Making sure every inch was cleaned. Rocco notice David scrubbed a little more aggressively than necessary. Was he taking his frustrations out on the walls?

"It's not right for the world to end this way," Rocco said. This was his fault, his mistake. He knew someone was following him last night and he came home anyway. He should have been more careful. David didn't respond. He continued to clean until all signs of the battle were gone.

Rocco sprawled out on the couch mulling over what David said. How could he think it wasn't right to kill monsters? Was it okay for them to kill their family?

"I don't think it's right your parents died. Or our little brother watched our mom and dad get shot before dying himself."

A fire started to burn in Rocco's chest. He didn't care what David thought all monsters deserved to die and was more than happy to kill them. The urge to yell or hit something surged through his body, but exhaustion prevented him from hitting anything, a verbal fight would have to do. Arguing with David wouldn't solve anything, yet he let his mouth run anyway. The battle that took place was completely his fault.

"I'm sorry I said anything." David dropped into the chair across from Rocco. "I'm not going to fight with you, so save your breath. I didn't know it was against the law to have an opinion other than yours."

Nothing would change the past. The enemy was monsters and it was okay to kill them. "You want to know what I think is right? Killing every last one of them." Rocco sat with a pistol in each hand. "I would be proud to put a bullet in every one of them." He gestured as if he were killing them.

Chapter 10

Ayden the feared leader of the monsters, peered through a crack in a boarded window. His face twisted and arms flung to his side. The men in the house were the two he had been searching for. How could his soldiers fail to carry out his simple orders? He only asked them to take these two men alive and bring them back to the camp. These two would continue to thwart him. But he would tear them down. He wouldn't let them win.

Should I go in and get them myself? He shook his head knowing he was I am empowered and these men were mere humans . *I sware if thouse to haddn't killed my men, I would have killed them myself. I will not be defeated. There's no reson to kill them. No, I need them alive. I have much testing to be doand I can't test a dead subjuct.*

Without a word, he turned and left.

Chapter 11

"We've got a lot of work to do in the morning." Tired of listening to Rocco's rambling, and knowing he was right, David stood. "We did all the cleaning but tomorrow we need to repair the house and make it secure."

David shook his head hating how the death of their parents and brother changed Rocco, yet he understood the change and dealt with it the only way he knew how he prayed. He found himself praying a lot for Rocco. Wanting to say more, but already regretting saying anything. He wished he could hate the monsters. Maybe they were still human and had good hiding inside. He wasn't going to feed Rocco's anger so he went to his room.

His Bible was on the nightstand. David sat on the edge of the bed and began reading. Not sure, what he was looking for, but needing to know he wasn't wrong in feeling the way he did. Longing for the peace reading the Bible gave him. His brain kept wondering about the diseased people and their families. Had he killed someone's father or brother?

The killing was self-defense. Knowing this didn't stop David's pain. He felt dirty and no amount of water would get him clean. Taking another man's life wasn't something he wanted to do and he had taken more than one tonight.

How could Rocco act so nonchalant with his comments? He was a coward. He let his mind wander to Jesus' death. How did those who killed him feel the next day? What was the weight of their guilt? He killed someone who deserved to die, but killing the King, was big. His thoughts gnawed at him.

"There is no judgment against anyone who believes in him. But anyone who doesn't believe in him has already been judged for not believing in God's one and only son." He read from John three. Verse eighteen wasn't as popular as the sixteenth, but still as potent. Jesus's death was a necessity. It was a death, which had to be so he could be saved, yet he wasn't going to be judged for it because he believed. The tight cords around his heart eased a bit. Killing the monsters had to be done for him and Rocco to live. He didn't like it but understood it. He justified the killing.

The light piercing through the slit in the curtain forced David's eyes open. He took the bible off his chest and placed it back on his nightstand. A busy day lay ahead. The repairs to the house would occupy his mind and keep it from wandering to darker thoughts. It was his body he worried about. His muscles begged him to stay in bed. Although he would love to, he couldn't, he needed to get to work. Dragging himself out of the bed he traipsed through the hall and down the stairs. Rocco was still asleep on the couch with one hand gripping a pistol while the other was lying limp on the floor.

"Wake up," David yelled on his way into the kitchen. "We have a lot to do today."

"I'm awake," Rocco groaned and rolled off the couch.

By noon, they had the glass cleaned and replaced some of the broken boards. They drug the bodies from the backyard and tossed them into the ocean. With all they needed to do they didn't want to spend the daylight burying them.

"They're trash, and don't deserve a proper burial." Rocco tossed the last body into the sea. "The sharks can have you," They watched the waves crash over the corpses.

David smiled with satisfaction. "They burst into our house and tried to kill us. Yeah, they got what was coming to them."

"Do you think when sharks eat them, they will become diseased?" Rocco plopped down in the sand.

David flopped next to Rocco. "I don't know. If I thought about it scientifically, I would say yes."

"So, you think we just created shark monsters? I like it."

"I thought you would. Sitting here isn't getting the housework done."

"You're right." They both stood and went back to the house.

The sun burned hot in the clear blue sky. Sweat dripped from their brows as they worked getting the house back together. This was the first time an attack happened at home, was this the last. They had stayed out of sight for a long time, but now the monsters knew where they lived.

Were there more monsters watching? Would they have to keep looking over their shoulder during the day to stay safe?

David was parched. He went into the kitchen to the food pantry to get water only to find they had two jugs left. He took one out and two cups. Rocco was sitting in a chair in the backyard looking out over the ocean. David poured the water and set the jug next to them on the table. "From this view, you can't tell the world is lost. The ocean gives me a sense of peace," David took a dink.

"Yeah, it's beautiful. Do you think somewhere out there a land exists without the diseased running around? Is there a place where the chaos is gone and people live normal lives?" Rocco mumbled downing his water. He stood and walked toward the ocean before David could answer.

"Yes Rocco, I do think there is," he whispered to himself. "Hey, we're running low on water. I don't want to tap into our reserves. I'm going to take the bike and go into town to see if I can find some," David shouted out at Rocco. They had the well and stocked food, but had agreed they wouldn't use it until their other resources ran out.

Rocco turned. "Get some canned goods if you see any. We have a whole well of water we can drink."

"Whatever." David ignored Rocco's comment. He couldn't help it he didn't like the taste of well water. When all other resources were gone he would drink it. "Do you want to come?"

"Nope." Rocco had his feet in the ocean. "I think I'll hang out here unless you need help."

"I'm a big boy. I think I can handle going to the store alone. In the daylight, anyway."

David road to the store with his shotgun out and loaded. He was ready for anything. He scanned left and right, searching everywhere for monsters. Seeing none, he started for the door. Every step he took he scanned checking, again and again, looking for any sign of them. He couldn't take any unnecessary chances. The attack on the house last night left him more jumpy than usual.

"Why didn't I make Rocco come with me?" he whispered.

A smirk broke out on his face. He had gone to the store a million times by himself and he didn't need Rocco to hold his hand.

The door wouldn't open. They never locked it; someone was in there. He tried three other doors. All locked. A movement off to his left caught his eye. His heart raced. Pointing the shotgun toward the front door, he blasted it with two shots. Glass shards glistened on the ground. This store always had what they needed.

"It looks open to me," he tried not to smile as he entered the store.

It took several minutes for David's eyes to adjust to the dark. A shadow of a man standing in the corner caught his eye. This man must have locked the door. The man was gripping a bottle as if he were ready to launch it, David.

"Drop it or I'll shoot," David yelled. He didn't want to kill this man, but he would if it would save his life. The man didn't move. "Put it down or I'll shoot." Still no response.

A shot rang out. The man didn't leave David any choice. Dying wasn't on the list of things he wanted to do today. Again the man didn't move. David shot once more before his eyes fully adjusted to the light and he could see he had been shooting at a cardboard man throwing a can of Mountain Dew like one would throw a football. David smiled at his embarrassment; thankful no one could see him.

He grabbed a cart and started his shopping. The stench rising from the frozen food section made his stomach churn. Flies covered the rotting meats. The store shelves were dust-covered and dirty. Broken glass lined the isles. Shelves toppled over and doors hung off their hinges. People had heavily looted the store yet a lot of useful things remained. David walked to the can goods section. Cans littered the ground under a shelf. He grabbed everything he saw. This would be the last time he would come to this store. The cans were dirty and dented, but the food inside was still edible. They didn't have many options and couldn't afford to be picky. The food at the house wasn't going to last forever.

David jerked his head toward the sound of shattered glass and readied the shotgun. Crouching, he crept through the aisles heading to the back of the store. A glance to the right showed him nothing, but the sound of glass-crunching steps caused him to dart to the left. His blood pumped faster and he listened intently for any sound. Glass sparkled on the ground in the dimly lit room as the sun shone through the slats on the back door. When he squinted his eyes, he could see a bloody footprint on the floor.

Last night's events flashed before his eyes he realized he would kill again; he couldn't let them follow him back home.

Two eyes pierced through the darkness David felt as if they were looking into his soul. The monster stood motionless. The skin of his face peeled away and a gooey discharge dripped from his lips and pooled on the floor at his feet.

The creature jumped onto David's chest and he fell to his back. Glass pierced his skin through his shirt. He cried, as his head crashed into the cement. The monster on his chest grabbed a piece of glass from the ground squeezed and so tight his hand started to bleed. The blood dripped onto David's arm. He held the monster by the wrist to keep it from stabbing him. The harder he pushed away the deeper the glass dug into his back. The pain was almost too intense for him to bear. He ground his teeth together and held his breath. A few more blood drops hit his forehead as the glass crept closer to his neck.

"God help me," David prayed. He couldn't win this one. A vase from the top shelf fell. David closed his eyes as the monster fell forward blocking the falling glass from hitting him. This monster was David's shield.

"Thank you, God." He smiled.

Throwing the unconscious monster to the side, David jumped to his feet. He had a choice to make. Should he kill this monster before he left? He couldn't chance it would awake and follow him, but he wasn't moving. If David ran, the monster wouldn't be able to follow him. He glanced at the ground. The gun lay next to him. He grabbed it and lifted the barrel to the motionless man's head. David's finger steadied over the trigger ready to rid the world of this monster then hesitated. How could he kill him?

There was another crash in front of the store. "I see you didn't come alone," David whispered to the monster. "You can thank your buddy. His clumsiness saved your life." Without hesitation, David drew up his shotgun and walked toward the sound. He could feel something watching him. His eyes scanned the store, roving back and forth. The stench of the meat section grew stronger as he got closer. "Please let me get out of this alive," he whispered.

A louder crash sent David jumping back. The crash came from behind the meat counter. He turned. A raccoon scavenged in the trashcan. He lowered his gun and breathed a sigh of relief. "Freaked out by a raccoon. Man, you need to get control," David laughed. Something hit him from behind and sent him flying forward face first in the rotting meat. David rolled to his back and looked at his attacker. The monster he didn't shoot earlier came after him. Rocco wouldn't have made this mistake. He would have shot first and asked questions later. *Why couldn't he be more like Rocco? Why did he have to have feelings?*

"What's wrong with you? You sick, freak," David shouted, as the monster jumped at him.

The monster chuckled. "You said it. I'm a freak, and I am going to kill you."

David tried to roll out of the way, but couldn't, it was too late. The man landed on him, grabbed his hair, lifted his head, and punched David in the mouth. The shotgun was out of reach. David kneed the infected man and tossed him on the rotting meat. He smashed the creature's face in the meat. Reaching in his side sheath, he pulled out his knife, and stabbed the monster over and over again, until it stopped breathing.

"I tried to let you live." He stabbed it a few more times to make sure it wouldn't come after him again. "This is your fault. I didn't want to kill you! Why did you make me kill you?" David jumped to his feet, grabbed his shotgun and the shopping cart, and headed home.

"Wow, the water sure handled you," Rocco teased when David got home. "I get attacked by a deer and you get taken out by water. I bet you'll start liking the well-water." Rocco droned on as he pulled the glass from David's back. "It looks like we need to stick together from here on out. No more alone trips, it is getting real out there. They are killing more. This is war, and we are going to have to start treating it like war." Rocco closed the antiseptic bottle and put the last band-aid on David's wounds.

"You're right." David agreed. "I hate all this killing, but you're right."

"I'm not going to quit! If I have to, I'll kill everyone on earth to save us."

"We're going to need a lot more ammo than what we have." David stood. He needed to be alone with his thoughts. Rocco was talking about killing and all he wanted was to forget it.

"Sorry I didn't go with you today. I should have been there. From now on we go together."

"Yes," David agreed.

David bounded up the stairs. "Good night."

"Night."

David couldn't sleep. He tried everything he could think of, but nothing worked. He lay in bed, staring into the dark till his eyes adjusted and he could see the ceiling. His head spun with thoughts and emotions. He tried to think about nothing, but it didn't work either. The fact was that life had nothing to offer him and he wondered why they were still here. He wanted to talk to Rocco, but he knew he couldn't. Rocco wouldn't understand.

David saw the outline of his bible in the shadows and picked it up and put it on his chest. He wanted to read it but had no light. He didn't want to move to get light. He was sore and tired. Why couldn't he get his mind to stop racing? When he closed his eyes, he could saw flashes of monsters trying to kill him. There was nothing he could do to stop them His solution was to keep his eyes open.

He was never a fighter. He kept to himself in school, even when others bullied him for being a nerd, he didn't fight back. Rocco was the fighter. David was becoming a fighter and it tore at his heart. He hated killing. It didn't matter what he called them animals, monsters, or diseased. He couldn't stop thinking about their families.

These monsters were once like him, before the infection. Did they still have feelings? David knew they had anger, but he didn't know if they felt pain. Were they trying to survive like he and Rocco were? Did they lay in bed thinking about the humans they had infected or killed? David thought about zombies and about the people who tried to save them. Those people were dumb; everyone knew zombies couldn't be saved.

"These things aren't the living dead. They are not human anymore either. What is it we are fighting?" he whispered letting his mind continued to race.

Chapter 12

"Get down here boy." Hue's father yelled struggling to get to his feet. He held the wall to steady himself. He needed the boy's help to get to camp. Aeyden, his leader, didn't tolerate tardiness. The group was planning its next attack. Aeyden called for everyone to be at the meeting. The longer the boy took the angrier his dad became. To Hue, he was a monster.

"Dang it," Hue said to himself. "I didn't want to play dead today." He went into the bathroom got his makeup kit and applied it to his face to make it look rotted and diseased. Hue didn't have the disease himself; only his father was infected. Hue had learned to imitate the disease so his dad and the other infected people wouldn't kill him. He didn't understand why but those with the disease were drawn to kill those without it. He hated these zombies. They weren't real zombies, but it's what he called them.

These once were normal humans who were turned into monsters by a virus. He wasn't sure where the virus originated from. All he knew was, it changed people. His dad had been one of the changed. These monsters were different than zombies. They could think and feel. The virus affected their skin and their mental status. It turned them into angry monsters wanting to infect the world. There seemed to be different levels of the virus too. Hue didn't understand it all. Some of the monsters were able to speak and function. Others were not. They were the ones more like zombies.

His hurried hands tried their best to make the sore look realistic. It was as good as it was getting. He examined himself in the mirror and hated what stared back at him. The makeup transformed him into one of them. No, it made him look like one of them. He was a survivor determined to make it out of here one day alive, not as a zombie. Playing dead worked for him. He would have to keep playing dead until the day he would kill every one of the diseased, even his dad. No. Especially his dad.

To him, the monster who had the face of his dad was nothing more than a walking corpse. His dad died when the disease took over his body. He hated this man and often dreamt of killing him.

Hue wasn't a killer or a violent kid, but he'd had enough. This man was evil and Hue didn't want to take the beatings he dished out on a whim. He didn't like the evil inside the diseased. There wasn't a time, in the twelve years, he had been alive, this man had ever been nice to him. With his mother gone, it was just him and his old man. His dad didn't just drink anymore, he liked to use Hue as his personal punching bag. Having no choice, Hue pretended to be diseased and go with his dad when he went to the camp. By doing this, he could gain the knowledge he needed to one day overtake the camp and kill all zombies.

He couldn't hold off his dad much longer.

His makeup wasn't perfect but it would do. He headed to the living room. His foot stepped on the last stair when something hit him and sent him sailing across the room. His body crashed against the bookcase and slumped to the ground.

"I called you ten minutes ago," his dad yelled, kicking him in the stomach. "I don't like to be kept waiting."

Hue gasped for breath as the air left his lungs. Without a sound, he picked himself off the floor. He couldn't let his old man know he was in pain. He took his dad by the arm and let him lean on his shoulder as they walked out to the road. They were both silent. Another blow would land on Hue if he said anything. He couldn't take any more pain. His chest was closing in on him. He had a broken rib for sure, but there was nothing he could do. He had no one he could run to.

The camp was a few miles from the house. They had to get there on time. If they were late, Hue would have more than broken ribs. It took all his strength to get his dad there.

A crowd of zombies already gathered around Aeyden. Fists were pumping in the air and growls erupted from the crowd. Aeyden took the floor and spoke his usual words of gruesome enthusiasm. The meeting itself was lengthy and mind-numbing once the pep rally ended. Aeyden talked about a house they were going to target. He had a whole route planned with roughly drawn maps of the house pinned to the wall, marked with points of entry and some other small notations Hue didn't understand. Aeyden had eyes watching the house for quite a while. There was a man he wanted named David, and he wanted him alive. Hue wasn't certain of the reasoning behind the kidnapping and not killing but when Aeyden wanted something he found a way to get it. This David guy wasn't diseased so he would be hard to apprehend. Hue knew this would prove to be a difficult task. When zombies attacked someone, they killed them, blinded by their rage. At the very least Hue figured they would change him into a monster like them. Aeyden didn't want him killed or changed, he wanted David brought to him safe and unharmed.

The meeting scared Hue, it got his dad excited, which meant trouble for him when they got home. His dad would need an out for his rage, and he knew he would be the out. Hue didn't take his eyes off him. The more Aeyden talked, the angrier the mob became. "I can't go home," he whispered to himself. "I won't survive if I do." His father had been angry enough without being fueled by this mob. His mind raced trying to figure out some plan to avoid going home.

He was deep in his thoughts when a stick came crashing on his back. "You listen when I'm talking to you boy," his dad yelled. He felt the warmth of his blood flowing over his cheek as his face met the dirt with an agonizing crack.

Why haven't I killed him already? I know I'd be better off without him. Why couldn't this monster die like mom did?

Hue hated this infected man with every fiber of his being. He dreamt of a day when his dad would no longer be in his life. It couldn't be today, not with all those people watching. No, not people, zombies. To him, they would always be zombies.

His plan would have to be flawless. If he made one mistake it would cost him his life. He had put it off long enough. His dad needed to die before Hue did. If Hue's dad knew he wasn't diseased, he would kill him. Everyone in the zombie camp would help. Maybe his father subconsciously knew he wasn't a zombie. Even in this rotted out world, Hue was a failure in his dad's eyes. The man never cared for him, even before he became a monster. He would rather cling to his bottle than to the hand of his son.

His dad took the stick and whacked him in the back again. The zombies didn't care. No, it was quite the opposite. They got a sick sense of joy out of Hue's pain. The mob cheered Hue's dad on, enticed by the sudden spike in violence.

"Kill the kid," they shouted.

The adrenaline in the crowd grew to another level as a zombie kicked one of their own kids off a balcony. The kid splattered on the ground, blood pooled around his body, he was dead. Hue stared. Good for the zombie kid. He was better off dead. Why couldn't he be lucky enough to die? Hue tried to stand only to see the bottom of his dad's boot come across his face. He didn't move. Blood from the dead kid flowed in a river straight for Hue. He wanted to get out of the way but knew if he moved another beating would follow. He lay as still as possible. His body ached. If he pretended to be dead maybe his dad would leave him alone.

A peculiar amusement struck Hue. He was playing dead like a dog; he played a zombie every day. He had to keep himself from chuckling, lest he gives away his liveliness. It worked, soon the crowd trickled away, bored at the sudden end to their entertainment. As the last of the crowd left his dad lost interest in beating him, and left too. Hue hated monsters. He hated all of them. He hated his dad.

Hue lay still until his dad rejoined the group. When alone, he crawled out of the camp. He despised this place. He started to walk home hoping his dad would stay at camp all night, as he did most nights after drinking. The heaven's opened and rain fell as Hue stepped out of camp.

"Thanks," he yelled to the heavens as if God was listening to him, or even cared about him. "Was there any way you could make my life any worse?"

Hue stumbled with every step. His back felt every blow. He needed to sleep, but he had nowhere to lie down. He struggled to fight off the darkness, only to fail and let it swallow him whole.

Chapter 13

Lena didn't know what to do. She stared out her living room window. A male figure. He looks to be between ten- and twelve-years-old trudging down the road. She couldn't tell if he were diseased or not. He was staggering as if he were hurt. Struggling, she fought the battle inside her. Everything within her told her to shut the curtain and pretend she couldn't see this boy. It could be a trap.

"He's just a kid," Lena said aloud. "What if he was in trouble and he needs help?" Before she was able to let go of the curtain and forget about him, he slumped to the ground. Her motherly instincts took over and she rushed out into the rain to help. Not having any kids of her own, might have been what pulled her to this kid. Helping him could cost her everything, even her life, but she didn't care. It was a chance she was willing to take. She couldn't stand by and watch him die, not when she could help him.

She found him face down in the mud. Lena rolled him over. She wanted to see his face needing to confirm he wasn't diseased. She could see what looked like sores, but the rain and blood were washing them away.

"You clever boy," Lena said. "It's makeup. You have thought of everything to fit in with both worlds."

"No, only at home," He sputtered. "I had to do it to fit in at home." He kept his eyes closed. "He would kill me if he thought I wasn't one of them. I think he killed my mother."

"Can you walk?" Lena wanted to get him out of the rain but didn't know if she could carry him. She was making it her job to help him.

"I can try," Hue slowly opened his eyes. "You're not a monster. I thought for sure you would be."

"Sorry if I disappointed you," Leana tried to make the kid feel safe.

She practically carried Hue into the house. He didn't say anything. Once inside she tended to his wounds. He had a huge gash across his back, which she thought needed stitches, but the butterfly bandages alone closed it. Her luck ran out with the one on his head, it would have to have stitches. To her surprise, the kid didn't flinch as she closed his wound.

"What's your name?"

They exchanged names. From the looks of his bruises and cuts, the kid had been through enough, for one night. She didn't ask him anything else. Lena stayed awake most of the night changing Hue's bandages and making him comfortable. As five in the morning came, she let her eyes close. When she opened them again, Hue was gone. He had left her a note.

I'm sorry I left. You were nice to me. I don't want you to think I'm not grateful, but I had to leave. I need to be home before my old man comes too, or he will kill me next time. I wish I could explain, but I can't. I'm sorry.

-Hue

Lena sighed. She thought she might have found someone to go through this nightmare she called life with. It was nice having Hue with her, even if it were only one night. He gave her a reason to live, someone she could care for and not be alone. Survival was hard enough on her own. Hue's absence reminded her of what life could have been like. Maybe she needed to look for other humans. Lena knew where two guys lived because she had been watching them through the woods, stalking them would be the correct term. Making sure they were trustworthy is how she justified her prowling. The attractive blonde may have had a little influence over her decision to talk to them. The thought of approaching him made her a little giddy.

"Get over yourself Lena," she said. "You don't even know them." No matter how much she scolded herself, it made her want to approach them even more. If it came down to life or death, she would choose life.

Chapter 14

David awoke sweaty and tense. He took a deep breath and looked around the room. Something wasn't right, he could feel it. He went to the closet, grabbed his shotgun, and pumped it, but it was empty. He tossed it on the floor and grabbed his pistol turned and got his rifle. His gut told him Rocco was in trouble. He opened the door to Rocco's room. It was empty.

"Rocco," he yelled running through the house. "Rocco, where are you?"

Out of the corner of his eye, he saw flashlights on the beach. His heart raced. Their lights illuminated on something in the sand. Terror paralyzed him. The lights were shining on Rocco. He watched not moving and trying not to breathe. The monsters were within twenty yards of Rocco. Without a sound, he slipped around to the back of the house. There had to be something he could do. He needed to save his brother.

Well hidden in the grass, he'd be able to shoot without anyone seeing him. With his rifle propped and ready to fire at the monster closest to Rocco, he watched the infected through the scope, ready to pull the trigger and end its pathetic life. One looked back at the others and put his finger to his lips to quiet them. They were not like any monsters David had encountered. These monsters appeared to have the ability to think for themselves. One of them stayed back in the trees as if guarding the others. There were too many of them for David to kill before they got to Rocco. He needed a plan of attack but didn't have time to think of one if he was going to get to Rocco before they killed him.

The monsters didn't appear to have any guns. David could see knives; this gave him and Rocco a little more of a chance. Taking a deep breath in and exhaling, he put the cross arrows to the largest monster's head and pulled the trigger. The ground shook when the monster fell to his death. The rest ran for cover looking around trying to find where the shot came from. They drew their guns ready for battle. Any advantage David thought they had was gone. He stayed hidden, as bullets flew around him. He held his breath trying not to give away his position. If he were going to save Rocco, they couldn't know where he was. He feared his shot might have cost Rocco his life.

Rocco's eyes popped open. Another bang echoed across the open space. Several monsters ran, scattering away from him. He rolled and started to inch his way to the house, trying to stay undetected in the commotion.

Another shot sailed through the air, and another monster fell to the sand. Rocco had to make it to the house. He saw where David was firing from and knew if he stayed low David would shoot anything trying to hurt him. Gunfire reverberated again and another monster fell. Guns were pointed at David, Rocco needed to act fast if he was going to save his brother. He pulled the pistol from his holster and fired. He hit his mark the diseased fell to the ground. He could see, from the trees, reinforcements were coming, and he was out of ammo. He did the one thing he knew to do. He ran.

"Rocco," David yelled and threw him the m16.

At least he would have a fighting chance. A loud cracking sound came from the front of the house. David met Rocco's gaze as he dove for the gun in the sand. He grabbed it, flipped onto his back, and shot one of the monsters in the chest. He stood and started toward the back of the house. Rocco went to jump over the two-foot retaining wall. A monster leaped and grabbed a hold of his foot, landing Rocco head first onto the cement. His gun went sailing in the opposite direction.

Gunfire continued, this time sounding like it came from the front of the house.

Two monsters attacked Rocco kicking and punching him until he couldn't breathe. Darkness tried to overtake him, but he couldn't give in to it. David needed him. Motionless on the cement he fought with everything inside of him not to give in to this pain and darkness.

67

"Try to keep him alive," one monster said. "I'm not sure if this is the one we can't kill."

"Why does Aeyden want them alive?"

"It's not for us to question. Our orders are to keep him alive."

"I think it's the other one. We can kill this one." Another boot to the head. "I want to kill this one."

"No. We keep him alive." He pushed his partner.

"I say we kill him." A fight broke out between the two monsters.

A boost of adrenaline shot through his body, as anger pierced his soul. Grasping a monster's foot, he rolled to his back and watched him fly into the air, hitting his head and slumping motionless on the ground. The second monster charged after Rocco. He ducked and turned, grabbed the rifle, and shot. He would show no mercy and wouldn't leave anyone alive to come back and haunt them.

The coast was clear. Rocco jumped to the patio table, grabbed a tree branch, and pulled himself on the roof. He ran toward the front of the house. Guns fired from every direction; he knew he needed to hurry. When he got in position, he fired, shooting the monster closest to David.

"I'll clear out the inside," David yelled to him.

"I'll cover out here," Rocco yelled back continuing to fire at those trying to get in. "They won't get past me."

Rocco shot until all the monsters fell back out of sight.

On the roof, Rocco fired more rounds into the trees, until he emptied the magazine. He heard a cry and feared the worst. Thunder roared and lightning flashed the night's sky. Rocco kept scanning the trees for anything to shoot. He couldn't believe his eyes. One of the monsters killed another one and ran off in the opposite direction. It was something he had never seen.

They didn't kill each other. It wasn't the way they worked. He had only seen their anger toward other monsters but they never kicked each other.

The raindrops rolled off Rocco's face as he sat on the roof. His gun resting on his knees and his head bent looking down the barrel scanning for monsters. He waited. He needed to make sure the monsters didn't come back. It was his fault they were there to start with. He should have been more careful when he brought the deer home. Rocco's stomach twisted in knots. His breathing slowed, into deep controlled breaths. When it was clear no monsters were coming back, he climbed down to find David. He hadn't heard anything from him in a long time. He prayed everything was alright.

It had to be.

One slow step at a time, ready for an attack from any direction. The house was a mess. Magazines and newspapers were strewn throughout the living room. There was a huge gash in the couch cushion, and the recliner lay on its side in the center of the room. Blood splattered the walls and floor, but there was no sign of David. The battle inside was worse than he thought. Rocco rushed to the kitchen. His heart stopped when he saw the frying pan lying in a pool of blood on the floor. Fear engulfed him.

What happened? Where was David?

Rocco couldn't control his thoughts as they raced through his mind. "It's not what it looks like," he told himself. "David's fine. This wasn't his blood. I need to find him."

He yelled for David as he ran through the house. Searching every hiding place, he could think of.

"Oh God, he's gone. How could you take him from me? He was all I had."

David was gone. Knowing this, Rocco didn't stop searching the house over and over again.

"You give and you take away," Rocco yelled. "Why can't you give instead of always taking? Take, take, take. Why can't you leave me be? Why do you always take anything which means anything to me? Why do you take everyone I love?"

He didn't stop yelling.

With each word, his fist made contact with the wall, then the door. He continued this path of destruction throughout the house. "Take, take, take. Why don't you take me? Take me, please take me.

God, how could you? How can I put my faith in you? How can my heart have comfort in you? You're supposed to be the shepherd, but you led my family to the slaughterhouse. Yet I walk through the valley of the shadow of death, and I'll fear no evil, it's all crap."

Rocco raged on.

"They were in the valley, and you were not there. No rod, no staff, and no comfort, unless you find comfort in death. You watched them die. You let my family die. You let them all die. You killed them. I want to take this opportunity to say thanks. What lesson are you trying to teach me? I'm not getting it. I don't get any of this world or this life. Open your eyes Rocco get yourself out of this dream, out of this nightmare."

The blackness in his heart now captured his soul, and he welcomed it.

Chapter 15

She wanted to meet them. Lena had been watching them on and off for months, and come to the realization she would never know if they were good if she didn't introduce herself. They were human, not diseased monsters, so how bad could they be. Lena was desperate for a friend who wasn't going to try to eat her. Tonight she would say hi.

Creeping to the tree she watched in horror as too many monsters to count attacked. She wanted to help the two strangers but didn't know-how. She didn't want them to mistake her for a monster and kill her. There had to be something she could do. Out of the corner of her eye, she saw a monster lurking in the shadows waiting for his opportunity to attack. Lena knew it wasn't much, but she had to try. Even though she didn't know these two, they were human and needed help. She took a pistol from her backpack, steadied her aim, and pulled the trigger.

I got him. One less you have to worry about.

She felt the cold stare of eyes watching her; she looked behind, then to the left and right. She saw no one but knew someone was watching her and it made her skin crawl. She fell silent and crouched in the bushes. She would be no good to anyone if she let them kill her.

"Aeyden wants him alive," Lena heard a monster yell. "Make sure you don't kill him."

The voice drew Lena to it. She needed to know who they were talking about. Was it Rocco or David, and where were they taking him? She needed to help them. Without a sound, she watched as the monsters as they tied David and dragged him into the woods. She followed close enough to know where they were going, but far enough behind they wouldn't see her. She could track, her father taught her how to shoot and track when she was little. Being in the woods was second nature to her, and today the monsters were the animals.

She missed her dad. Being alone sucked.

For a moment, she let her thoughts drift back to her parents. She missed hunting and fishing with her dad and, doing everything else with her mom. Lena never dreamed she would go through life alone. She had to block the thoughts of her parents from her mind. She couldn't dwell on the past. Nothing she could do would bring them back.

The corners of her mouth rose as she let her mind wander to Rocco. She knew from watching the two of them he was the rougher of the two brothers. David was quieter and gentler.

For months and months, Lena would watch them as they worked and lived their lives. In her mind she lived with them, she would tell herself, so she didn't feel so alone.

She found herself attracted to Rocco. This was her love story she played over, and over in her head. Lena liked his bad-boy attitude. She wondered if there could ever be anything between the two of them. In her mind, there always was, never her and David, always Rocco. Things were not different for her than any other girl. She dreamed of her wedding day. Her first kiss. The day one knows they've found their soul mate. The day they find the man whom they're going to spend the rest of their life with.

Lena couldn't help but wonder if Rocco could be her man. *Could he be her knight in shining armor? Would they live life together and turn to stars when they died in each other's arms?*

Lena wanted a normal life. She longed for the kind of life they had before the disease. A life where people married their high school sweetheart, had kids, and lived happily ever after. She wanted to be the princess in her fairytale world.

Instead, she lived alone in a nightmare with no prince charming to rescue her. Again, her mind drifted back to her dad. Lena's heart sunk to think he wouldn't get to walk her down the aisle on her wedding day. *Who would if she married Rocco? Maybe David would.*

She shook her head. She couldn't marry Rocco. The truth was they didn't know she existed. Would there even be an aisle to walk down?

Her mind raced to another place. Was it even possible? There would be no doctors to deliver a baby. Would she even want to bring a child into this world? She thought about the boy she found last night. He deserved a better life than the one he lived in. Would she want to bring a child to live in this nightmare? *No.* She didn't think so.

Who was taking care of Hue? She would have taken care of him if he had stayed. She could be a good mother, not as good as her mother. No one would ever be as good as her mom was. Lena would have loved Hue as if he were her own. The way things were, he might not have had many material things, but he would have known love.

Lena missed her mother she made life better. Her mother never let a cut go un-cleaned or a night end without a good night kiss and a bedtime story. Did Hue have anyone to give him good night kisses? In her heart, Lena wanted to pray for Hue but doubted it would do any good. Was there a god out there? If there were, would he listen to her prayers?

Her mind drifted to the world around her. Did God care about any of them? He couldn't. With everything happening in the world, she was sure God had left them.

No matter how hard she tried, she could not shut her thoughts off. She needed someone to talk too. She stayed silent as she followed the monsters to wherever they were taking David.

What did they want with him? Why did they want him alive? Lena had a thousand questions but no one to ask them too. She could only follow and listen.

"Thomas why can't we kill him?" One of the monsters questioned.

"Aeyden wants him alive," Thomas answered. "Do you want to go against Aeyden?"

"Nope." They kept walking.

"It'd be easier to kill him, but we can't. He must have information Aeyden needs."

After miles of walking, they reached camp and went in. There was nothing more Lena could do for David. She knew where he was, and could tell Rocco. As she turned to go she ran right into someone.

"I can get you in to talk to him," the boy stated.

Lena's heart stopped. She didn't recognize the kid in his makeup. It must be Hue She stood speechless.

"I can get you in," he repeated.

"How?"

"All you have to do is to put makeup on like I do and stay away from the smart ones. You have to only interact with the ones who can barely speak. It's easier for them to accept me because of my dad. I fooled him for years. When they start to question, you have to get their scent too."

"How?" Lean was intrigued.

"With their blood or decaying flesh. It's gross but it works, then bam, you're one of them. I can tell you which one's are the most violent, those ones you need to stay away from. It's not much, but I'll help you if you want me to. We will have to wait a few days for them to get this David guy settled in. I'm the one who brings the prisoners food and water. I'll be able to get you as close as you want."

"You would do this for me?"

Lena didn't know why she was questioning this kid; except she wanted a friend. She was much older than him, old enough to be his mother. Still, a friend in a world like this was always a good thing.

"You helped me without question" Hue smiled. "I thought I would return the favor."

"It's nice to see you're okay." Lena returned his smile. "I worried about you."

"No need to worry, I'm a survivor. The old man passed out when I got home, he didn't know I was gone."

"Would he miss you tonight?" Lena could sense Hue didn't want to be alone and neither did she. It was nice to talk to someone other than herself.

"Yeah, I think he might."

Lena wanted to take Hue in her arms, hold him and tell him everything was going to be okay. She knew she couldn't. She had to let him go. He could help her get close to David. He knew what he was doing.

"The offer's always open. If you ever need or just want a place to get away you can come to my house."

Lena wanted Hue to know not all adults were out to hurt him, some of them cared.

"Thank you," Hue said. "I'll take you up on it, but tonight I need to be home. I have to make sure I get in good with Aeyden so he lets me take care of David."

Walking home alone Lena wished she could have taken the kid with her. She had a bad feeling about tonight and wasn't sure how safe Hue would be. She did the only thing she could.

"Lord," she prayed. "Please, if you're out there. Keep Hue safe. I'm not sure what his future holds, but I think you know. I'm asking you to protect him and keep him safe."

She paused, hoping to get an answer, as she was desperate for conversation. She remembered reading Bible stories when she was little. God talked to people in them. She wanted to be one of those people.

Why didn't she make Hue come with her? The least she should have done was walk him to his house to make sure he made it home safe. Why didn't God talk to her?

"Lord" Lena continued talking. It couldn't hurt if God were out there. "Would you make a way for me to tell David and Rocco I was here tonight? I want them to know I helped them the night the monsters took David."

Chapter 16

Hue's dad was gone when he got home. He couldn't get Lena out of his head. Was she what a mother was supposed to be? His mom was nothing like Lena. Something inside him wanted to please her. David was important to her, so he would make it appoint to help her save him. Not wanting to have a run in with his dad he went to bed. He figured he wouldn't have any trouble if he were asleep when his dad came home.

"I'm going to teach you a lesson you won't forget," his dad yelled from the bottom of the stairs. "I didn't give you permission to leave this house. You do not make a move unless I tell you too."

Hue scrambled to the bathroom to get his makeup on. He had taken a shower when he got home and forgot to re-apply it before he went to bed. It didn't matter much to his dad. He was drunk and wouldn't be able to tell.

"Get out here, now!" His dad pounded on the bathroom door.

Chapter 17

Rocco's heart stopped as he got to the back door. He knew what had happened. The blood trail, which led outside and to the beach told the story.

"Oh God, oh God, please no," he cried out. "Let me wake up."

He ran following the trail of blood out the back door. When he hit the trees, the trail ended. It was too dark to see any blood. Rocco feared his brother was dead, and he was to blame.

How could he have let this happen? His chest tightened, as his mind raced with thoughts of David. He imagined the horrid things these monsters would do to him. They got off on torturing their prisoners. Even if he found David alive, he feared he wouldn't be the same. These monsters would at least infect him. Infecting him would be worse than killing him.

"Give him back to me," he cried out. "I need him," his eyelids could no longer hold in the tears of pain, so he let them fall.

His wet hair fell over his eyes. Anger filled his heart making him feel like a killer.

Rocco ran into the trees, "David," He screamed.

His body shook as he realized he was alone. David was gone.

"David," Rocco shouted again. Time passed and the rain ceased, still, Rocco didn't move. He stayed on his knees in the woods. He couldn't bring himself to move. He'd lost everything he cared about only this time it was his fault. Monsters had taken everyone he ever loved, his parents, Kyle, and now David. Rocco was cold, hurting, and alone.

"Am I the last human on this planet?" He whispered, "Am I alone?" The night sky grew lighter. Rocco sank into the ground, as the dirt became mud. Even the animals were silent.

Not knowing how long he had been there, he struggled to his feet. There was nothing left for him in life. Walking almost as if he were dead himself, he made his way back to the house. All hope had left him. He had no reason to live. What would the last person on earth do anyway? His face was blank as he sat on the couch looking at the mess in front of him. He didn't care about his safety anymore. He liked the idea of the monsters coming back to get him. He left the front door wide open, welcoming them in. He cared about nothing. He sat on the couch staring at the walls. The thought of never seeing a normal person again killed him. Alone in the world, left with demons who hated him and haunted his dreams. These demons would torment him night after night.

The sunlight snuck into the house throwing its rays onto Rocco's face. The warmth from the sun woke him from a deep sleep. Time swept past him. Before he knew it, afternoon crept in on him. His stomach growled at him. Rocco didn't pay attention to it. *Nothing mattered.* He couldn't think of a better way to go out of this world than by starvation. He opened his eyes again, still alone.

Why couldn't the monsters have come back for him?

He grabbed the side of the coffee table and flipped it over. Glass from the top showered the living room floor. Feeling a sudden surge of energy, Rocco jumped to his feet, welcoming the rage building inside. It felt as if the hand of hell wrapped around his heart and held on tight.

"Am I diseased, too?" he questioned.

The diseased had an uncontrollable rage within them. It must be what he was feeling. Anger seeped into his bones like a disease. His heart beat faster. His breathing grew heavier he knew he should contain his anger, but he didn't want to. *No.*

He welcomed the rage, even encouraged it, letting it take its hold of him. He had no desire for it to leave. His muscles tightened. His eyes narrowed. He couldn't control the shaking in his body as his rage consume him.

He hurled a chair through the sliding door.

"Come and get me." The glass sprayed across the ground. "Why did you leave me here? If you weren't going to take me, why couldn't you have killed me?" Nothing mattered anymore. "I said come and get me!" Rocco continued to rant into the void. "I'm the one you came for, not David. Are you too chicken to come after me? I said, come and get me."

He needed an outlet for his anger. He walked over to the punching bag and slammed his fists on it. A small piece of his anger released with every punch. He continued punching long after his knuckles drenched the bag with blood. It felt good to hurt. He hit the bag one last time with everything inside of him. The bag flew off the chain and sailed across the room crashing the lamp to the floor. He wasn't done. The anger still burned within him, he searched for a way to release it.

Memories of his friend were in every room of the house, reminding him David was gone. The blood and the frying pan were still on the floor in the kitchen.

"Why did you take him?" Rocco's hands went through the drywall with ease and his head followed suit.

His mind numb, nothing mattered anymore. His eyes swollen, his hands and forehead bloody, yet he continued to let his anger control him. In the dining room, he smashed a wooden chair into the wall turning it into kindling. He left nothing in one piece, yet his rage still wasn't tamed.

Rocco grabbed his m-16, bullets, a few pistols, a wagon and headed out the door. He had a plan, it wasn't a well thought out plan, but it was a plan. He needed to avenge David by making every monster pay for what they did. There would be no mercy shown to anyone. Rocco lost everything he loved and now he wouldn't only kill them, he would make them suffer for what they did to him.

His first stop, the neighbors.

He kicked the door open and walked in. He shouted profane language as he asked if anyone was home, and fired a few shots into the ceiling. He had no reason to be there, but it didn't stop him. He was looking for monsters. He wanted someone to hurt as he did. He let his anger guide his footsteps.

A sound from the kitchen startled Rocco. He turned and shot. Upon closer look, he saw it was a cat. He shrugged and continued through the house. His eyes widened and a smile crossed his face. He found a fully stocked bar in the dining room. He took each bottle of alcohol out and put them on the bar.

There were five bottles of hard liquor and three bottles of wine. He set his gun on the bar and poured himself a glass, mixing all five bottles. He downed it, shook off the taste and went in for a second shot. Out of the corner of his eye, he saw a small cigar box, on the side, read "Cuban's".

"I do believe this is my lucky day."

Rocco opened the box and took out a cigar. He lit it with the matches beside the box and inhaled. He held the smoke in his mouth and sighed as he exhaled rings of smoke. After he finished the cigar, he found a crate and loaded the remaining bottles of alcohol and the cigar box in the wagon. These would help him take his mind off the pain; he headed for the next house.

He was hoping to find things, which would make him happy. He needed something but wasn't sure he would find anything to fill the emptiness in his soul. What he wanted was to eliminate every monster who crossed his path. He went through house after house shooting the windows out and knocking furniture over. He collected anything he thought would make him feel better.

The sun was setting. Darkness would take over soon. His wagon was loaded with liquor, cigars, matches, and a few fireworks he found in his looting.

Chapter 18

To Hue's disappointment, he wasn't dead. He opened his eyes to find himself drenched in a thick pool of blood. His head pounded. He knew what he needed to do. Tonight would be the last time this monster touched him. He grabbed the hockey stick his old man beat him with the night before. He would beat his dad until his breathing stopped. Never again would this monster hurt him. He fought through the darkness, which threatened to engulf him. He couldn't give in to it no matter how hard he wanted to. He had to finish this.

Tonight, the zombie would die and Hue would do the killing.

A noise stopped him in his tracks. Someone besides his dad was in their house. He had to make sure his makeup was on before he went downstairs, he couldn't take any chances. If it were a monster with his dad, they would kill him if they found out he wasn't a monster. He looked in the mirror. He didn't need any makeup this time. Thanks to his dad, he looked diseased already. Hue hated him even more.

Chapter 19

Seeing a light on in this house excited Rocco. He wanted to kill someone. He needed someone to pay for what happened to David. He kicked the front door, it didn't budge. He tried a few more times, still nothing. Anger rose inside of him, burning with more fire than he had ever felt before. He wanted in, he wasn't sure why, but he knew he had to get into this house. He tried the doorknob the door was locked. The windows were boarded shut. There was someone in there and Rocco needed to find out who, and kill them. He took his pistol, stepped to the side, and fired at the knob, shattering it. He kicked the door one last time and it opened, inviting him in.

"Honey, I'm home," he yelled, letting his anger and the alcohol take control of his actions. The alcohol burning through his veins fueled the rage inside of him.

"Good to see you," the owner of the house, a diseased man, greeted him wielding a metal bat in Rocco's direction.

Diving to the floor, Rocco ducked out of the way. Another swing came at him, hitting inches from his leg. He scrambled on his belly, trying to get away from the monster with the bat. He made it to the kitchen and hid behind a counter. He tried to get his thoughts together. Rocco wanted this man to pay for everything the monsters had put him through. He pulled himself to his feet to peek and see where his attacker was. A surge of pain shot through his hand driving him back to the floor.

The monster jumped on top of Rocco and kicked him in the chest, sending him flying across the kitchen. Rocco lay on his back planning his next move. He had two options, he could lay here and let the monster take his life, or he could fight back. Rocco didn't know which he wanted to do. Feeling his m-16 on his shoulder, he made his choice.

This was for David.

He grabbed his gun and pointed it at his attacker, who was starting to swing the bat at Rocco again.

"Not this time," Rocco shot the monster's hand and the bat dropped to the floor.

"Now we're even."

Rocco stood to his feet, getting high off the monster's cries of pain. This must be how the disease worked. Rocco was sure he wasn't diseased, but he was beginning to understand how it worked. He wanted this monster to feel pain like he felt when they took David from him.

He placed the barrel of the gun to the man's forehead, "Get on your knees," he commanded.

His adrenaline pumped. This was no longer about David. He needed to kill this man to fuel the fire burning inside of him. No, this had to be for David. How could he justify it if it weren't? This monster had to pay the ultimate price for what they did to his family.

On command, the monster dropped to his knees.

"Do it. Shoot me. I didn't ask for this life," The diseased begged for death. "If you let me live I promise you I'll find you, and I'll kill you. I'll finish the job you should have."

"I've made this mistake a few times already." Rocco let out a laugh. "I have no intention of keeping you alive. It would be easy for me to shoot you and get it over with but," Rocco let out another laugh.

"But look at you, you're already dead."

A sharp pain rushed through Rocco's back, causing him to fall forward firing the gun and killing the diseased man. He turned to see what had hit him, in front of him stood a diseased kid with a hockey stick ready to hit him again.

"Is this a family of jocks?" The kid was eleven or twelve. "First a baseball bat, now a hockey stick."

Rocco's eyes opened and the memory of his little brother filled his head. Kyle was about this kid's age.

Lost in the memories of his past, Rocco could do nothing. He tried to forget Kyle, but how could he? This kid's eyes brought his past back to life. He needed to get his head back into the present.

What was he going to do with this kid? He grabbed the hockey stick and threw it to the side. Out of anger for Kyle, he pointed the gun at the boy. They stood there for a few brief minutes motionless. There was no way he could pull the trigger. This boy was a kid and Kyle was a kid. He couldn't kill him any more than he could kill Kyle. He knew this wasn't his brother, but he didn't have the strength to kill him.

He was, after all, just a kid.

Amongst the anger and hatred, which filled Rocco's heart, love began to creep in. He couldn't explain it, but there it was. He hated everything about these monsters. His mission in life was to rid the world of every last one of them.

How could he want to hold this kid, to comfort him and promise him everything was going to be alright. He wanted to play ball with him and do all the things he regretted not doing with Kyle. Rocco's mind was betraying him, playing games with him. His eyes deceived him, and his heart tricked him. He had never seen a diseased kid before. *Why did he want to comfort him? How could Rocco see Kyle standing before him?*

He knew this kid wasn't Kyle. He didn't want to believe it. He wanted Kyle to be there. He needed Kyle. He needed his family. He needed David.

"You're a lucky kid, or monster," Rocco said. "What's your name?"

"Damned," the boy said, swinging his fist at Rocco.

Rocco ducked, and then hit the kid with the butt of his gun, knocking him out cold. He hated to do it, but if he didn't do something to stop him, he would kill the kid, and he didn't have it in him. Rocco's head filled with memories of his family. Visions of the bullet, which pierced his father raced through his head.

His eyes started to water, then shaking his head as if to shake the memory free, the second bullet hit his mother. His tears grew heavy, almost more than he could handle.

"NO," Rocco yelled, trying to shake the memories before the last bullet came. He hated the last bullet. It ended a life before its time. All his attempts failed. The last bullet went through his little brother and gravity took hold of Rocco's soul.

Rocco walked through the kitchen and grabbed his half-smoked cigar, which had fallen from his mouth earlier. He inhaled the cigar for a long time and took his time exhaling small rings of smoke.

He turned and walked away.

"Please kill me," the kid whispered. "Don't make me go through life like this. Please kill me."

Chapter 20

"What am I supposed to do?" Hue sat on the bottom of the stairs shaking, scared and alone. "Why couldn't you kill me?" He wanted to cry for the loss of his father but couldn't. He had no feelings for him. No sorrow, only regret. The regret he hadn't killed the man. "Why did you let me live?" Hue yelled. "You were a psycho. You came in here and shot my dad, but you forgot to kill me. Come back and kill me."

There was silence. Hue was alone.

He looked over to where his dad's body lay. He wished he had killed him when he broke into the bathroom. He was angry at his dad for dying in the dining room. *Why couldn't he have crawled outside and died?* Now, Hue had to figure out what to do with his body. He hated he looked diseased.

Would the madman have helped him if he had known he wasn't diseased?

"Why couldn't you have taken me with you? I wouldn't have been any trouble. I need you." Hue hated these feelings.

No, stop it. The guy killed your dad and you want him to take you with him? Maybe you're a monster.

His eyes cut back to his dad's body lying on the floor.

"No," Hue said to him. "I'll do nothing with you. I'll leave you to rot right here on the dining room floor."

He stood, and kicked his dad's body. He was dead for sure; half of his head lay plastered on the wall behind the table.

Sore and tired, Hue crept up the stairs to his room. He needed to sleep and get his head straight. He would have to figure out what he was going to do with the rest of his life. Everything within him wanted to go to Lena's house. He didn't know if he should.

Once Aeyden found out his dad was dead, he would come looking for Hue. He would expect him to stay at camp. It was the last thing he wanted to do. Hue would have to pretend to be dead forever, he hated to put on the makeup.

Of course, he would do it if it were the only way for him to survive. *What choice did he have?* This was the hand life dealt him. He could either play it or fold. Hue decided he was going to play. He vowed to kill them all. He hated every one of the zombies. If he lived at camp with Aeyden, he could kill them easier. When they were dead and David was safe, he could stay with Lena. He couldn't go now, not knowing Aeyden would be looking for him. He wouldn't put Lena's life in danger.

His mind wandered back to the last night with his mom before she became diseased. The two of them were alone at home. His dad had been gone a few days, looking for food. They were in the living room, while his Mom read a book, and Hue played with his toys. She wasn't an affectionate woman. She hated when he would try to hug her or even hold her hand, he never felt safe with her and he needed to feel safe. Hue's dad came home without food but he had bottles of alcohol.

"Where is my dinner? When I walk through these doors you have my dinner ready," he commanded Hue's mom.

"Did you bring home food?" She asked. His dad's fist landed its first punch on her cheek. "We only have enough for the boy."

Hue's dad's foot landed hard in his stomach. He couldn't breathe, he could not move. He knew he was going to die, he wished death would hurry and engulf him. The kicking didn't stop.

"He isn't going to need any food by the time I get through with him." His dad turned to his mom. With one swing he caught her by the hair and flung her to the ground next to Hue.

"You don't ever put him before me. I'm first."

He took the book and threw it into the fireplace. Hue watched as his mom stood to her feet, went into the kitchen, fixed a plate of food, and set it on the table. She then turned and walked up the stairs. His dad went to the table and ate. Neither one of them cared what happened to him.

Finally, his mom came back. She had a large bag in her hand. Hue smiled. They were going to get out of there. He would never have to worry about his dad hurting him again.

"You be a good boy," she whispered in Hue's ear, before walking out the front door. She didn't care about the blood trickling from his forehead into his eyes. She left him alone to die by the hands of the man he called dad.

He fought hard to erase these memories. Hating how they made him feel unloved. How could a mother not love her child? What could he have done to make her not love him? Mothers loved and protected their children; it was their job. Even animal mothers protect their young. *How could a human mother not care?*

Hue's eyes started to water.

"No," he mumbled. "You aren't going to shed a tear for those people. They didn't shed any for you."

He let the pity he felt for himself, turn to anger toward the zombies who took his parents from him. His mind drifted to the kid killed at the camp. He may have been a zombie, but it didn't give his dad the right to kill him. Hue didn't care if the kid died. He hated zombies and everything they stood for.

He hated the man who came into his house and killed his dad. He wasn't a zombie but he hated him. Hue was the one who should have killed his dad, not this stranger. The man was no better than his dad. He was as evil as the zombies were.

No, he wasn't. He didn't kill Hue. Did it make him one of the good guys? Why did he spare Hue's life? He didn't care.

He was going to kill them all.

Yes, he would infiltrate the camp, gain their trust, and then blow every one of them away. He could feel his adrenaline as it pumped through his veins. He was going to rid the world of zombies, but first, he needed sleep. Aeyden would be looking for him. He went to his room, shut his mind off closed his eyes and gave into the night.

Chapter 21

Rocco tried to open his eyes, but the sun's rays and last night's drinking made it almost impossible. He didn't want to move or think. He wanted to die. His stomach ached. It took all his might to keep the contents of it down by swallowing hard. His head spun with thoughts of his little brother. He prayed last night was a dream, he didn't move. The pain shooting through his head told him he hadn't been dreaming.

Shielding the light from his eyes for a few minutes, he sat on the edge of the bed. He took a deep breath and lunged forward; his face met the floor. Pain shot through his body. He wished he hadn't drunk as much as he had, yet he wanted another drink. He wanted the pain gone.

The welts on his leg confirmed last night was real. He felt it coming. He tried to move, but the pain in his legs just gave way and he fell again. It was too late, the contents of his stomach ended on the floor next to him. Now the dry heaving started, he couldn't stand, so he had to crawl through the vomit to the bathroom. He had to get clean and a hot bath might help his aching muscles.

The water hitting the tub, echoed through his already pounding head. His hand throbbed. The alcohol wore off and pain took its place. His swollen hand hit the side of the tub, he jerked and his head hit the faucet, the water continued to run.

When his eyes opened, he darted to the surface and gasped for air. He turned off the water and lay there trying to get air into his lungs. The bathroom flooded.

"This was stupid. I'm stupid."

He wanted his pain to end. He put his head back under the water and laid still. His chest was heavy from the weight of the water crashing in around it. If he stayed under long enough, he would pass out and his pain would end. A few minutes passed and his head lifted from the water again.

"Coward. Do it," he yelled.

This would be the only way his pain would end, both the physical and the emotional.

Be a real man and end your pain. End it now.

There were a few more failed attempts; he couldn't get himself to stay under the water. He drained the tub, dressed, and left the room. He found a crutch in the closet to help him walk. The growling of his stomach sent him downstairs for food. He took mental notes of the damage done to the house on his way to the kitchen.

The wagon filled with alcohol sat in the corner where he'd left it. The site of it made him feel like vomiting again. He grabbed the handle and dragged it into the closet. He didn't want to throw it out, but he didn't want to see it either. His stomach couldn't tolerate food.

Sleep, he wanted to sleep. He stumbled to the couch and flopped on it. The cleaning would wait until he rested. He laid his head on a pillow and let himself drift to a place where there was peace.

Not knowing what time or even what day it was when he opened his eyes didn't matter to him. The house was still a mess. He started in the living room, hating himself for destroying everything. Just once, he would like to be able to control his anger and not destroy everything in his path. His mom used to call him Taz He wished she were here. He wished anyone was here, He hated being alone. Cleaning had taken Rocco most of the day.

He sorted out the broken things from the things which were still usable. He threw the broken stuff into a pile outside and put the good stuff away. Knowing he would have to replace the sliding door with one in the shed but not right away. He patched the hole with broken dressers, shelves, and electronics parts. To cover the new wall from the inside, he took old DVD cases and glued them to the wall as if they were wallpaper. It looked neat for the time being, but he knew it was a temporary fix.

He left the kitchen for last. It was the one room Rocco didn't want to go in. The monsters got David there. Everything in the room brought back memories of David.

How could Rocco live without him?

Staring at him from the floor was the blood-stained frying pan. He could never use it again, not with David's blood covering it. He threw it into the trash. He wished he could throw the blood-soaked floor in the trash too. David's blood was the only thing he had left of him. It took several bottles of bleach to remove all the stains. With the job complete, Rocco went back to the couch and looked at his house. Everything reminded him that David was gone.

Days melted into weeks. Rocco's body started to heal, but nothing seemed to help his emotional state. He could move his hand, thankful it wasn't broken, as he had feared. The welts from the hockey stick were lightening in color and not as sore. Drinking was the one thing, which eased his emotional pain.

He wanted to die. He had no fear of dying.

The pain he would feel before death terrified him, though. Rocco's stomach continued to remind him alcohol wouldn't sustain him forever. He could feel himself starting to get weak and he didn't care. He had nothing left to care about. He moved from the couch to the table. He sat holding his gunslinger winning desert eagle in his hand. This could be his answer to everything?

Just do it. He begged himself. *One pull and it's over. You can end this pain yourself. You don't have a problem killing the monsters. Pretend you're one of them. It would be better for this world if you were not in it. Just do it! Put the gun to your head and pull the stupid trigger. The only difference between you and the monster is you don't have the disease. You're no better than they are.*

Why was this so hard for him? He knew it would end his suffering.

"Aim, point, and shoot. It's simple."

He poured another glass of whiskey and downed it, and again held the gun only to set it back on the table. He didn't want to be alive. He wanted to be with his family. He wanted to be dead.

Why couldn't he pull the trigger? Why was he sitting here staring at the gun?

Once again, he had the gun in his hand and dropped it as if it were a heap of molten metal.

"What's the matter? You don't have the guts to do it, do you?" Rocco yelled. "Grab the gun and do it. Be a man. Rid the world of yourself. Pull the trigger."

Rocco's thought taunted him. He put the gun to his head and this time he pulled the trigger.

He did it.

He found the courage to end it all. The gun clicked, but nothing happened.

Was it empty?

He opened the chamber and emptied the bullets. There were still six unused bullets in the gun. His heart raced. He finally got the courage to end his life and the stupid gun didn't fire.

"What's next?" He threw the gun at the wall. "Why can't you do anything right?"

He smashed the bottle in his hand, shattering it on the table, and stormed out of the house. He had no place to go but knew he couldn't stay there. The hours passed, he continued to walk. His mind was blank. He didn't want to think about anything.

When he let himself think, Kyle and David were the only things in his head. He didn't want to remember either of them. He didn't want to remember any of his family.

Why didn't he save David?

He was there on the roof and didn't save him. He couldn't save Kyle either. He was useless. Rocco stopped at a big white van parked on the edge of a steep hill with the keys still in the ignition.

He smiled. It didn't matter if it has gas or not.

The van was on a hill, he could get it moving. He got in the driver's seat, put the van into neutral, and hopped out to give it a push. When it started to roll, he jumped back in the driver's seat. The van increased speed as it raced to the bottom of the hill heading straight for a building. When faced with it afresh, Rocco didn't want to die.

He jammed on the brake, nothing happened. His hand darted for the door handle a little too late. The van crashed into the building.

Disoriented and confused, Rocco opened his eyes. He was still in the van, and he was thankful to be alive, or was he? Dying would have solved his problems. Instead, he walked away with a few scrapes and bruises.

"I can't die when I try to kill myself. I can't die on accident. "I'm a loser," he grumbled. He would have to make the long walk back home. "It would be nice if I had gas for the van," He complained.

The walk home seemed longer and more painful than the walk there. All he wanted to do was sleep. Many more days passed. Rocco wasn't sure how long he stayed in bed. He remembered seeing the sun through the window a few times. His body ached, but his stomach wouldn't leave him alone. There would be no more rest until he complied with its needs and gave it food.

The cabinet in the kitchen was empty. How could he let this happen? He slammed the door shut. The garden was just as they left it, empty.

They had meat. He went to the garage. He could feel vomit lurking in the back of his throat as the stench of rotting flesh filled his nostrils, and no cool breeze greeted him when he opened the freezer door. The stench of rotting flesh filled his nostrils. He slammed the door and kicked the wall. David was the one who maintained the freezer and with him gone so was the freezer.

"No," Rocco could not believe he had forgotten the freezer.

Defeated, Rocco went outside and sat looking out at the beach. From this view, he couldn't tell the world was in chaos. It even gave him a little peace. Looking out into the ocean had always calmed his spirit. He could still hear David's voice.

"You need to find peace. Let the chaos go and find your peace."

It did look peaceful, he thought. He smiled as his mind thought of the bodies he dumped in the ocean. It looked peaceful because he threw the chaos into it. He lay there watching the waves crashing on the ocean's shore letting the feeling of peace wash over him, only to have it interrupted by his stomach begging for food.

"I hear you. I'll find food," Rocco said as if speaking to his stomach would quiet it. He closed his eyes and slept until the warmth of the sun's rays woke him.

The trail where they drug David was visible from where Rocco lay. He stood to get a closer look. To his surprise, there wasn't as much blood as he had thought. There had to be a logical reason they took him alive. If they wanted to infect him, they would have done it right away, and watched, as he became one of them. If they were going to kill him, they would have done it and left his body. They would have wanted Rocco to feel the pain of losing David. Something else was going on. Rocco had to figure it out.

Could David still be alive? Rocco started to feel hope. *Could this be a reason to live?*

David might not be dead or infected. Rocco knew they had David prisoner, somewhere. He didn't know why or where they were holding him. He ran to the bedroom snatched his guns, loaded them, and grabbed a few extra magazines.

He would be ready for anything.

Chapter 22

For the first time in Hue's life, he was alone. He had dreamt of this day for so long and now he feared it. At least with his dad here he had protection from the monsters. *What would he do now? Would Aeyden take care of him, or have him killed?* Despite everything he had gone through Hue wasn't ready to die.

He bounded downstairs to get something to eat. His dad's body blocked the entrance to the kitchen. He hated the man who lay on the floor. He hated, even more, he wasn't the one to put him there. The stench of death filled his nostrils sending a sickening feeling to his stomach.

"I can't stay here," he mumbled.

Where could he go? It didn't matter, he had to leave.

He stepped over the body and went into the kitchen, took out garbage bags and packed all the useful food he could find. He had to take everything with him, as he would never return.

Upstairs he packed ever piece of makeup he could find. The makeup was more important than clothes, or food. Without it, he would die. He filled the rest of his bags with clothes. He wanted nothing more than to get out of here.

It was time for him to make a clean break from this house and his past. Out of the corner of his eye, he saw it, a picture of his mom and dad. Their wedding picture. He slumped to the floor with it in his hands.

What are you doing? He asked himself. *Why are you holding on to a past you longed to get out of?*

These were his parents. *How could he not want their picture?* They didn't want him. His dad would have killed him if the crazy man hadn't killed him. He owed them nothing and didn't need to take anything to remind him of them. It was time to start over, a time to leave the past, where it belonged, in the past. He would leave them behind like they left him.

Hue smiled. "I don't need you, I never needed you." He dropped the photograph and watched the frame shatter on the floor.

The unknown didn't stop him from going. He hated the thought of running to Aeyden, yet living at the camp was better than living alone. The drawback was he would have to play dead for the rest of his life, or at least until he killed all the zombies.

Hue liked being human. He wanted someone to love him. He wanted to be able to love someone else. A girlfriend maybe and a normal life would be ideal. It would never happen if he lived with the zombies, but he could kill them easily if he were there. He would rid the world of zombies. *What a better way to do it than from within?* His new focus would be to become the zombie killer.

Hue, *the zombie slayer*, he liked the sound of it.

He stood shaking off his crazy thoughts. The zombies would come looking for him soon; he needed to get out of the house. His thoughts raced to Lena, she would gladly take him in, he knew it, and he would love it, but he couldn't go there. It would put her life in danger. He didn't know her very well but he liked her enough not to burden her with his problems.

Living at camp would be no better than living there. Maybe he could find an empty house close enough to camp. He could work for Aeyden and go home at night, being a zombie by day and human by night.

First, he needed to get out of his father's house. Then do whatever it took to accomplish his goals. Hue the zombie slayer would soon be born. He grabbed his bags and walked out into the sunlight shutting the door on this part of his life.

"This sucks," Hue mumbled.

He dreamed of staying with Lena, even though he knew he couldn't. She was everything he thought a mother should be, someone who would love and protect him. A real mother would have never let anyone hurt her child, and would never leave them alone. Lena would be this kind of mother. She would sacrifice her world for the life of her child.

Sadly, Hue was not her child; he was no one's child. The truth was he's nothing to her. Maybe he could find the crazy man, who killed his dad, and live with him, he at least owed him that much. He remembered the look of love in the man's eyes. Hue had to remind himself the love was for someone else, not him, but he wished it were for him.

Why couldn't someone love and care about where he went and what he did? He hated himself for his thoughts. *Did he want to live with the animal who murdered his father?*

Yes, Hue sighed and kept on walking.

He didn't want the man to be his dad. No, he wanted the man to love him. He wanted anyone to love him. *Why did he want this man's love?* Hue fought back these thoughts. He needed to stay focused and figure out where to go. If he were going to live with Aeyden, he would have to get dead.

He laughed.

Yes, he would like to be dead, but not while he still breathed. He snickered and continued to walk, not knowing where his final destination would be.

"Care to share the joke?" a voice from behind him asked.

Hue froze.

He had no makeup on. If it were a zombie behind him, he was dead. His hand hovered over the knife in his pocket. He wasn't going to lie down and die. He would take out as many zombies as he could. He was, after all, the zombie slayer.

"Hue," he felt a gentle hand on his shoulder. "It's me, Lena. I didn't mean to frighten you."

He sighed. Maybe life would get better.

"Are you okay?"

"I'm fine."

His mind filled with emotions. He didn't know if he could control them. *How did she know where to find him? Did she care about him, and if so why?* He knew he could trust her, but didn't know if he wanted to let himself get attached. *Would she be safe if he stayed with her?* He couldn't live with himself if Aeyden hurt her because of him.

He had too many unanswered questions.

Lena turned him so he faced her. "Are you okay," she asked again.

He said nothing.

"I have an idea." Lena took his bag. "You don't have to say a word. I t's getting late. I don't want you wandering the streets alone after dark. Tomorrow you're free to go wherever you want to." She gestures for him to follow her.

He silently followed her to her house.

He liked she didn't give him a choice but to go with her. This was where he wanted to be anyway, but he would have told her he couldn't stay if she would have asked him.

Once in the house, Lena headed down the hallway. "I'm going to put your suitcase in the spare bedroom." She returned and went to the kitchen. She came back to the living room with a hot plate of food and a tall glass of water.

"You don't have to tell me anything, but I want you to know I'm a good listener if you need to talk." She handed him the plate of food. "After you're done eating, we need to get your wounds taken care of."

"He's dead," Hue took a bite of food. "I'm alone."

He was kicking himself for saying it. She didn't need to think he was a charity case. He didn't need to think he could stay here either. He had to be with Aeyden to become the zombie slayer.

"What happened? You don't look okay?" Lena crossed the room and grabbed a medical kit.

"I'm going to be." He smiled at her. He needed to tell her what happened so he could get this behind him. "My dad went nuts last night." He knew once he told her he would never have to talk about it again. "I was in the bathroom, trying to put makeup on, he crashed through the door. He beat me with a hockey stick until I was

103

unconscious. I thought he was going to kill me. No, I prayed he would, but he didn't.

"When I came to, I decided I wasn't going to let him do this to me again. He was the one who was going to die. I heard some commotion. When I got to the bottom of the stairs, I saw a crazy man in the dining room with my dad. They were both drunk. The crazy man was a human, not a monster. I don't know why he was there, or what he wanted. I'm not even sure how it happened, but he killed my dad.

"I was angry. I wanted to be the one who killed him. It had taken me a long time to get enough courage to do it, and this stranger took it away from me. I went crazy myself, hitting the guy with the hockey stick, wanting him to kill me too, but he didn't."

Hue paused fighting back emotions he didn't expect to have.

"You're welcome to stay here." Lena smiled. "I would love the company." She finished cleaning Hue's sores and gently kissed his head. "You're going to be okay. We both, will be."

He couldn't stop his emotions. He gave in and let the tears pour from his eyes. Lena sat silently holding him until he fell asleep.

When morning hit, Hue knew this is where he wanted to stay. He would still work for Aeyden, but at night, he would come home to Lean. She showed him something he had never knew, motherly love. He and Lena unpacked his suitcase, and she made her home his. He worried about her safety, but couldn't leave her. She needed him as much as he needed her. They would somehow figure out how to make this work.

Over the next few weeks, they talked about everything, their hopes dreams, and fears. Hue told Lena about Aeyden and the camp. Lena told him about the two guys. She had heard them talking and yelling their names. The one taken was David. The one left behind was Rocco.

They tried to go to Rocco's house on numerous different times to tell him they thought David was alive. They could never find him home. Together they made plans to get David out of camp and back home to Rocco.

Hue would contact Aeyden to make sure he had access to David, then he would bring Lena in. Lena didn't like it but said she thought it would work, and she didn't have any other plan.

She showed Hue how to cook and Hue showed her how to play dead. At night, Lena would sit on the bed next to Hue and read to him. He knew how to read, but liked the sound of her voice. Reading is the only thing he learned from his mother. She loved her books. Lena helped him by challenging him with more difficult words.

"Thanks for letting me stay here," Hue said.

"You don't have to thank me," Lena tousled his hair. "I'm here for you, and you're for me. Maybe there is a God, and he knew we needed each other."

"I'm not one to believe in God, but if I did, I would agree."

Hue liked being with Lena, he felt safe, but he knew he would have to go to the camp soon. He couldn't wait too much longer or Aeyden might not accept him back. Playing dead wasn't something he looked forward too, but he had to do it to find David. He needed to do it for Lena. He would play dead.

The day came when Hue's wounds healed, and it was time for him to go to Aeyden. He hated the thought of leaving the safety of Lena's house, but wouldn't become the zombie slayer if he didn't go to the camp.

"Hue you don't have to go." Lena put her arm around him. "You can stay here with me forever."

"What about David?" Hue wasn't sure he wanted to go.

He feared he would get caught playing dead. Nor did he want to leave Lena. He'd found someone who he thought of as a mother and he didn't want to lose her. Yet this was something he had to do. As much as he didn't want to leave, he wanted to kill the zombies. They had to die and he needed to kill them.

Who else was there to do it? No one.

"We will figure it out. I don't want you to take any unnecessary chances."

"I have to do this Lena. I can get to David. I'll kill all the zombies, what better way to do it than to become a double agent. I'll be the zombie slayer. I can't kill them if I'm not with them"

"You know they're not the living dead."

"Yeah, but they're dead to me. They are the walking dead."

"Okay, zombies it is." She cracked a grin. "I don't need you to get David. I can tell Rocco where he is when I see him. He will figure out how to get him out."

Hue knew Lena was trying to protect him, but he didn't need her protection. He had to admit it was nice to have someone care enough about him and want to protect him. He would do anything for her.

Hue had known Aeyden almost all his life, and he didn't fear him. Aeyden hadn't figured out he was playing dead so there would be no reason for anyone to panic. Hue knew what he was doing when it came to the zombies.

"No, I need to do this. Aeyden will know I'm missing and I don't want him to come looking for me."

"You don't have to do this," Lena again stated.

"Lena, this is the best way to help get David out of there. I'll be fine." He smiled to himself. "I'm a double agent. It's not the first time I've done this. I have fooled them for years. They don't scare me."

He was afraid if he didn't go, they would come looking for him and find Lena. Hue knew what the zombies would do to her if they found her. It was his job to protect her. She was the one person in the world who cared about him.

"Tomorrow when I talk to Aeyden I'll find David. I'll be fine."

"Make sure you're home for supper." She fought the large lump forming in her throat. "If you aren't, I'll come looking for you. Trust me, you don't want me to come."

"Yes ma'am, I'll be home." Hue closed his eyes to sleep. He didn't remember a time in his life he slept this sound.

******

Lena didn't get much sleep; she couldn't help worrying about Hue. *Would he be safe?* She wasn't sure why she cared so much about this kid, but she did. The first time she saw him, she knew her job in life would be to protect him. He had lived through more than most adults had, and she would show him he could be happy. She didn't know how, but she knew she had to try.

******

"Where's the kid?" Aeyden yelled.

"We don't know? We found his father dead," one of them responded.

Chapter 23

At noon Rocco reached the library. He chained his bike at the bike rack, it wasn't necessary, but he didn't want to walk home. The thought of taking the bike in with him crossed his mind. No one would stop him. He imagined his high school librarian's face as he rode up and down the aisles and smiled. It was nice to know he could do whatever he wanted, yet he chose to lock his bike on the bike rack.

A vending machine full of chips and snacks next to the front door caused his stomach to rumble. Desperate for chips, he reached his hand in the open tray and tried to grab a bag of chips from the bottom. He couldn't reach anything. His stomach growled loud enough for all to hear. If there was anyone to hear. He tried to shake the food lose. Nothing worked.

Hunger won.

He unlocked his bike and shook a bar on the bike rack until it came loose. With a hard swing the glass shattered and his path to junk food heaven opened. He pulled everything off all the shelves and sat in the middle of the pile and his junk food binge began. The chips may have been stale, but they were still chips.

From his seat on the ground, he could see two more vending machines, one filled with soda and the other with water and juice. Again, he hurled the pipe at the machine. The plastic front acted as a shield and the pipe bounced back toward Rocco, ducked out of the way. He needed something sharp and heavy to break into this one. A rock sat in the flower garden, he snatched it and smashed the lock until it broke. The first thing he grabbed was an orange juice.

Even though it was warm, he wanted it. He couldn't remember the last time he had juice. It easily popped open and took a big gulp then gagged until he almost spewed. The juice had fermented and curdled in his stomach. Working as fast as he could, he opened the lock to the other machine and downed a bottle of water.

"What was I thinking." He laughed. He felt a little less alone when he heard his voice. "Of course, the juice would be bad. I bet the soda is still good. Funny how it works, soda lasts and juice doesn't."

Rocco longed for someone to talk to. He grew tired of talking to himself like a crazy man. He opened a sprite and drank it. Even flat warm, it was refreshing. The grocery store had been out of soda for at least a year. With the world the way it was, there wouldn't be more anytime soon. He didn't know why these machines weren't already broken into but didn't complain. Finding them felt like Christmas. He ate what he wanted, and left the rest of the soda and food on the ground to collect later.

A noise startled him as he opened the library door. It wasn't human. It sounded like a bird chirping. He looked back. A small bird stood before him. Its color amazed Rocco. The bird was bright blue with an even brighter yellow chest. The tiny creature was flying around a red oak tree. The bird flew past him and landed on a branch. It chirped twice, looking toward Rocco.

"I think I'm losing it," Rocco said. "Are you talking to me?" The bird tilted his head to the side and again chirped twice. The bird was talking to him. "What is it little one?"

Rocco attempted to mock the birds chirping. After Rocco's last chirp the bird took flight, it flew toward him and hovered in front of his face for a long time. Rocco stood motionless. This bird intrigued him. With nothing else said the bird turned and took flight again. It flew over the building and out of sight.

Rocco made a mental picture of it.

He glanced over to his bike and smiled. There was no one around to tell him he couldn't and he felt rebellious. He took his bike with him. He rode the bike around and parked at the front desk. For the most part, the library was nice, a lot nicer than the other abandoned businesses he had been to. There were books on the tables, some on the floors; everything had a thick layer of dust on it.

109

"I guess during a zombie apocalypse, the library isn't a looting hot spot."

The room had two staircases on either side, connecting at the top floor. The top floor wrapped around the wall the center opened to offer a view of both the top and bottom floors. Books lined the top walls. The oversized windows let the sunshine in making a circle on the first floor, where Rocco stood.

The light shone on him like a spotlight. He was an actor in a play and the books were his audience staring at him as he spun around in a circle with his arms spread out and his head leaning back. He stood in the center taking in the applause for his outstanding performance. The books cheered him on.

A painting of an angel with its wings spreading out fully caught his eye. In front of the angel was a long-haired man in a white robe. The man knelt on a rock his hands folded, and head bowed. It was breathtaking. The thing which grabbed Rocco's attention was the bird resting on the shoulder of the longhaired man. The bird looked like the one outside, the same color and size.

Could it be the same bird?

"I just saw you outside," he felt a little crazy talking to the painting.

Rocco had come to the library for a reason, talking to birds and dancing, wasn't it? He came to get information to help him find David, but something kept drawing him to the painting. There was something special about the bird, but he couldn't figure out what.

He bounded up the stairs to get a closer look. The closer he got, the more impressed he was. The tree had so much detail he could see the bugs in the bark. He could even see the tiny hairs on the bug's back. The bark itself was detailed with many layers and colors. Rocco's gaze landed again on the bird. Its eyes looked at him no matter where he stood. No, they did more than look at him, they peered through him into his soul.

"What is it, little buddy? Why did you come to see me? Did you need something?" Rocco felt a little more foolish but didn't stop. "What's going on? I think I'm going crazy."

Rocco sat on the top step and closed his eyes. When he opened them again, the sun had moved. He had to get what he came for and leave before dark. First, he wanted to find out what kind of bird was in the painting.

He found six books on birds and put them on a table. Then he went to find the books he had come for. Maybe if he researched war books, it would give him insight on how to look for David. This probably wouldn't do him much good, but it made him feel like he was doing something. He needed to save his friend. Despite all his efforts, he couldn't concentrate on war books. His mind drifted to the bird.

In ten minutes, Rocco found the bird it was a Tanager.

The text read, *Blue and Yellow Tanager*

Thrupis bonarien sis shulzei

"You're a tanager." Rocco gazed at the painting. "I'll call you Thrupis." Rocco tore the page out of the book folded it and put it in his pocket. "Thrupis, is there any way you can help me find out why they took David and what they are doing with him? Please help me find David?"

Time passed quickly as Rocco poured through the war books. Nothing he read brought him any closer to making a plan. He read about prisoners of war and their captors, but nothing applied to David or the monsters who took him. He learned nothing of use. Some captors took prisoners to get an upper hand in the war, they weren't at war, not anymore. Humans as far as Rocco knew where nearly extinct.

He learned they interrogated the prisoners and beat them to the point of death. Sometimes they did kill them. *Were they doing this to David? Did they think he had some useful information? Why did they take him?*

Rocco wouldn't be able to live with himself if something happened to David.

"What do you want with him?" Rocco threw a book at the wall.

The familiar feeling crept inside him. He knocked over the table and books crashed to the floor. He stood to his feet and smiled, looking at the mess he made. He imagined the library full of people staring at him. To his right, he imagined his high school librarian telling him he needed to be quiet and clean his mess. In school every time he was in the library he seemed to get in trouble. He had no intention of cleaning anything.

After several moments, his conscience got the best of him. He turned the table back on its legs and stacked the books in a neat pile on the corner. He looked around for someone, anyone. Loneliness overwhelmed him.

Why did they take the one human he knew? Where did they take David?

Having no answers, he trudged down the stairs.

To the left of the stairs, he spotted a table with books open and papers scattered about. The books and papers weren't unusual, but the fact they were dust free was. Someone else had been there.

Maybe he wasn't alone. Who else was out there, and were they still here?

Rocco looked around every aisle. There was no sign of another human. Curious about what they were doing, he sat at the table and pawed through the books and papers. They were anatomy and weapon books. The anatomy books were open to pages containing information about arteries. It appeared someone was learning how to kill.

He took out his m-16. He wasn't taking any chances. He got into firing position. These books dealt with ways to kill humans. Only the diseased would conduct such research. And they were there with him.

He craved it to be someone not diseased. He longed for a friend but dared not hope.

Still, on his knees, Rocco felt eyes piercing through him. He's not here alone. Someone was watching him. His killer instincts took over.

"This one's for you," he whispered and rose to his feet ready to fight.

He didn't understand why he didn't see them when he came in. *How did they have time to hide?* Breaking the vending machines and racing his bike through the aisles gave his enemy plenty of time to hide. He couldn't help his embarrassment as he looked to the center of the room. He saw himself there spinning and someone watching him.

Rocco took slow controlled breaths, trying to calm his heart. The realization hit him. Whoever was in the library with him hid behind the desk. They had to be, it's the only place to hide. He jumped to the desk counter and scanned the area behind it.

To his surprise, there was no one there. He turned his back to the desk facing the door to his left. With the cross arrows of his gun locked on the door, he tightened his right index finger. The bullet entered the doorknob and it shattered. He kicked the door open and entered. The only thing in the room was a library cart.

Where could the monster be?

"Could the books on the table be from when college students studied here?" Rocco looked over at the table again. No, the table was dust-free. Everything in him; told him he wasn't alone. Whatever was out there was learning how to kill more efficiently.

What, or who would be studying those books?

He strode back to the table with an anatomy book in his hand. The picture was a human neck, the veins and a big artery had circles around them. The artery had a line going to the name with a description.

Carotid artery: *carries oxygenated blood to the neck and head.*

"If someone cut your artery, you would bleed out." Rocco knew if he were to cut someone's neck, they would die. Now he could sound educated next time he slit someone's throat. "Stop or I'll slice your carotid artery," he yelled, laughing at how crazy it sounded. He should have just said cut your throat.

"Is there anyone in here? If you're uninfected I'm here to help you. I don't want to hurt you. I'm loaded with protection." Rocco sat on the table.

What was he doing?

He knew he should leave, but if someone was here Rocco needed to find them, and kill them so they didn't follow him home.

Rocco's stomach churned. The chips and juice were revolting. He took his gun from the table. The bathroom was on the other side of the room diagonal from where the table of books sat. He opened the door enough to peek in; it was safe.

He finished and washed his hands. It was time for him to leave the library. He needed to get home and find David. He pushed on the door; it wouldn't budge. It wasn't locked, something was blocking it. This proved he wasn't alone.

If he used force to break the door down, it could be a trap or worse, it might end with a knife in his carotid artery. He couldn't stay in the bathroom forever, and couldn't see any other way out, no windows, no back door, not even a cleaning closet. He put his back to the wall and slid to the floor.

Maybe a bookshelf fell over when he shut the door. In theory, it was plausible, but no way had it happened. He would have heard it fall.

Rocco stretched out on the floor and stared at the ceiling. A vent in the ceiling gave him a brilliant idea. He sprung to his feet, climbed onto a toilet, then onto the stall dividers, barely reaching the vent cover to take it off. His plan had failed even before he had it figured out. The vent was too small for him to climb into.

One of the war books he read said you need to make diversions to distract the enemy. If he could get them to look away when he forced himself out the door, he could run to the back wall for cover. He had the firepower and wasn't afraid to use it. His hand slid to the three grenades in his pocket. He always carried them; he never knew when they might come in handy. The vent duct lay perpendicular to the door.

It would work.

He pulled the pin and tossed a grenade through the vent then dropped to the ground, and ran to the door. The grenade exploded aways away as he reached the door. Pushing with all his might, the door opened. He ran out of the bathroom and reached the back wall to safety. His plan worked; he escaped the bathroom. Now, he needed to know who was in the library with him, kill them, and get home before it got any darker.

The grenade had exploded between the first and second floor near the stairs. Rocco could see the smoke and fire coming from the opened hole where the vent used to be. A monster hung half on the floor and the other part of him on the second floor. He counted six more, but he only counted two guns. He crept with his back against the wall toward the desk. When he got to it, he would use it as cover.

He's going to the front, said one of the monsters. The two monsters with guns turned and fired in his direction, as they ran toward him.

Rocco was a bookshelf's distance from the desk. He sprinted the last few feet and dove over the desk; as bullets flew past him. The top half of his body made it behind the desk when a bullet grazed his calf. He landed in a roll, with his butt and his back against the desk. The bullets didn't stop. They buzzed like angry bees around his head.

"I got him," one of the monsters yelled in excitement.

Rocco popped his gun over the desk aimed in the direction of the voice and fired. Direct hit. He merely needed to wait for the next one to do something stupid so he would know where to put the next bullet.

"You got it wrong, he got you," another monster said.

Again, these monsters' actions let Rocco know where he was. He was thankful he'd taken an arsenal with him this morning. He hoped he wouldn't need it, but was thankful to have it. Rocco loaded his grenade into the launcher. He stood long enough to aim and launch death to the next monster.

"Target hit," Rocco said, proud of himself. He ducked back behind the safety of the desk.

Rocco took in deep slow breaths, trying not to think about the fire burning in his leg. He reached into his pocket and retrieved a flask of vodka, took a sip, and poured the rest on the leg. He bit his teeth together, holding in his pain. When the pain subsided enough, he stood to peak over the desk to see if he could see where the rest of the monsters were.

A fist flew toward his face. Instinct kicked in, Rocco moved his gun and the monster's fist came in contact with the steel of the barrel. Rocco jabbed the gun to the side of his attacker's face causing him to fall back a few steps giving Rocco enough room to shoot.

Rocco started this morning out longing for death, even tried to end his own life, but nothing worked. For a split second, he thought about doing nothing, letting the monsters take his life. No, he couldn't die, not yet. Not while there was still hope, David was alive. He had to find him.

Only one monster remained.

This one seemed to be smarter than the rest. He saw Rocco, turned, and darted toward the stairs trying not to get killed. He reached the steps, to save time, Rocco slid down the stair rail and got to the floor the same time the monster did. It was a race to the door. They sprinted, jumping over the dead bodies and books.

The diseased man reached the door first. Rocco got to his bike, pulled the chain off, and threw it at the man. It smacked him in the back and gave Rocco the time he needed to hurl the diseased into the door using his own body. He drug the monster and drug him to the librarian's chair, and used the bike chain to chain him to the chair.

Rocco tried to control the rage burning inside him. "Where is David?" He was on the verge of unleashing a demon of his own. "Your kind makes me sick. Tell me where David is. Where have you taken him?" Rocco was ranting like a mad man. He needed answers, and he needed them immediately. He wasn't going to let this man die, not without getting his questions answered.

"Who?"

"Don't mess with me. I'm not in the mood."

The monster spit in Rocco's face. Rocco reloaded his gun and pointed it to his head.

"Sorry, sorry, sorry. I sneezed," the thing chained to the chair pleaded for his life.

"Where is he?" He asked again. He waited for a response, but there wasn't any. Rocco placed the muzzle to the man's shoulder and shot. "Do you like my games? They are fun, aren't they? Where is he?"

"I can't move my arm," the monster cried in pain.

"I'm sorry."

"Please, I didn't want to fight you, they made me." Tears covered his face.

This was something Rocco had never seen. He didn't think monsters had feelings. There was still no answer. Rocco shot him in the knee. "Where's David?"

"Okay, I'll tell you where he is," the man said between gasps of breath.

"Now."

"It's me. Look. They infected me. It's why I don't want to fight you, and I was trying to leave. You stopped me."

"Oh my God, David I'm sorry. I'll unchain you, just don't kill me." Rocco said with all the sarcasm he could muster. Rocco saw the monster was clearly not David, but he was willing to play along.

"Yes, of course, I won't."

Rocco took the chains off the monster.

"Thank you." the disseized claiming to be David, stood his back still turned to Rocco.

Rocco Took the M-16 from around his shoulders and reloaded it.

"What are you doing?" The diseased asked.

"Protecting myself."

Rocco shot three more times landing the bullets in the monster's other shoulder his foot and leg.

117

"Good luck getting back. If you make it back tell the rest of the damned, I'll be coming for David."

Rocco hopped on his bike and rode out of the library. He once again left a monster alive. This time he was sending a message to their leader. He wanted them to know he was coming for his brother and would kill anyone who stood in his way. He was going to set David free.

On his way out, Rocco grabbed everything left in all of the vending machines. He wasn't going to pass what might be his last chance at junk food. On his way home, he stopped at a few abandoned houses, stocking as many supplies as possible.

In one house, he found a kitchen stocked with can goods, more than he could carry. He hurried home, unloaded the bags, grabbed the wagon, and started back to the empty house. Maybe his luck was turning around.

Finding supplies was never this easy. There was no fighting or killing. He loaded the food and left; in less than five minutes he was back on the road to home. This was his lucky day. The only thing missing was meat. He would go hunting again soon, but the canned goods would sustain him for months. After stocking the pantry with his new supplies, he took the two things he had missed, a can of soda and a bag of chips. He sat on the couch and toasted to finding food.

This small victory was a reason to celebrate.

Chapter 24

Why are they keeping me alive?

David didn't understand. There were so many reasons for them to kill him, but he couldn't think of one reason for them keeping him alive. He had been in a glass cell for days. They gave him food and water once. He was tired and hungry.

Where was Rocco? Had they taken him too?

David didn't think so. He would have heard someone talking about it if they had captured him too.

Did they kill him? No. They wouldn't kill Rocco and leave him alive. None of it made any sense.

"Where are you," he said. "Do you even know where I'm, or why they took me? Do you think I'm dead? Are you ever coming to rescue me?"

He hated being alone and longed for someone to talk to. He would even talk to one of the monsters if they would listen. He tried to stay positive, with every passing day he was losing hope. The monsters didn't interrogate him. They didn't try to find out anything from him. The reason he was there was a continued mystery. Left alone to his thoughts brought on sad memories.

"You're not shooting it right," Rocco took the gun from his friend. "I don't know why your dad lets you carry one of these."

David smiled at this memory. He and Rocco were ten. Their dads were taking them hunting. Rocco was used to firing guns. David wasn't. He would get great at it, but in this memory, he was still learning.

"I bet I get the first kill," David replied assure of himself, snatching his gun back from Rocco. "I may not have as much practice as you, but I know I'm a better shot than you are."

"I bet you don't." Rocco tried to grab the gun back. David held on to it tight, he wasn't letting it out of his hands.

Rocco always had to be the best at everything. David could tell it bothered Rocco when he didn't come in first, even when he was a child.

"Boys, neither one of you're going to get to shoot if you don't knock it off." David's dad said as he rescued the gun from David.

"I don't ever want to see you two fighting over a firearm," Rocco's dad added. "These are not toys. Guns can kill you. We thought you boys were old enough to come with us but the way you're acting, I think we might have been wrong."

"You weren't wrong." Rocco frowned. "Sorry," he said to David. "I think we will both be lucky today."

"Yeah, I'm sorry too." David didn't agree with Rocco about the kill.

He was hoping Rocco wouldn't get anything. Just once David wanted to be better than Rocco at something. He was smart and got better grades in school, but when it came to competitions and physical challenges Rocco always won.

David's dad handed him back the rifle and without a word, they walked to the edge of the woods where they parted ways. David and his dad went to the right while Rocco and his dad went left. The waiting killed David. They couldn't talk or even move fearing they would scare off the wildlife. He had drifted off to sleep. He wasn't sure how long he had been sleeping when he felt a tap on his shoulder. His dad motioned for him to get ready.

A large buck grazed in the distance. David steadied his gun. He had one shot. He would have to make it count. Looking through the scope broke his heart. The buck looked directly at him.

How could David kill him?

He was a beautiful creature. He stood tall and proud showing off his huge rack of horns, which meant he was older. This was the biggest buck David had ever seen. He could feed both his family and Rocco's for a long time. His entire body started shaking, he needed to

121

calm down and kill the deer. He would never hear the end of it from Rocco if he didn't. He took a deep breath and let it out as he pulled the trigger.

He did it, one shot and the buck was his.

"Great shot son," his dad embraced him. "I'm proud of you."

David walked with his head hung low behind his dad toward the buck he killed. He knelt next to it and looked into its empty glassy eyes. *How could he have taken the life of such a magnificent creature?*

The guilt, which engulfed him, was more than he could bear, and it seeped out through his eyes.

"It's okay son." His dad put his arm around his shoulder. "We kill for food, not sport."

"Don't tell Rocco," David begged, not taking his eyes off the deer. "I don't want him to think I'm a baby."

"Your secret is safe with me."

Rocco never found out, and his dad never asked him to kill anything again. David went hunting with them but didn't kill anything for years after. He couldn't help but smile at the memory. He longed to be back in time safe in his dad's arms, free from fear and worry. He had to remember more from his childhood. He couldn't let the memories of Rocco fill his thoughts. He needed Rocco, and he had left him out here alone.

David and Rocco were a team and they needed each other. There were jobs each of them had to do, and David feared Rocco would forget to do the things he did. *Would he remember the freezer?* He knew he should have made a list of what to do if something went wrong, but he never got around to it.

"Stop thinking," David told himself. "You can't dwell on the, what if's." Tired, scared, and alone, he yearned to get out of this prison. If they were going to kill him, then he wished they would hurry and do it.

"I want out of here." There was no one to hear him. He remained alone in the cell. The days passed and still, he was alone. Once a day someone would slide food under his door but they never talked to him. They never responded to any of his questions. He needed answers, but instead, he got silence.

He even tried singing an annoying song which repeated itself over and over again. He and Rocco used to sing it to bug Kyle on road trips.

"This is the song that doesn't end."

David sang louder with every word. He sang it for hours until his throat was sore and scratchy. Still, nobody came, nobody cared, he was alone. Nobody even told him to stop.

He couldn't think about Kyle. It hurt too much. He pushed those memories out of his head. His mind thrashed with thoughts of pain from the devil himself. He feared he would never be set free.

Footsteps brought him out of his thoughts. They were coming for him. There was a lot of talk amongst the monsters about the games.

"Get out here," the guard barked, as he opened David's cell. Would he finally get to see what they were all about? He followed the guard to a large arena. "What am I doing here?" David questioned. Pain surged from his back and raced to his leg.

"No one told you to speak." The guard struck him again across the back. David winced as the metal bar once again crossed his back. "Watch and learn. You'll be playing soon." Fearing more pain, watching was exactly what David did.

The arena held four women and one man. The women were bloody and bruised. The man stood motionless locked in a cage. David fought hard not to rush to their rescue.

One of the guards introduced the women to the crowd. Then, the games started. Rebecca grabbed the rusted rebar and rushed another woman stabbing her in the back.

This was unreal. *How could those women do it?* They were killing each other. He realized the purpose of the game. The caged man would be awarded, as a prize to the last women alive.

The 'game' was barbaric and not anything David wanted to watch or participate in.

He turned away.

"I said watch."

Another blow to his head, a second before he crashed into the wall. The warmth of blood trickled over his face. His knees started to buckle underneath him.

Come on, he begged his body, please don't fail me.

The announcer gave play by play details of the event. David could see clearly what was going on.

Rebecca yanked the rebar out of the other girls back and hesitated but only for a second. With the rebar high in the air, she let it fall on her victim's skull, over and over again until there was no doubt the girl was dead. She turned and looked at David.

"You're diseased," he whispered.

Rebecca clung to the rusty rebar lifting it high above her head. She stared bug-eyed at Tabitha, who was attempting to open the cage and free the man.

"You're weak," Rebecca hissed. "You're giving us empowered a bad reputation. You have strength. Why are you not using it? It is your time to die."

David was surprised he could hear the monsters in the arena, he supposed they might have microphones too.

Rebecca's scowl grew darker as the crowd cheered. The crowd hooped and hollered. David's stomach rolled. They wanted more. The diseased seemed to feed off it. They began chanting.

"Rebecca! Rebecca!"

With the crowd shouting her name, she ran toward Tabitha and speared the rebar into the back of her head with a strike. Tabitha fell to the ground. Again, Rebecca looked crazed with power. She continually struck Tabitha until her skull was unrecognizable.

The third girl's eyes widened and scanned the arena. The man in the cage knocked her to the ground. She tried to crawl away. The man grabbed her leg and pulled her back.

"My name is Gerald," he stated. "Kill me."

"Why? I plan on winning you as my prize. I'll kill this Rebecca and make you mine." She broke free from his weak grasp.

"Please lady I have a daughter and wife and I need to get them."
He begged.

"I do not care about your wife or your daughter. I had a husband too and a son. We can't live in the past. We need to think about our future." She stood only to meet a rebar to the throat, ending her life.

"Too much talk and not enough action," Rebecca said as Ashley's body hit the dirt.

Rebecca knelt next to Gerald.

"I do not need a prize. I do not need a man in my life. Do you want to find your family? It will have to be in the afterlife." Rebecca shoved the rebar down Gerald's throat.

"Shhhh. No more talking."

David rolled over and vomited.

******

Rebecca pulled the rebar out of Gerald's body and lifted it to the crowd. This was her prize. The crowd went crazy. Aeyden had never seen this reaction before. He was losing control. Rebecca had killed the prize and was defying the game.

Or was she redefining it? Did it matter?

She was taking his glory. He wanted to shoot her but feared the crowd. They loved her. He stood to his platform and spoke to the people.

"Today we have witnessed 'Rebecca the Backstabber' emerge from a slave to a warrior. She needed no prize. Three days ago, she was a weak human. Today she is a favorite among us. Rebecca the Backstabber I give you access to our kingdom."

Chapter 25

"**B**ring the prisoner to me," someone bellowed over a loudspeaker. Shortly after, two monsters opened David's cell door.

"I don't know why we couldn't have killed him, why does Aeyden have all of the fun?" the first monster hissed at the second one.

"I wouldn't let anyone hear you, or you will be the dead one." He grabbed David's arm. "Get to your feet."

David punched the monster and kicked him with all his might. The monster didn't flinch. David continued fighting. Both the monsters laughed as they dragged him out of the cell.

"You're lucky he wants you alive." A blow to his gut doubled David over. "It's funny what you can live through."

Despite all his efforts, David couldn't getaway.

"Where is Rocco, and where are you taking me?"

"Your buddy is dead," the second one laughed. "We at least got to kill one of you."

"It was a fun kill. I don't think I've seen someone fight to stay alive more than he did," the first monster chimed in.

This couldn't be true. Rocco wasn't dead. He had to be alive. He wouldn't have let them kill him. No, David needed Rocco alive. They hauled him to a room; which looked like some scientist's lab. He froze staring at a photo on the wall. Where was he and why did the monsters have a portrait of his dad hanging on the wall as if it were artwork? So many questions flooded his mind yet he stood speechless. He missed his dad. If he were alive, he would save him.

Why was he standing in this room alone? Where was Rocco? Could he be dead? Was David truly alone?

"Strap him to the table," the monster who appeared to be in charge barked. Despite all David's efforts, he couldn't getaway. In mere moments he lay unable to move strapped to a table.

"I can't get your dad, so I have the next best thing, you," the leader said and started laughing. His laugh sent chills down David's spine. His voice was pure evil; it was what David had envisioned Satan's voice sounded like.

"What do you want with him?" David's eyes darted to the monster who dared to question the leader. "Why didn't you let the boys kill him?"

"I'm trying to purify the virus and create followers with strength speed and still have skin. We don't have Joseph anymore. If I find I can't use him, I will enjoy torturing him like his father did us. I'll turn him and then enjoy watching him suffer in a cage-like an animal."

"His dad didn't," one of the monsters standing next to Aeyden spoke in a whisper. "We did this to ourselves. We volunteered for this."

Within seconds, Aeyden had the monster pinned to the wall with a knife to his throat. Tiny drops of blood fell from where the tip of the knife dug into his skin.

"Thomas, don't you ever cross me again. I'll kill you where you stand."

"I'm not trying to cross you. I'm just stating the facts."

Aeyden pushed the knife in further. "I'm almost to the point I can't control myself. You need to back off Thomas."

Thomas raised his hands in surrender. "I'm not crossing you."

David wanted to look away. He feared for this monster's life. He wasn't sure why Thomas was trying to defend him, but he was thankful the diseased man had tried.

"Don't ever contradict me." Aeyden shoved Tomas to the ground. "I don't care who you are, I'll kill you next time." He turned toward a desk with a bunch of vials on it.

"Congratulations Thomas you get to inject our young friend."

Thomas said nothing; he took the vial and the needle from Aeyden and walked over to David. He mouthed the words I'm sorry as he cleaned David's arm, readying it for the injection.

David struggled, but couldn't loosen the straps. With every move, they tightened. "Stop, why are you doing this to me? I did nothing to you. Let me go and you will never see my face again." He continued to strain against the bands.

"Do it," Aeyden commanded. "Infect him just as we were infected.

Thomas closed his eyes and took a deep breath. He opened his eyes and jabbed the needle into David's arm.

"What are you doing to me?" Burning filled his veins. He felt as if he were on fire from the inside. "You're killing me," he yelled. "Why are you doing this?"

Aeyden leaned close to David's ear.

"Your father is the reason I look like I do. I was his first human lab rat. I'm just repaying the favor."

"Dad," a normal looking guy, in his late teen's early twenties stood in front of Aeyden. "Why are you doing this again?"

"Noah, after the stunt you pulled with Joseph you are no longer aloud near my prisoners."

"Then, stop torturing them."

Aeyden hit the kid and sent him sailing across the hall. "One of you take him to the basement. Clearly, he hasn't learned his lesson."

"Just kill me and get it over with." The kid yelled as a few of the monsters' drug him away.

"You're my son I won't kill you."

"I'm going to kill you," Noah yelled back.

Aeyden turned toward David.

"Get him back to his cell before his strength comes." He left the room.

"You have to help me," David begged Thomas. "Make the burning stop."

"I can't help you," Thomas said as he followed Aeyden out of the room.

The monsters who'd dragged David out of his cell were the same ones to take him back. This time David didn't fight them. He had no energy or desire to fight. He sat in the far corner of his cell not knowing what to expect next.

He concluded they injected him with a virus, which would change him into a monster. He might as well be dead. There was no going back to Rocco or life as he knew it. He scanned the room for anything he could use to end his life. He didn't want to live as a monster. He wanted death, but they'd left him with nothing.

Aeyden had chosen death for him, but a different kind of death than he wanted. This death was a death to the human race. He was officially a monster.

As the days continued, Aeyden came often to check on him and would leave angry because there was no change. David himself didn't know when the change would happen, he could only assume from Aeyden's anger it should have happened already.

Something was different. Aeyden brought four monsters with him, and the one he called Thomas wasn't one of them.

"Hold him tight," Aeyden commanded. "I guess if you want something done right you have to do it yourself."

He pulled a syringe filled with a black liquid, from his pocket. He took the cap off it and jabbed the needle into David's arm.

"This amount will either kill you or turn you, and at this point, I don't care which."

David waited for the burning, which never came. He did not react to the injection. The next few days they left David alone. Not even Aeyden came in to see him.

Why hadn't he turned?

They injected him with the disease twice and he was still human. *Could it be possible for him to be immune?*

He had never heard of someone who had an immunity to the disease. His next few weeks were filled with giving blood and having tests run on him.

"He doesn't show any signs of the disease." Aeyden smiled at David. "What did your dad do to you? This might be better than I hoped. I think we have found our savior. We have found our second Joseph." He turned to the monsters with him. "David's blood might have what we are looking for."

Once again, David found himself strapped to a table with tubes and needles running through his veins. Aeyden lay on the table next to him. David struggled to pull the tubes out. The monsters were giving him a blood transfusion. They were taking his blood and putting it in Aeyden's and giving him Aeyden's blood.

Almost instantly, Aeyden yanked the tubes from his arm. Aeyden's arm had bleeding sores forming all over.

"Make it stop." Aeyden howled as he stormed out of the room slamming the door behind him. The monsters took David back to his cell.

"I guess I'm not your savior," David yelled. "There is only one savior, and I am not him." He lay on the floor in the corner of the cell David's mind raced for a reason he was immune. He remembered a time when he and Rocco were around nine or ten. Their dad took them to an office on the base and gave them a flu shot. David could remember his dad telling him he'd done it to keep them safe. The world as they knew it was changing and he had to protect his family.

"Thanks, Dad. You kept me safe."

Chapter 26

It was still dark when Rocco's eyes opened. He turned to his side and groaned. The pain in his ribs was excruciating. He rolled onto his back and sighed.

"This cannot be good. I had the decency to let one of you live, and this is how you repay me."

Rocco sat in bed. His head spinning. Still feeling a little groggy, and not having a reason to live, he stretched back out on the bed. His body needed time to rest and heal.

The next time his eyes opened the clock said it was four. The sun was shining bright in the sky. Four in the afternoon, he surmised.

His stomach growled. He stumbled into the kitchen, grabbed a few cans of food, and made himself some breakfast.

After eating, he went to the door and looked out at his front yard. The grass was about three feet high and the tree were overgrown.

"Looks like someone should do yard work."

They'd always kept the yard looking nice. David said it was one way they could have some sense of a normal life, not this one, but the one their parents lived in.

They did the yard work together once a week. Having both being raised in military homes, they pretended they were in a contest for the yard of the month. It was more of a joke since all the neighbors were gone or infected.

David had made a sign. "Yard of the month Stinson village." Rocco had laughed when he saw the sign weaved with long lush grass. He looked at the other houses and chuckled again. His yard was still the best looking.

Sighing, he turned back to the house. It looked like a tornado had gone through it. He had some after the drunken rage he still needed to clean. The bathroom floor would need repairing. He never soaked the water from the floor when he overflowed the bathtub. Water spots were forming on the ceiling in the kitchen. If he didn't make the repairs soon, the bathroom would fall into the kitchen. He was ready for the task ahead of him. He couldn't have David coming home to such a mess.

The rest did him good. He could breathe easier and felt stronger. The desire to drown himself in jack and captain had left. He went to the kitchen. He glanced at the cabinet loaded with liquor. A chill ran down his spine and vomit crept in the back of his throat.

With a bottle of vodka in hand, he strode to the bathroom. "I'll put you to good use," he said. Grabbing a washcloth he dumped vodka on it and wiped the mirror and the sink. They sparkled. "Yes, this was a good idea." He needed to get his house shiny again. "David, you would be proud of me."

The shower rod and curtain were lying at the bottom of the bathtub. He hung them and from there he soaked the water off the floor. To his surprise, he only had to replace one board and was thankful for the perfect one in the shed making it an easy fix. After the bathroom, he tackled the upstairs. The first thing he needed to do was take out the trash. There were four bags full of empty alcohol bottles.

"Just because you're not here, doesn't mean I'm free to trash the house and live like a pig. I know you're out there and I'm going to find you. You'd kill me if you came home and saw the house like this." Rocco needed noise, so he continued to talk to himself. "Things are going to be different. There will be no more drunken rages. I'll start cleaning after myself. Yes, things will be much different," he promised David and himself. "I'll be different." He moved to the next room.

Darkness had taken over outside by the time he finished the house. The house was starting to look like a home again, and he was feeling good about himself. His body was sore, but it was a good sore, not from fighting but honest work. There were more repairs to make, but the progress he made pleased him.

He went to his room to close his eyes for a minute but slept the rest of the night. When he woke the next morning, he jumped out of bed eager to start a new day. Joy simmered deep within him. There were no words to explain it, but in his soul, he knew something good was about to happen.

David was alive and he was going to find him.

First, Rocco needed to get the rest of the house and yard fixed. He got out the bike mower and chuckled to himself thinking about how David built it. When they were kids, they had a lawn mowing business. Rocco suggested they stop using their hard-earned money on gas. David thought for a long time, and took an old reel mower and a mountain bike and made a bike mower.

He was the brains of the team. He took off the front bike tire and welding the reel mower to the spot where the front wheel had been. In doing this, they cut out the price of gas and increased their profits, which was the part Rocco liked. The bike mower was easier to use and cut grass faster than pushing a gas-powered mower.

Rocco missed David more with each row he cut.

In a little over an hour, the grass looked fabulous. Rocco trimmed the trees and pulled the weeds until the front yard deserved David's yard of the month sign. It was one of the many things in their house, which reminded Rocco's life was good. At least David thought so. He had told Rocco every day they needed to be thankful they were alive. Some people would kill for the life they'd been living. He didn't know how true the statement was. The monsters proved it the night they took David.

With the yard work finished, Rocco got a jug of water and rested on his well-groomed lawn.

"This is for you." He lifted the jug in a toast to David. "I'll find you, and bring you back home."

They had a ton of old doors, windows, and boards they collected from other houses and stores in the area. David had been in charge of storing them. The boards were stacked in sections according to size. There were boards precut to the sizes of each window. They were stacked and labeled, for easy access. The doors and windows were marked. David had made sure if something ever happened to him Rocco would be set.

He sauntered to the shed and found the things he needed to repair the house. Rocco patched the holes in the walls and put in a new sliding door in the back to seal the house from the outside. It took Rocco about a week to get the house back into shape.

The day after he finished, he went to his attic and took out an old box labeled photos. The time had come to make the house their home again. He hung family pictures throughout the house. He used to hate looking at them because they made a fire burn in his soul. David had removed them to keep his sanity. Now they gave Rocco hope. He didn't know why, but they did, he was going to display them in every room.

The last picture in the box wasn't a family picture. Rocco held it and studied it for a long time. This was one of his mother's favorites, a picture of Jesus walking on the water. The water was clear and Rocco could see the fish swimming below Jesus. There was a dark brown boat with a man getting out of it. He had one foot on the water and the other still over the boat. The sun was bright and the clouds were little. He looked at the artist's initials E.B. This triggered a memory of David's grandma. She had loved painting, and her name was Ellen Banenger. The painting was one of hers.

Looking at the picture calmed Rocco's inner beast. He had never envisioned the story this way. He had always thought it to be an overcast cloudy day with the water murky and dark. He never visualized the man getting out of the boat being careful. Every picture he saw was of the man standing on the water. Everything takes a process, he thought. Faith wasn't the man standing on the water. The act of faith was the man getting out of the boat. He had to have faith he wasn't going to sink, but instead, he was going to stand on the water.

Rocco could imagine as Peter eased his foot into the water. Peter believed his foot was going to touch a hard surface. When his foot hit solid water, he stood confident he wouldn't sink. Peter must have been thinking to himself as he turned to the other men in the boat. Look I'm walking on water. When pride came in the solid water broke under his feet and he began to sink.

Rocco smiled, and hung the picture in the living room, then sat on the couch. His mind wouldn't shut off. He gazed at the picture again. The message from the picture would forever be etched in his mind.

"The act of faith wasn't Peter walking on water," he said aloud. "But him being willing to take a step out of the boat. This act allowed him to have the chance to stand on the water." He gave it a thought for a long while. "I need to start stepping out of the boat. I need to step out and go look for David. It's the only way to find him. If Peter never had faith to step out of the boat, he wouldn't have walked on the water. I'll step out and find you, David. I promise you I'll find you.

Chapter 27

"It's been long enough, Lena," Hue said. "I love being here, but I have to go to Aeyden and find David. This is the only way we are going to get close enough to David to figure out how to rescue him. We tried to get to Rocco and have failed every time. If we wait much longer, I'm afraid of what they might do to David."

"I don't like it."

"I don't like it either, but we have no other option. I'm the only way you're going to be able to get into camp. By now Aeyden knows my dad is dead. It hasn't been too long. I can still play off the grieving son. He'll let me into the camp and I'll take my job back as his runner. I'll have access to David when I bring him his food. Lena," Hue begged, " you have to let me do this. We need to get to David. He has to know we are out there. You know he will die if he loses hope."

"You're right". Lena paused. "I can't help I have a bad feeling about this."

"I know what I'm doing." He gave her a sheepish grin. "Are you forgetting I've been doing this for most of my life?" He had to do this for himself as well as for David. He was still determined to kill every zombie in the camp, and become the zombie slayer. No one, not even Lena was going to stand in his way.

"No, I haven't forgotten." Lena frowned. "I haven't forgotten, and just because I remember doesn't mean I have to like it."

"Thank you for caring about me, I don't remember anyone ever caring." He had to go and no one would stop him. He didn't want to ruin things between him and Lena. Hue liked he had a family to come home to. There was no other way he was going to be able to get close enough to David and get him out of camp unless he went in. He told himself he needed to do this for Lena and David, but he had other selfish motives.

Hue spent the next hour getting his makeup on, making sure it was perfect. The masquerade had to last all day and maybe all night too, depending on if he could get away from Aeyden. He took extra glue and hid it in his jacket pocket in case he had to spend a few nights. He couldn't tell Lena. He didn't think she would understand but made sure he was prepared. He wrote her a note and left it on his bed in case he didn't come home right away. The last thing he wanted was for her to come looking for him. There were things he needed to do which might take longer than a few hours.

After his makeup was perfect, he went downstairs to say his goodbyes. His heart ached he hated to leave this safe house, but he had a job to do. "You know I'm going to be okay, don't you?" he asked walking into the living room.

"In my mind, I do, but my heart is telling me different." Lena tapped her chest.

"This isn't a big deal. I have been there a thousand times. I can do this."

"You better be home before dark," Lena warned. "If you aren't, I'll come looking for you."

"Promise me you won't," Hue said terrified she might come looking for him. He didn't want anything to happen to her. If the monsters found her, they would do terrible things to her. She was pretty and they liked to torture pretty women before mutilating and killing them.

"Honey, it's okay." Lena reached over and took his hand. She cringed, then relaxed her face.

"You don't understand." Hue tried to stay calm. "I know what they will do to you if they find you." He took a deep breath in and out. "Please let me do this, and you stay here until I get back. I can't let anything happen to you. I wouldn't be able to live with myself."

"Hue," Lena said, "I also know what they would do to me." She smiled, taking in deep breaths. "I promise you I'm not going anywhere. I'll stay right here and wait for you."

139

"Don't come, even if I don't make it home tonight." There, he had said it. He didn't need her coming and blowing his cover. "I don't know what Aeyden will want me to do. If he asks me to do something, I have to say yes. No matter how big the job is. It might be too late for me to come home. Don't worry, I'll be safe. I can't let them suspect anything. They are going to know my dad is dead and might make me stay there for a while."

"I don't like this," Lena confessed.

"I know. Don't worry about me." Hue hated, he was leaving her scared and alone. He wished someone was around to stay with Lena while he went to find David.

"Hue," Lena stood. "Don't worry about me. I'm going to be fine. I promise you I won't come looking for you if for some reason you don't make it back tonight. I'll give you a few days before I freak out and come find you."

"Thanks," Hue returned her smile. "I think I might be the luckiest kid in the world. You're the best."

"I think I'm the lucky one." She knew she had to let him go, but she didn't want to.

"I promise you I'll do everything in my power to be home before dark." Hue turned to walk out the door. "Maybe when I get back, I'll teach you how to be dead, so you can come with me next time."

He didn't wait for her reply but hurried out the door. He needed to make it to camp as fast as he could. He had to make sure David was alive, and more importantly, he was still welcome there. He needed to figure out how to accomplish two things. First, he needed a plan for getting David out of camp. Second, he needed to figure out how he was going to kill all the zombies.

Hue found Aeyden in his main meeting room. "I saw what happened to your dad." Aeyden didn't turn to look at Hue, a map on a table had his full attention. "We thought they might have gotten you too. Where have you been? I had someone stay back at your house, and you never showed."

140

"Couldn't stay there. It was time to move on." Hue wasn't expecting this kind of questioning. "I'm not a kid." Hue had to think on his feet. "I thought it was time I got my own place."

"You're right." Aeyden turned and faced him. "You're almost a man. I think it is time you started working with the men." He turned to one of the monsters next to him. "Thomas, are you and the men going out this afternoon?"

"Yes sir, we are."

Aeyden turned back to him. "Hue, you are to go out with them."

"What about the prisoner?" Hue needed to know if he would see David. "Am I still in charge of bringing him his food and water rations?"

"Yes. As you said, you're not a kid anymore." Aeyden turned back to the map he was studying. "You will handle both jobs." There was a pause. "I hope you aren't still standing there? I told you what I expect you to do, now do it before I decide I don't need you anymore." Aeyden grabbed his gun and turned toward Hue and Thomas.

They knew what would happen if they stayed around. Aeyden wouldn't hesitate to kill them. Dying wasn't high on Hue's list for the day. He promised Lena he would be home before dark, it wasn't going to happen if he let Aeyden kill him. He was the one who would do the killing if there were any killing to do.

After going to the kitchen to get a plate of food Hue went to find David. He needed to talk to him and let him know they were going to get him out.

They were holding David in the inner cell. The cell itself was a glass room with a barred door. With it being glass anyone who wanted could watch everything in the cell. He would have to be careful. He needed to get close to David. He had to talk to him without anyone else knowing what he was doing.

A giant zombie stood at the entrance. He was the keeper of all prisoners.

"Where have you been, boy?" hissed the giant. "I have had to feed this one myself and you know how much I hate it."

"Sorry, I'm here."

"Good," the giant tossed Hue the keys and stepped aside to let him through.

It was easier than he thought it would be. He even had the keys. Was he going to have free reign with the prisoners? Hue needed to play it cool, he didn't know if this was a test from Aeyden or not. He would tell David as much as he could without being too obvious.

"David," Hue said in a hushed tone, knocking on his cell door. It seemed like the right thing to do, even though Hue could see David.

"I'm not hungry," David's stomach growled loud enough for Hue to hear.

"Listen, I don't have much time, and I'm not sure who is listening to us. I know you might not believe me, but look at me and listen. Lena and I are going to help you get out of here. Lena told me to tell you she saw the fight and knows they took you from Rocco."

"Who are you?" David's narrowed his eyes. "I don't know any Lena's."

He opened the door. "My name's Hue." He held out his hand for David to shake.

"It's nice to meet you, Hue," David shook his hand "What kind of plan do you and Lena have?"

"No plan yet," Hue confessed. "It will be my job to bring you food every day. I think between the two of us we will figure something out. They aren't hurting you, are they?"

"No kid, they aren't." David drew his lips into a thin line.

"It's not kid," Hue smiled. "My name is Hue."

"Then, Hue it is." David grinned. "You're not like the rest of them."

"I'm glad you noticed." Hue smiled.

"Wait." David stepped back in his cell. "You're human."

"And you must be a rocket scientist; I told you I was here to help you. If I were a zombie, I would want to kill you not help you."

"So, do you act infected often?"

"Every day." Hue hated he had to put on this makeup, but he wanted to eliminate every zombie, and to do it he would need to play dead. "Listen, I'm going to teach Lena how to act diseased, or 'play' dead. I'll bring her in to see you as soon as I can get the okay. I wanted you to know you're not alone. We are here and we are trying to get you out."

"What about Rocco?"

"I don't know. I haven't seen him. Lena said she saw him the night they took you. He is alive."

"It's all I need to know." The wrinkles in David's forehead relaxed.

"I've got to go. Aeyden has a job for me," Hue said.

"Praying I'll see you again, soon."

"Thank you." Hue turned to leave. "I'll be back tonight."

"I'll be waiting for you." David chuckled. "It's not like I'm going anywhere."

Hue went in search of Thomas. He wasn't sure what the big job they were going on was, but he knew he had to let Thomas know he was with them. Hue was sure Aeyden would be questioning Thomas about him.

"I'm ready," Hue said, standing before Thomas. "I have taken care of the prisoner, and I'm here to help."

Thomas frowned. "You're coming with us to watch how we get things done, nothing more. Stay in the back, and for god's sake don't get yourself killed. Stay out of the way kid."

"Yes, sir." Hue didn't say anything else. He was thankful Thomas didn't want him in the action. Staying out of the way and safe were the two things Hue wanted to do. He was there to learn all he could so killing them would be easier.

Twenty zombies left camp heading for a small village. Hue was under the impression it was an abandoned village. He didn't recognize the men they were traveling with. He knew Thomas, but none of the other guys. They were different. These men were more like real zombies. Hue laughed to himself. These diseased didn't talk. They

143

even walked a little weird as a zombie might. He stayed back behind everyone a good ten, maybe twenty feet, but he wanted to stay in the front with Thomas. It was funny, he felt safer with him than he did back here with these stupid zombies. He knew Thomas didn't want him near him, so he stayed safe in the back like he was told to do.

Every house in the village had people in them. They were humans like Hue, not monsters. He crept around back to try to warn the people. He didn't want anyone to get hurt. He had cleared the humans out of three houses when it happened. He came around the front of the fourth house and heard a blood-curdling scream. His eyes locked on to a little girl's eyes. She had seen what Hue thought to be her father, beheaded. The look in the little girl's eyes would haunt him for the rest of his life. She hovered over her mother who was vomiting profusely. Hue could do nothing. He was too late. The man had died trying to protect his family, and nothing Hue could do would change it.

He stood frozen in time staring at the angel. He wanted to protect her from what she had seen, but couldn't. The girl's mother got to her feet, took the girl by the hand, and ran. Hue waited until they were out of his sight, then he gave in to his body, he knelt on the ground and puked. He couldn't believe the poor girl was going to have to live with the image of her dad forever. He wanted to cry, he wanted to scream, but he couldn't. He couldn't let the infected see him.

Compassion would be a sure sign he wasn't a zombie. Zombies didn't have any emotions but anger. If Hue had been a zombie, he would have been angry seeing the look in the little girl's eyes. He would have tried to kill her and her mother. The mere fact he didn't, would show Thomas and the other monsters he was human.

"Get it together," Hue whispered to himself. "You need to stay calm for Lena and David. You won't do either one of them any good if you get found out now." Hue stood to his feet. He wished he had a toothbrush. He couldn't let Thomas know he puked. Hue went into the house, rummaged around in the kitchen, and found some bottled water and a can of fruit. He opened the can and sat in the corner and ate it. He washed it down with the water. When he finished, he listened for the zombies, making sure they were nowhere around him.

He looked out the front door. They were heading back to camp. He needed to do one thing before he left. Hue walked over to the body he believed to be the little girl's dad and knelt next to him. He searched him for anything he could find which he could save for the girl. He vowed he would find her again and tell her how brave he had thought she was. The difference was this girl loved her father, and Hue was angry he didn't get to kill his.

He found it, a letter with the word Jezzy on the envelope. Hue didn't know what it was, but it looked important, so he kept it. The other thing he found was the wedding band on his finger. The symbolic object wouldn't do him any good now, but the girl might want to have it.

"Yes," Hue said to himself. "I promise you I'll find you one day, and give these to you."

With this said, Hue stood to his feet. He slipped the ring on his finger, folded the envelope, and slipped it into his pocket for safekeeping, then hurried to get back with the group heading back to camp. If he played it right, he would be back at camp, and feed David in time to arrive home to Lena before it was too dark. He didn't think it would be long before Aeyden would trust him with bigger jobs. He was determined to get in as tight as he could with the leader of the zombies, and then kill him.

"David," Hue almost whispered. "Are you awake?" He had hurried to the kitchen to get his food so he could get home.

"Yeah, I'm awake." David crawled over to the door.

"I brought you food. I'm sorry it's late."

"Don't be sorry." David scrunched his nose. "Are you okay?"

"I'll be fine." Hue tried to be strong. He couldn't get the girl's eyes out of his head. She would haunt him forever.

"I'm sure you will," David half smiled at him. "I'm a good listener. You don't have to wear the weight of the world on your shoulders."

145

"Thanks, man, I might take you up on it someday. Right now, I need to get home. I promised I would be home before dark."

"Will I see you tomorrow?"

"Yes, and every day until we get you out of here," Hue stood. "I'm sorry I have to leave you here. Maybe tomorrow I can stay longer. I'm going to try and bring Lena with me."

"I'll be here waiting for you Hue." David shoveled the food into his mouth. "Thank you for risking your life to help me. I appreciate it."

"Of course you will be waiting for me, you're in a cell you can't go anywhere." Hue chuckled, as he shut and locked the door behind him. Hue left the camp as quickly as he could. He didn't want Lena freaking out because it was getting dark.

Chapter 28

The days passed were long and the heat was harsh. Rocco had no idea where to find David. His food supplies were low and, it was time for him to get the wagon ready for a long trip. He modified it by adding bigger tires for rougher terrains. He also added rails to the sides and made shelves so he could haul more things. In the front, he added handles and a bar with straps to attach his bike so he could pull the wagon. When the upgrades were finished it was time for a fresh coat of paint. Rocco chose camouflage and named the wagon Hank the tank.

"Hank, are you ready? Oh, I agree. I think you need self-defense." Rocco hated being alone. The silence drove him crazy. Hank was all he had. He hammered nails inside the wagon so they stuck out on the outside like spikes. He painted a clear gloss over the wagon, protecting Hank from the elements. The final step was to attach the bike to the wagon. Hank was ready to go.

With the sun starting to set, Rocco put the bike and Hank in the garage. He locked the doors and went inside. In the kitchen, the calendar showed it was Thanksgiving. "Some holiday this turned out to be. I worked all day in the hot sun, and now I'm eating turkey soup without the turkey." He couldn't help but laugh. This wasn't how he had envisioned spending his Thanksgiving. David was the one who remembered all of the holidays. It didn't matter how little they had, he always made them special. He missed David a little more today.

Rocco closed his eyes. He thought of past Thanksgiving tables full of food and family. The fragrance of fresh deep-fried turkey filled the room. Freshly baked pies offset the smell of the turkey giving a sweet aroma in the air. The sounds of giggling girls and laughs of guys filled his ears. The football game was on in the background. Children played and chased each other as the adults made conversation.

148

He ate and remembered his family. He could see his mom cooking in the kitchen, with David's mom. Their dads were arguing about the football game. He and David were in his room watching the same football game and making bets on which team was going to score next. He could see Kyle running into his room begging him and David to play catch. Kyle wanted to play professional ball and he needed the practice. Rocco and David dismissed him and continued to watch the game. Tears filled his eyes with thoughts of too many things he regretted. Why didn't he play catch with Kyle? He would give anything to turn back the hands of time and throw the ball with Kyle one last time. He never got to tell him what an awesome little brother he was. He wasted the time they had together. He had to push the thoughts of Kyle out of his mind. He wanted only happy thoughts today. It was Thanksgiving and he wanted to be happy.

After eating, he took out a map from behind the closet door and placed it on the table. David had marked each house. It was marked empty or infected. He also marked where stores were and if they had anything left in them. Rocco got a phone book and looked in the yellow pages for gun stores and ammo stores. He looked through a few different cities, so he could mark them on the map. He remembered when David started collecting phone books from different cities. Rocco thought he was crazy. Now he could find lumberyards, ammo stores and other places they might need. How would Rocco survive without David? He couldn't help smiling as he remembered the day David started collecting phone books.

"You do know the phones don't work, don't you?" Rocco said. "Those aren't going to do you any good."

"I know, but I have a way to make them work. They will be running soon."

"Really?" Rocco was impressed with most of the things David had shown him. David was the one with the idea to use solar panels. It was also David who created their freezer. Rocco wished he would have paid a little more attention to the things David did.

"No," David laughed. "You would believe anything I told you, wouldn't you?"

"I know there's nothing you can't do if you put your mind to it," Rocco said, feeling a little silly for believing David could get the phones running again. "I have complete and total faith in you, David. If you tell me you can make it snow in July, I'll get my snow pants out."

"Faith," David turned and looked at Rocco. "I don't want you to put your faith in me, I'm only a man. You need to put your faith in God. He is the only one who can save our souls."

"It's not my soul, I'm worried about." Rocco knew David meant well. After watching his family slaughtered, he stopped putting his faith in God. "There's no hope for my soul, it's damned already. I'll put all my faith in you, brother."

"We need phone books so we can look find places of interest. Kind of like a video game where they point to where the ammo and guns are. We will need to get maps of all the cities around here. Then we can research the places we deem important," David explained to Rocco. "When we find the address, we pinpoint it on the map and know where every store, gas station, and the house is."

"This, my brother, is why you're the brains of this operation."

He folded the maps as he folded his memories, and placed them in his pack next to the door with his guns and supplies for the next day's trip.

In the morning he prepared the wagon and bike for the hunt. He knew he would have to go further away than normal. They had already looted all the nearby stores and houses. Taking out the map, he went over the route he was going to take.

Well, the route he hoped to take. With the roads overgrown with vegetation, he didn't know what roads he would be able to travel on. He put the map away and placed a rifle, shotgun, and an assault rifle on top of the wagon on the gun rack. Rocco wasn't taking any chances. On the front of the wagon, he made a place for his pistols. After loading the wagon, he filled his camel pack with water, got on his bike and headed off.

Time passed slowly as Rocco pedaled. The weather was chilly, but the workout had kept him warm. He stopped a few times to look at the map and to get water out of the wagon. Then it was back on the bike. He needed to get to his first stop before the sunset.

A few hours into the trip, it was time to rest. The tree leaves were bright yellows, reds, and brown. Where the sun hit them, they glowed.

"This is beautiful." He said. "I had forgotten how much I liked the changing of the seasons." He could see an old abandoned gas station.

Rocco unlocked the top rack of the wagon and grabbed his shotgun and a box of shells. Then he loaded the gun and put the rest of the shells in the side pocket of his pants. He was ready to go. As he got closer, he could see a sign on the window.

The road I travel is rough.
The star I was following shot off.
The path I seek is gone.
The time I can no longer count.
The space is full.
The emptiness is crowding.
The searching is found.
The lost are here.
The pain is under medication
The words are foreign
The dammed rest here
The life I had is the life I lost...

"Real encouraging," Rocco said as he pumped the shotgun. "Does this mean I'm not alone?"

He couldn't help hoping whoever wrote these words was still alive and human, not a monster. He wanted the companionship of another human. He wanted David but would take any healthy person.

151

The door was easy to push open. He walked in listening for any movement. When he heard nothing, he relaxed. He was a little disappointed there, but weren't any humans there, also thankful he didn't find any monsters. The gas station was a truck stop with lots of room. The only thing Rocco saw on the shelves were bottles of alcohol.

He shook his head no and continued looking around. He saw no food or ammo, nothing of any use. As he turned to leave, he grabbed a few bottles of vodka and put them in his bookbag, he didn't want to leave empty-handed.

A fist came toward him, but he blocked it with the bottle. It crashed against the wall. Vodka went sailing everywhere. Monsters surrounded him.

"Now you die," a bloody monster howled as he pulled bits of glass out of his knuckles.

Instinctively Rocco grabbed the top of the broken bottle and thrust it into the monster's throat. "Any more false predictions?" he asked. "I think I might have just sliced your carotid artery. I did learn something at the library," he laughed despite himself.

"Leave now, we don't want any more fighting." Another one of the diseased said, holding the body of the dead monster.

"He killed Pete! He needs to pay with his life," another yelled.

"Yeah, let's kill the rat," a third joined in. "Get him."

Rocco had slipped out amid the commotion. He pulled a bottle of rum off the shelf, opened it, and made a trail of rum from the store to where he was standing outside. "Fools, now you all die." He lit a match and flicked it on the rum.

The fire raced toward the monsters. Their eyes grew wide. As the fire reached the bottles of alcohol in the store, it died. The fire wasn't hot enough to make the other bottles burst.

"Well, it didn't work like it does in the movies." Rocco had to admit his disappointment. He looked forward to seeing the boom.

"Real life sucks?" Rocco reached for his pistols and headed back to the gas station. He needed to finish the job. They weren't going to let him ride off into the sunset on his bike as nothing happened.

They would follow him and kill him.

The monsters darted toward Rocco. "You guys are making this too easy."

He fired four shots and four fell. He put his pistols back and continued on his way to the ammo store. It was another hour before he got there. He hid his bike, grabbed a gun, and went to the door. With the doors locked and the windows boarded there wasn't much he could do. Thoughts of trying to shoot the lock or kicking in the wood crossed his mind.

If he did, he would forfeit the element of surprise. If there were anyone or anything in there, he wanted to surprise them. At the back of the building, there was a ladder, which led to the roof. Rocco decided this was his chance to make a surprise attack. He wasn't going to let the monsters surprise him. If he didn't get smarter, he would get himself caught, or killed.

Who would save David then?

The latch on the top of the roof had a lock on it. He had found his way in. All he needed to do now was to break the old rusted lock. With one twist, the lock broke open.

"No way did this just happen. Maybe the things in the movies do happen sometimes."

He sat on the roof and took a long drink of water. His mind raced with thoughts of the terrible things, which could be waiting below him. He had to go in. He hoped there would be no fighting. Just once, he wanted something to go right. He knew David would be praying if he were here. Rocco didn't see the use in prayer. He relied on his strength to get him through whatever was waiting for him.

He blindly opened the latch. It led to a ladder on a brick wall in a back hallway. It was dark, with no windows for light. Rocco's nerves twitched and his stomach tightened, his heart pounded. He couldn't shake the bad feeling he had. Lowering the gun, his eyes shut as his body tumbled to the ground.

Chapter 29

Rocco's eyes flickered open, only to see nothing. "Am I blind?" Rocco whispered. "Where am I?" He felt around him. There was only cold hard rock. "David! David! Are you there? Of course, you're not." His voice echoed against the walls. A musty smell filled his nostrils. "What am I doing?" Rocco whispered. "They wouldn't put David in the same cell as me."

Rocco sunk with his back to a wall. He still had his pack and water. He took a sip, but then spit it out. "What if they poisoned it?" *His mind raced. He wanted to know where he was, and why they were keeping him. Heck, who was keeping him here. There were so many questions and no one to ask them too.*

"We all have to die sometime," Rocco said as he closed his eyes. He could do nothing else. His throat was dry and he craved water. "If the water is poisoned hopefully, I die sooner than later." Rocco sipped his water again. He took in tiny amounts over an hour. He was getting bored. He hadn't moved from his seat on the floor.

"Where's a toilet, or do they want me to go anywhere?" Rocco felt around the cell for anything. He felt the door. He got a little excited, reached for the handle, but it didn't turn. He pulled with all his might but the door didn't budge, he was trapped. He found the corner of the cell and relieved himself. "I hope this room isn't on a slope or I'll be sitting in my waste. Rocco crept back to the other side of his cell. His stomach hurt; he was hungry. "I need some food. If you're not going to feed me then kill me."

He got no reply. Once again, he felt his way to the door and proceeded to beat it with his fists while he yelled to get his captor's attention. The door opened a little. "What? It wasn't even a locking door. Why hadn't he tried to push it? A little light filtered in. It was too bright for Rocco at first. He hurried and shut the door to get the light out of his eyes. He had been in the dark for a long time he needed to let his eyes adjust to the light. When they had adjusted, he could see he was in a hallway. When he fell off the ladder, he must have hit his head. He was thankful he wasn't, in fact, a prisoner, but felt stupid for not realizing he wasn't in a locked room sooner.

He opened the door all the way so he could see. He needed to find his gun. The gun lay right where he had peed. He couldn't dwell on it. He needed to make sure he was alone. He thought about all the noise he had made earlier and came to the conclusion he must be alone.

He retrieved his new improved gun and continued his journey into the light. He was in a gun shop and it was full. Anything he wanted to be was there for the taking. Rocco ran through the shop examining all the weapons and gadgets. This was the best shop he had ever seen. He couldn't believe it was all there and no monsters around to fight him. He was like a kid in a candy shop. Finding the supplied would help them fight the monsters.

His mind raced to David. He needed to continue his search for him. He would do two things. First, save David, and second eliminate the monsters. He would have no more mercy. No more letting them live. He would send a new message of fear. They would know if they come in contact with him, they would die, no questions asked. He would kill them just for being monsters. The sooner the world was rid of these creatures the better of the humans would be.

He made sure the place was secure and sealed so no one else could get in. The front was blocked off. Even if someone managed to make it through the front doors to them, it would appear to be empty. Whoever owned the store had done a good job of protecting it.

Had Rocco not gone in through the top, he would have passed by when he walked in?

There was a fake wall built to hide and protect whoever was inside. The windows were sealed in cement and bars. The doors were barred, chained, and locked. Rocco continued to look around the shop. There was a section with locks and took one so he could replace the one, which rusted away on the hatch.

In the hall, there were two other doors and a shelf a foot taller than he was. On it sat screw gun screws and sheet metal, along with a toolbox. Rocco took a few trips, but he got the sheet metal and tools on the roof and started to make a cover for the lock. He drilled and screwed the sheet metal to the latch. Then, with the overhang, he drilled screws at an angle to add three walls covering the lock like a box. He put everything back on the shelf and locked the latch. This was a good place to hang out. He went out to the bike and unloaded everything into the shop, leaving the wagon and bike outside.

This shop would be his home for a while. He could defend himself from anyone or anything with the guns and ammo. He liked how protected he was in here. Yes, this was his home away from home. Rocco locked the hatch from the inside to seal himself away from the outside world.

The shop was getting dark as the sunset. Rocco could see sunlight through crakes in the concrete which covered the windows. He still had one more room to look in. Rocco wanted to see what was behind the second door. He pushed the door but it didn't budge. He then turned the knob and still nothing. Out of frustration, he took out his pistol, pulled the trigger. The bullet ricocheted off the lock and hit the wall behind him.

"Oh God, I'm an idiot," Rocco yelled, and his heart raced.

He almost shot himself. The excitement of the day left him exhausted. He made a bed for himself in the hallway and slept.

Rocco awoke sore. His back hurt and his neck felt tight. His eyes took a few minutes to adjust to the sunlight. He stretched and went into the shop. There were still a lot of things he wanted to do before he continued his search for David. He took a large bookbag, which had a ton of pockets to store weapons, ammo, and other items of his choice.

He went through every aisle grabbing anything he thought was cool or felt he might need. By the time he finished, he had anything he might need to survive. He walked back to the backpacks and filled each one with survival sets of the basics: flashlights, batteries, handguns, bandages, alcohol, and ammo.

He had six bags of the same stuff inside and put them in the back room on the shelves. He wanted them so he could grab one and go if he needed to. Even with six bags full, the store was plentiful. He hadn't even put a dent in it. David was going to love this store.

Rocco lit a kerosene lantern and set it on the shelf in the backroom and went back to the gun cabinet. He opened the glass case where the handguns were and pulled out all of the Glocks. He had always wanted to own one, now was his chance. The store had the 17,19,21, and the 23 in stock with bullets for each of them.

After many hours of deliberation, he chose the Glock 19. He could have taken them all but chose only one. The Glock 19 was thin, accurate at long range and very comfortable to carry. This was a solid weapon and he felt it was a good choice. When he brings David back, he would switch out to another one, but for now this would be his.

He got a cot. Pillow. Sleeping bag. He was going to get a good night's sleep tonight.

He would continue his search for David tomorrow. Rocco stretched out on the cot; he couldn't help staring at the doorknob he had shot earlier. Something compelled him to the door. It called to him. He tried to shake the feeling, but couldn't. After a few minutes, he ran to the other room and grabbed a hatchet. Something behind the door wanted Rocco.

They were calling out to him to open it.

As he held the hatchet ready to swing down on the handle, he stopped. What would he find behind the door? *I bet it's a gravesite of the family who lived here.* Maybe they took their own lives so they didn't have to deal with the world. Rocco lowered the hatchet. The door was locked from the inside. Could there be someone in there? What if they thought he was a monster? What if they were hiding to save their own lives? He hadn't heard a word from the other side. He had to know what was behind the door. Rocco put the hatchet back into swinging motion and hacked away.

He beat at the handle with anger. Wondering if he would find something, of worth or a tomb.

Chapter 30

Someone once said history repeats itself. Rocco couldn't remember a time in history like this. A time where monsters roamed the earth slaughtering humans. They didn't eat people or anything like a zombie would. If they bit someone one of two things would happen. The person would either die or get the disease. Why would they want to exterminate the humans? He didn't have any answers. He knew he didn't want them to bite him.

When a person became infected, the sickness didn't hit all at once. They didn't sink their teeth into someone and they would magically become diseased. No, the disease worked like no other disease or virus. Some people could be around it and never get sick. Others could hide from it for years and get infected by someone simply sneezing and shaking their hand, but even then, it wasn't instant. One day a person could wake up and out of the blue, the virus hits them. First, their skin started peeling away from their body. After they looked like death, anger kicked in.

"I don't need anger issues." Rocco laughed. "I think I'm angry enough."

He couldn't imagine him, of all people, having a hormone boost to make him three times as angry as he already was. The world isn't ready for a diseased Rocco.

He didn't know what he would find but he had to look. He took another swing at the door. Everything within him was telling him to leave it alone. He couldn't get the little voice out of his head, the one urging him on. He had to know what was calling to him behind the door. He raised his arms over his head and hit the doorknob with so much force it broke into three pieces.

Finally, the door creaked open. With squinted eyes, he peeked around the door. It was too dark to see anything.

"Hello, is anyone there?" Rocco yelled as he took the lamp from the shelf.

Thankful he hadn't rushed into the room when he broke the knob, as it wasn't a room, it was the opening to a staircase. He held the lamp out in front as he took his first step into the darkness. A strange odor filled his nostrils. The stench wasn't of the dead. He paused, closed his eyes, and took a deep breath. He thought if he concentrated hard enough, he would be able to decipher the smells; he could not. He knew the smell was familiar, but couldn't place it.

"Anyone there?" Rocco yelled again drawing his pistol from his side and continuing down the staircase, still no answer.

On the last step, he stopped, scared at what he might find around the corner. He took a deep breath and released it steadying his pistol and his nerves. It was now or never. Rocco turned the corner. He couldn't help grinning. He set the lamp on a box to his right, and he put his pistol back in his holster.

Rocco was happy for the first time in a long time. At the back of the room was a desk with an old computer on it, an open box of Cuban cigars, and a bottle of Gewurztraminer. The year on the wine bottle was 2005 meaning it was over twenty years old. There wasn't much left in life to take pleasure in.

He'd have to take them when he found them.

These were pleasures Rocco was proud to take. He stumbled into a gated wine cellar filled with over a hundred bottles of wine. To the left were metal barrels. Rocco went over to them to investigate. With one whiff he knew what was in the barrels, and he knew what the smell was.

"Gasoline?" Everyone had said it ran out six years ago.

He unlatched the lid and lifted the cylinder cap and to his amazement, it was gasoline. He didn't know how well old gas would run in a car, but he was willing to try. If it didn't work in a car it would start a fire just fine.

"David," Rocco proclaimed at the top of his lungs. "To answer your question, all the gas in the world isn't gone." His smile left his

163

face. "I wish you were here with me." He needed to find a car and try the gas. He would no longer have to plan long trips to find food or water he could drive wherever he needed too.

To celebrate Rocco rolled the desk chair out and sat down removed the cigar cutter and a lighter, from the drawer. With one flick, he had a flame and enjoyed the cigar. His dad didn't smoke, but his grandpa did. The memories of his family filled his head. Flipping the glass over, he blew the dust off and poured himself wine. He hesitated, remembering how he acted the last time he drank. With the glass in this hand, he circled the wine around the inside of the cup. The sweet aroma filled his nostrils. This wasn't hard liquor; he would be alright. He took a sip. It was warm going down and gave him chills.

In the desk drawers, there were a few notes and note pads, he thought nothing of them. There was also a picture, a family of three, a father, mother, and a baby girl standing in front of the building he was in.

"I wonder what happened to you." He stopped his thoughts.

He wasn't going to let anything ruin the moment. He put the picture and the papers back into the desk and closed the drawer, then leaned back and relaxed while he finished the cigar and the wine.

Rocco puffed one last time, put the cigar out and traipsed upstairs. At the top of the stairs, he saw the six-book bags on the shelf and had a sudden urge to go home. He needed to refocus on what he had set out to do. His job was to find David and then rid the world of monsters.

Rocco packed his wagon with supplies and took the six bags. He would leave at first light. Traveling at night wasn't wise. The shop had been good to him, and he welcomed another peaceful night.

When morning hit, Rocco headed for home. He found random places to bury his backpacks, making sure if he needed them, they would be available. He marked where they were on the map so he wouldn't forget.

The ride home was uneventful. Life was looking better. He felt good. At the house, he unpacked the wagon, looked around making sure no monsters invaded while he was away. When he deemed it to be clear, he sat on the sofa. Being alone in the house-made him sad. He missed companionship. With nothing else to do Rocco started toward his room. He would welcome his soft mattress.

Tears filled his eyes as he passed David's room. As he turned away, the family picture caught his eye. He wasn't angry at his memories, this time he embraced them. His heart ached to have his family back. Again, he looked over toward David's empty room. He dropped his head, closed his eyes, and let his tears fall. He needed to pull himself together. There wasn't time for tears. He brushed them away.

This wasn't a time for him to feel sorry for himself, it was a time to find David. He couldn't let himself get derailed. He needed to stay focused on his mission, and not let his emotions get the best of him. He went to his room. David was out there and Rocco, more determined than ever, would find him. He wasn't sure when his thoughts turned into dreams.

In the morning he fell back into his routine. He ate nuts and an apple for breakfast. Then trudged to the living room to read a book. He jumped to his feet; the book fell to the ground. "What was I thinking? I had gas and I didn't try it on a car. The wine must have been good to make me forget about the gas. It's been like ten years since I have even seen gas. I happen to have it, smell it, touch it, and then I leave it behind.

"I didn't even take any with me. To think the monster murdered my family for a tank full of gas, and I left barrels of it. I know what my plans are for today. I'm going to go get me some gas, find a car, and go for a drive. I wonder if I still remember how to drive. It should be like a bike, once you learn how you never forget. I can't believe I'm going to drive a car today. This is going to be epic."

He grabbed a bag, packed it with supplies and started to go back to the shop. He decided to walk today. When he came to one of his spots he had placed a book bag he checked on them. They were still there. He was learning the path to the shop. He found a shortcut, which cut his travel time in half. He still scanned the areas for any monsters, not wanting any surprise attacks.

When he reached the shop, he unlocked the latch and entered. Heading straight for the basement. He looked around for a gas can. With no luck, he went upstairs to see if he could find anything to put the gas in. On an island in the front of the store, the shelf had a tag, which read:

"NO GAS NO CAN!"

"There was plenty of gas in the basement. I like this guy's sense of humor. It's kind of sick humor, like mine. I think if things were different, I would have gotten along well with this man."

The only thing he found was a bottle of wine. It was a large gallon size jug with one glass of wine left in it. He emptied the bottle into his glass. It was too good to waste. He cut the tip of another cigar, sat in his chair, and enjoyed himself again. Rocco dipped the wine bottle into the gas barrel, then went on a quest to find a car.

There had to be something in the town, he could drive. He walked to a neighborhood nearby and hoped to find a car with keys. He was in a once rich housing area. He saw a few BMW's and Honda's, but he couldn't find any keys for them. His plan wasn't working out as well as he had hoped. Rocco thought it would have been easier. It made sense the keys were not in the ignitions. They would be in the pockets of someone dead and buried, or a monster had them.

Rocco kept moving and checking every car for keys. He wished David were here with him. to hot-wire the car, Rocco didn't know-how. The sound of a tin can hit the ground echoed in his ears. With pistol drawn, Rocco went toward the house. A Doberman pinscher darted out across the yard. Holstering his gun, he kicked the front door open.

Lounging on the sofa thoughts of the dog rushed in his mind. Could it be diseased? Could animals get the disease? He didn't know but didn't think they could.

Rocco wished he would have stayed. He would welcome the company. Dogs are, after all, man's best friend, and Rocco wanted a friend.

Out of the corner of his eye, he saw the wine bottle on the table and remembered what he was doing in the first place. His mind was easily distracted. He had always been able to count on David to keep him on track. He grabbed the bottle and looked around the house. Since he was there he might as well see if they had anything he needed.

In the kitchen, he looked through the cupboards. There wasn't anything he could use. Rocco went to the garage. The area was clear of clutter and looked spacious, minus the car under a car cover. As he walked closer to the car, his heart beat faster. He hoped the car was as nice as the garage. He couldn't stand the suspense any longer. He grabbed the cover and pulled it off. His heart stopped. Sitting in front of him was a Lamborghini embolden. The car sparkled and shined even in the garage with bad lighting. The cover and the owner took great care of this car.

"Dang, I hope this will run off of this old gas. God, please let this start for me. Please, please." Rocco opened the door and the smell of the car was like new. "Wow still smells good. I wonder if the owner is still alive, upstairs thinking I'm a monster and he is hiding. No, he wouldn't be alive, he has no food in there. I don't care. I'm taking this bad boy if it starts. Please God, let it start for me."

He sat in the driver's seat and looked at the ignition to see if the key was in there. He didn't find the key. He found a few CDs in the glove box. He hadn't heard music in ages and wished he could listen to some. He got out of the car, looked around the garage and spotted a set of keys hanging on the wall.

I hope those are it.

He took a deep breath in and out then, said a quick prayer, which was more of a plea for the car to start. He turned the key and nothing. Rocco hung his head. He needed something to go right. A smile crossed his face. He didn't put any gas in the car. Darting back in the house he snatched the gas can and headed back to the car. After pushing the gas button to release the gas cap, he filled the tank.

This was the big moment. He flung himself into the driver's seat. With one turn of this key, his life could change. He had gas and with a vehicle, he could go anywhere. The key turned and the engine rumbled a little. He tried it a few more times giving it gas and then the rumble became a holler. His heartbeat was hard and fast. Hope rushed through his veins. Rocco put a CD in the player and opened the garage door.

He backed out of the driveway in a tail whipping spin, shifting to first, squealing tires and smoke everywhere. He smashed into second gear and was off. Third, fourth, fifth, and then sixth gear. Rocco was at speeds of 120 miles per hour. He headed back to the shop since it was getting dark and he only had a small amount of gas with him.

The bass in the car was banging and bumping, Rocco was in heaven. The car was in a desolate world. Reaching the shop fairly quickly, he parked the Lamborghini by bushes and covered it with a tarp. He went to the basement to sip a glass of wine and sleep. He would fill the car with gas in the morning before he drove her home.

When morning hit, he gathered a few more supplies and as much gas as he could. He drove to his house, but not before taking an hour joy ride. He parked the car in the garage and made a list of things he needed to do. First, he would have to stock the house with all the essentials. He needed meat. Before he could get the meat, he would need to figure out how to get the freezer running again. The garden was in sad shape, it would take a few days to get it the house back to par.

Rocco planted seeds, pulled weeds, and dug trenches. In a few short days, he started to see some growth. Although he hated it, he was getting used to being alone. He started to accept he would be alone until he died or became diseased. He didn't like either one of his choices. He hadn't forgotten about David. He didn't know where to start looking for him. The daily routine kept him going.

He had made a checklist of the things he had to do and things he wanted to. At the end of the day, he would look at his list to see what he had done. It made him feel accomplished when he checked things off it as if he had something to live for. The first two items on his list always remained unchecked.

Number one, find David. Number two, kill the diseased.

Chapter 31

"**Y**ou can argue with me all you want to Hue," Lena stated. "I told you, you aren't going if I don't go with you."

"What if we get caught?"

"Then we get caught together." Lena wasn't going to back down on this one.

She had been putting on the makeup just like Hue did for a few weeks now. It felt natural to her, not awkward. She perfected how to walk and talk as if she was one of the monsters. She was ready to go with him to camp. In her mind, it was now or never.

They could not wait much longer to get David out back to safety. Hue was in good with Aeyden, he could explain Lena away if he needed to. She had to see David. She would need his help to get to Rocco and devise an escape plan.

"Hue I'll be fine," she said after a long silence. "You don't need to protect me."

"Fine," Hue stomped his foot and crossed his arms. "We need to go. Stay with me," he snapped as they started walking toward camp. "I don't know why Aeyden is watching my every move. I can't let him know I left." He glanced over at Lena. "I don't want anything to happen to you."

"Hue, I'm the adult, it's my job to worry about you."

"Go ahead and worry if you want to." Hue didn't want to admit it, but he liked it when she worried about him. He felt special like he belonged to someone. "I'm a big boy. I can take care of myself." He had been learning all the inner circle things about Aeyden, like when he ate his meals and where he slept at night. He was gaining the knowledge, which would help him when it was time to eradicate the zombies and become the zombie slayer.

Lena kissed the top of his head. "I think I can take care of myself, too."

"Seriously," Heat rushed to his cheeks. He was trying to become the zombie slayer and she was treating him like a baby. He ignored her comments. He had to stay focused. "I have it all set. You're going to be the maid. I have you scheduled to clean the cells. David is the only prisoner on this block, so you will have all day to talk to him. The giant isn't going to be there today I'm taking his spot."

Hue was proud Aeyden trusted him enough to take charge of the prisoner all day. This showed him Aeyden had faith in him. He wasn't sure why having Aeyden's approval mattered to him at all, but it did.

"I'll do my best. Did I tell you I'm proud of you?"

"Yeah, but you can say it again."

"I'm proud of you Hue. You have proven you can handle yourself, but if it is okay, I would still like to take care of you."

"I wouldn't have it any other way." When they reached camp, Lena followed Hue into the kitchen to get food for David. Hue got a cleaning cart ready for Lena. He was on edge. It was okay when it was just his life he was risking, but he wouldn't forgive himself if anything happened to Lena. What would he do if something went wrong? He would fight every zombie here to keep her safe.

"I'll stand guard at the gate," Hue said to Lena. "You take the cart and go in and talk to David. You will have a few hours so make sure you talk to him about everything. I don't know if I'll be able to get you another huge chunk of time like this again."

"I could kiss you right now."

"Don't," fear gripped Hue's soul. "They will know you aren't one of them."

"I know kiddo."

"Stop talking," Hue was getting anxious. "Zombies don't make small talk." She silently followed him.

"Get in there before someone sees you." Hue sighed. He had gotten Lena in to see David.

171

Chapter 32

Lena pushed the cart into the tunnel, making sure she walked just like Hue had taught her. Her heart pounded against the walls of her chest. She was almost there. David was at the end of the tunnel. What would she say to him? She didn't even know him. How could she explain she was a stalker and not have him freak out? She would have to figure it out fast. Reaching the end of the tunnel, there was no turning back.

She could see David sit and scoot closer to the door.

"David," Lena spoke softly. "I know you don't know who I'm, but trust me when I say I'm a friend."

"Lena?" David questioned. "Is it you? Hue said I should be expecting you."

"It's me."

David moved away from the door as she opened it. "The kid thinks the world of you."

"The feeling is mutual, he's a great kid," Lena said. She started her cleaning while they talked. She wasn't sure if Aeyden would inspect her job or not.

"Don't get freaked out, but I have been watching you and Rocco for a long time, months. I'm not a freak or anything, I was trying to determine if you were good guys or not. I was going to come and talk to the two of you the night they took you." Lena looked at David. "I did manage to take out one of the monsters before they got you. When I realized they had taken you, I followed them. I wanted to know where they were keeping you so I could rescue you."

"Is Rocco okay? Does he know I'm alive?" David asked.

"I don't know. I have tried, but haven' exactly seen him. I mean I have seen him, but I have not talked to him. What am I going to do, knock on his door and say hi I'm Lena? I've been stalking you, and I want you to know, David's alive?"

174

David laughed.

"Yes, it's what you say. He would understand it better than anything else. Rocco's a real straightforward hot head. You need to get straight to the point or he might explode."

"I'll keep it in mind."

Lena and Hue spent their days with David and at night, Lena tried to get to Rocco. Although she hated leaving Hue home alone, they had no choice. She needed to get to Rocco. Hue had learned why Aeyden wanted David alive. He wanted him to star in the games. Aeyden had a sick, twisted sense of humor. He devised a game to put human against human. It was never the same game twice.

Sometimes it was as simple as a race, but it always ended the same. The winner would kill the loser, and if he refused, Aeyden was there to finish them both off. Aeyden once told Hue the games brought his men closer together and gave them a reason to bring humans in alive. After Aeyden interrogated the prisoners, they competed for their lives.

David had escaped death twice. Both times his opponent died before they commanded him to kill them. They had reserved him for the big game, the tournament wherein the end all humans were fated to die. The monsters named it the big purge. All the prisoners would die, leaving the prison freed for the next batch of humans.

Lena brought the cleaning cart into David's cell. "Hue and I are thinking we need to get you out of here soon. Aeyden is planning something big and I'm afraid it includes your death." Lena turned and looked at David. "I'm going to go tonight to talk to Rocco. I know I have gone many times and he hasn't been home, but this time will be different. If he isn't there I'll stay until he gets home. I need you to keep Hue safe for me while I'm gone."

"How? If you have not noticed I'm kind of in a prison cell here."

Lena sat next to the cart. "I'll leave your cell unlocked. If you hear anything go help him. I couldn't stand it if anything happened to him. He's been through enough in his life." She desired better than the life they led to him.

"You don't have to worry about Hue, I'll take care of him. You make sure you take care of Rocco for me. He isn't always the easiest person to get along with."

"I think I can get around it," Lena remembered how she felt every time she stalked him. Rocco was the one she thought was dreamy. She hated to admit she was looking forward to talking to him. She had a good feeling about tonight. She needed to get Rocco so they could get David out of the prison.

"When you talk with Rocco you need to make sure he doesn't try to storm this place like a mad man."

"I have an idea," Hue said, standing in the doorway.

"Fire away kiddo," David said.

"When Lena gets Rocco here, you lure the guard to the cell, take him out and I'll lead Rocco to you. We will take the zombies by surprise. Lena, you need to make sure Rocco has guns. I'll take as many of the bullets out of as many guns as I can here. I think we can do this if we stick together and follow the plan."

"I'm impressed." David laughed. "You have this all planned out."

"It's all I have been thinking about," Hue confessed.

"I hear you," David said. "Thank you for what you have done for me so far."

Hue nodded.

"Hue," Lena said. "Are you sure you won't stay here with David. I don't like the thought of you home alone. You never know what is out there at night."

"Right, and I'm so much safer in here in a camp with hundreds of zombies." Hue said sarcastically. "What do you think is out there, stalkers like you?" He chuckled.

"It's not funny. I need to know you're safe."

"Yes mother," Hue mocked.

"Good boy." Lena realized she did sound like a mother hen. She couldn't help herself. "I hate you're right." She gave in. "We can't have Aeyden getting suspicious of you. We need to make sure everything

176

stays the same until I get Rocco back here." She turned to David. "You don't let anything happen to him."

"He's safe with me."

"Rocco will be safe with me." There was another pause before she turned to go. "Be safe David." Lena left camp and waited for Hue at their designated meeting place. She always left an hour before him. This gave her time to rest while she waited for him before they made the long walk home.

"This is it," Lena said to Hue as she got ready to leave the house. "I have a good feeling about tonight. I'm going to talk to Rocco."

"Be careful," David said. "He's the type of guy who shoots first and asks questions later. I don't want anything to happen to you."

"I'll be okay." She put a jacket on and turned toward the door. "I'm not going to lie to you. I'm a little scared. If I don't make it back tonight, don't come looking for me." She looked at the boy sitting on the couch. He was so young to have this much responsibility.

"I know we have been over and over this. I'll go to the camp like I do every day. If Aeyden asks about you I know nothing. Lena, I don't think anyone at camp has made the connection between the two of us. We come and go at different times. I'm going to be fine. I know even if it takes a few days you're going to be okay too. We need to stick to the plan; David doesn't have much longer. Aeyden is planning the big tournament. He is waiting for one more human."

"Be careful, I worry about you."

"I'll be waiting," Hue said in

"I love you." Lena leaned over and kissed his forehead. "You be safe."

"I love you too," Hue said as Lena shut the door behind her. She was off in search of Rocco.

Chapter 33

There was a knock on the front door. Rocco jumped, startled at the sound. He had been sitting in the living room reading an old newspaper. He set the paper on the end table and with caution got to his feet.

"I didn't know death started knocking before it came in. At least he had the decency to knock."

Rocco chuckled as he grabbed his shotgun from the coffee table and headed for the door. He took his time trying not to make any sound. He didn't want to scare who or whatever might be there. No one had knocked on his door in years, which gave him an uneasy feeling. He paused for a second, thinking he might have imagined it.

It wasn't the case. This time, they banged harder. He wasn't sure if he should see who it was or just shoot. When he got to the door, he lifted the shotgun. He would shoot first and ask questions later. The monsters knew where he lived. This could be a trick.

"Rocco," a female voice said. "I'm kind of freaking out here alone, open the door. Please, Rocco let me in." The voice continued to beg. "David said if I told you I was human, you would let me in. He said you would either let me in, or you would shoot me. Please don't shoot me."

A flood of emotions filled Rocco's heart. She could be diseased or just a killer. He slumped back to the wall next to the door and took a deep breath. She was probably diseased, he told himself. He needed to be strong and not fall for this trick. He grabbed his gun again and aimed it at the door.

"Let me in before the monsters see me." The female's voice echoed from behind the door again. "For God's sake, don't shoot me. David said if I knocked, you wouldn't shoot. He said monsters don't knock. Please don't make me stand out here much longer"

After a long pause, she spoke again. "Rocco, please don't shoot me. I don't want to die."

Why couldn't he tell whether she was playing him or if she was telling the truth? He crept outback and circled to the front of the house to see if it was a trap.

"I know you're in there. Let me in, you bully." Lena stood and pounded harder on the door. "I know you aren't one of them and I need your help. No, David needs your help. Please don't leave me out here to die."

Rocco stopped.

She has been watching him; he thought she might be a freak. She might be a handful. He looked around the corner to see if there was an entourage of people waiting for him. To his surprise, there was no one there. He continued to the front of the house and peeped around the corner to observe the voice.

She stood there alone yelling at the door. He thought he was safe. Before she had time to comprehend what was going on Rocco leaped and tackled her to the ground. He had his revolver pointed at her head and he looked at her. She was one of the most beautiful women he had ever seen. The tears in her green eyes glistened in the moonlight. This was all too much for him. He must be dreaming.

Dropping his gun, he stood to his feet and walked into the house. There was no way any of this could be real. She was gorgeous. Rocco slapped himself and looked out the window where he tackled her. He wasn't surprised she was gone. He went to the kitchen to get a drink of water. How could he have thought any of this was real? He turned around and stared deep into her eyes.

"Is this the way you treat all your guests Rocco?"

Rocco's glass crashed to the ground.

"I must be dreaming." He walked to the living room and sat on the couch. He closed his eyes and took a few deep breaths. "Wake up," Rocco repeated a few more times, as this woman walked into the room and sat next to him.

"You're not asleep." She smiled at him. "I'm Lena."

181

He couldn't bring himself to say anything. *How could this be happening?* Her voice was soft and soothed his spirit. She was amazing and everything he could have ever dreamt of. He had lifelike dreams, but this one felt real. She said something about David. Did she know where he was? He needed to find David.

Warmth filled his body as he looked at her. If this was a dream, he wanted to kiss this angel. He lifted his hand to her head and brushed her hair off of her silk face. She felt real. He longed for her to be real.

Her body shivered at his touch, her face flushing. She opened her mouth, but no words came out. She leaned in closer, meeting him as his lips brushed against her forehead.

Her soft skin felt like silk under his lips. His lips ran across her cheek, and fire surged through his body as their lips touched. This was perfect. Rocco opened his eyes and stood.

Lena smiled again.

When he realized he wasn't dreaming, he jumped back.

"I'm sorry." What else could he say? He hadn't even met the girl before and he was kissing her. Even though he said sorry, he was not.

"Don't apologize." Her smile grew. "I liked it too."

"If I'm not dreaming then I must be dead," Rocco said.

"You're very much alive." Lena stood, reached both hands to Rocco's face. She kissed him again.

"After this kiss, you want me to believe I'm not dreaming, or dead?" He raised one eyebrow.

"It's what I'm saying."

"If this is the case, I'm the luckiest man in the world."

"I'm not complaining, but this isn't why I'm here. I'm here because David needs you."

"What," Rocco grabbed her shoulders. He had forgotten about David. She knew where he was.

"You're hurting me." Lena wiggled under his arms.

"Sorry." Rocco let go of her. He sat on the couch again. "David's alive?"

"Yes. Which is why I came here. We need your help."

182

"Wait, how do you know?" He was suspicious, thinking it might be a trap after all. He had to admit he liked it if it was.

"I saw them take him the night you were fighting the dead."

"What? The dead, is what you call them?"

"Yes, they are dead to me. They fight and kill, for what? They are monsters all of them. Even the kids are sick and kill. Their anger's outrageous. The things they do to the ones who aren't diseased is shameful. It's sick, repulsive, and inhumane. They tried to...."

Tears filled her eyes. She swallowed as they flowed over her cheeks.

"How did you stop them? How did you get away?" Rocco paused; he was starting to feel uncomfortable.

He didn't like the way the conversation was going. He couldn't decide if he were angry someone would try to hurt her, or if he were sad the whole thing might be a trap. He could feel the fire starting to burn within him. He didn't understand his feeling, they were clouding his judgment. For all he knew, this chick was a trick of the enemy. He smiled again, a welcomed trick.

Stop it, he told himself. He needed to keep his mind clear. Think only of David. If the girl knew anything to help, he needed to listen. This wasn't about him, it was all about David.

Rocco couldn't help looking at Lena. He wished he was kissing her again, or... he stopped his mind right there. She knew about David and nothing else mattered. He couldn't let his feelings turn this into anything else.

"With this." Lena reached down and grabbed a gun strapped to her leg.

"So is this where you shoot me?" Rocco knew this was too good to be true. It was like a love scene in the movies, where the gorgeous girl magically appears to help the hero. He wasn't a hero and they weren't living in a movie. Rocco couldn't think of a better way to die.

"Why would I shoot you? If I wanted you dead, I could have killed you weeks ago. I carry this for my protection. Do I need to protect myself from you?"

"Only your heart." Rocco couldn't believe what he had said. *Could he be any cornier?*

"I think it's too late."

"Do you know how to use it, or is it just for show?"

"I would show you, but I don't want to waste the bullets. I'll save them for someone else."

"I guess you would have to know how to shoot in today's world." Rocco started to feel at ease. It was getting easier talking to her. "You saw the fight me and David had with them?

"Yep. I had been watching the two of you for a few weeks..."

"What? Why?" Rocco interrupted her.

What he wanted to know was why it took her so long to tell him about David. He was thinking of all the long lonely nights he had spent since the monsters took David.

"Let me finish. Keep the questions for later."

"Sorry." He leaned back on the couch pillow and listened.

"Like I was saying, I had watched you two for a few weeks to see if you were part of the dead, or not. The night they took David I was going to come and talk to you. I heard shooting and took cover in the woods. There wasn't much I could do without being killed. I couldn't risk coming out shooting. You wouldn't know I was one of the good guys and you would have shot me." Lena stood and started to pace.

"The leader of their army's name is Aeyden and he is as nasty as they come. I waited and watched. I did manage to kill one of them for you. When they left, I followed them back to their camp. It's where David is." She paused, stopped pacing, and met his gaze. "There's a boy, his name is Hue. He knows how to look like the diseased, but he isn't sick. He tricked the monsters, so he can work at the camp. He got me in to see David. I was able to talk to him and tell him I would help get him out. He told me I needed to tell you he was alive." A smile brightened her face. "He told me to be careful. He said you could be dangerous. He was right. I should have been better prepared. You did throw me to the ground like a linebacker."

Lena grinned, then took a deep breath. "David wants me to tell you all about the camp. He said you would help me figure out how we are going to get him out without getting us, and him, killed." She paused, lowering her gaze. "He also said I can't let you go in guns blazing. We need some sort of a plan before we go."

Rocco stared in disbelief. This morning it was just him against the world. He was trying to figure out a way to find the camp and David. Now he wasn't alone. This girl claims to know where they are keeping David.

Who was she and why was this the first time he has heard of her? Better yet, why was she helping them, risking her life for them?

None of it made any sense to him. On a positive note, she hadn't killed him yet.

"I don't have any secret word to tell you to help you believe me." Lena sat next to him. "All I have is my word. I don't know what else to say. Hue and I are willing to risk our lives to help you and David. I can't help you if you don't trust me."

"I don't know anyone named Hue. Why would he help us?"

"He's a kid with a heart to help. David said you will know it was Hue if you look in his eyes. I'm not sure who Kyle is but David said Hue had Kyle's eyes. He said you would understand. Maybe I do have a secret word maybe it's Kyle, I don't know. I do know I want you to believe me and not freak out and try to kill me again."

Rocco sunk a little further into the couch cushions. Everything she said sounded like something David would say.

"Who's Hue again?"

"He's a kid who has been helping us. It's hard to explain. His dad was a monster and he played like he was too, he showed me how. Without him, I would have never gotten in to see David."

He shook his head trying hard to understand what she was telling him. How could someone play dead, better yet, why would they want to? Why would a kid who he didn't know want to help him? There was something about her story that didn't make sense to him. How could he go on faith and believe her? How could he risk not trusting her? If she knew where David was, he should follow her.

"Listen, Rocco, I told David I would find you and tell you. This isn't the first time I've been here. You're a hard man to track down. I have tried several times to tell you. Every time I looked for you, you were nowhere to be found. I even slept in your house thinking you might come home, but you never did. I came one night and the house was destroyed.

"I told David what the house looked like and I couldn't find you. He wasn't surprised and said, 'He's alright, it was probably him. Keep trying to find him. I don't want him to do anything stupid.' So I kept trying and here I'm"

"I have been doing stupid things like David feared." There was a long pause. Rocco wasn't sure what he should say or do next. They sat in silence for a long time. "Can I see him?"

"I'm not sure it's a good idea."

"You come in here and tell me David's alive and needs me to rescue him. You tell me you know where the monster base camp is and then you tell me I can't go see him. What kind of a fool do you think I am? Is this a trick to get to me?"

"You've got to be kidding. David didn't tell me you were a jerk. I risk my life to help David. Heck with it, I risk a kid's life and all you can do is think we're out to get you." She stood. "Forget it. We will get David out ourselves. You can thank me when he is home." She stormed out the front door. "I don't know what I was thinking about kissing you. I guess I thought you would be my knight in shining armor, I was wrong."

He hesitated for a brief second before going to the door. Everything inside of him was saying he should believe her. Everything but the little voice. The voice saying if he followed her, he'd die. It was a trap. If David were alive, somehow, he would have contacted him. Rocco shut the door.

186

He couldn't let her go. *What if she were telling the truth? What if she was who David was sending? When he opened the door there was no sign of Lena or anyone else. What had he done? Had he pushed the only person who could lead him to David away?* He grabbed his keys and headed for his car. He needed to find her and apologize. It didn't take long for him to reach her. He saw her duck into a house when she heard the car. He turned the engine off and followed her.

"Lena," he whispered. "I'm sorry. It's not safe for you out here. Let me at least take you home."

"I'm safe enough. I'm probably safer here than with you." She swung a pan at his head.

His head pounded when he opened his eyes.

"I come here to save you and this is the thanks I get?"

"Save me? I don't need anyone to save me. I'm done risking my life for you and your friend. All I have tried to do is help you. I get it you don't want my help. You don't need to tell me more than once."

"Whoa, slow down a little." Rocco sat rubbing his head. "I came after you to apologize. I came to thank you for helping me and David. I'm ready to stop being a jerk and listen."

"Really?"

"Yes."

"Maybe it's too late. Maybe I've decided you are a jerk and I don't want to help you anymore." She bounded for the door.

"Wait," he rubbed his head. "I said I'm sorry."

"Oh, I get it." She stopped and turned back towards him. "Because you say you're sorry I'm supposed to forget everything you said?"

"There is nothing more I can say." He pulled his keys out of his pocket.

The corners of Lena's mouth slightly rose. "Were you driving a car? A real car?" She darted out the front door to check out the car. "You have to be kidding me, it's a Lambo. Wait, you have gas." She was bouncing around laughing.

"Yeah, I know, I'm awesome,"

187

"I want to ride in it."

"My pleasure. I can take you anywhere you want to go."

After they drove around for a little bit Rocco let Lena drive. She took him to her house. She was hoping Hue would be there. She thought if Rocco could talk to him, maybe he would believe her about David.

Hue wasn't home. Lena showed Rocco how Hue played dead. He seemed quite impressed by it all. She showed him some of her family pictures. They talked and got to know each other a little better. It was getting late. Hue still wasn't home. Lena assumed he'd stayed at camp. She wasn't worried about him. If she didn't hear anything from him tomorrow, she would start to worry.

After a long debate and a few threats from Rocco, Lena agreed to go back to his house and stay the night. She left Hue a note on the table and told him she was going to be with Rocco. If he got the note, she asked him to write back before he left for camp again.

She stayed in Rocco's room. He knew it was crazy. One of them could have stayed in David's room. Rocco couldn't picture anyone but David in there, he grabbed a blanket and curled in a ball on the couch.

Chapter 34

Lena lay in Rocco's bed thinking about her day. She liked the way she felt when she was in his arms. She thought about her future. Life for her and Hue would change after they got David out. Lena hoped Rocco and David would be a new part of their lives. She couldn't picture her life without them in it. She had gotten to know David in their long talks and she wanted to get to know Rocco better. She liked what she had known about him so far, she could only imagine it would get better as time went on.

She replayed their first kiss over and over in her mind. She liked the way she felt when Rocco touched her. She had never had electricity flow through her as it did with just one touch from this man. She dreamt of a different world. A world where her parents were still alive. One where she and Rocco could be husband and wife. She knew her mother would love Rocco but she wasn't sure about her dad.

She could picture her dad saying, "Lena I think you can do better than this hothead. You need a man you can settle down with. Does he have a job? Did he go to college? What are his plans for the future?" Lena laughed at her thoughts.

Plans for the future. Did they even have a future? Jobs. No dad, he doesn't have a job. No one has jobs anymore, it is a, fend for yourself kind of world. She smiled.

"You would like his car," she said aloud. "I'm sure he would let you drive it. I wish you were here Daddy; I miss you and Mom." Lena rolled over and let her tears fall. She let the many different emotions flow out on her pillow.

She needed sleep before their lives changed forever.

Chapter 35

The next few weeks were full of talking and planning. Lena and Hue brought messages to David from Rocco. They didn't think Rocco would do well at playing dead so he didn't go to see David. Rocco and Hue never met either. When Hue was home, Rocco was out doing things for the rescue. David didn't want Rocco to storm the camp. Everything had to be planned out down to the last detail. They would have only one chance to infiltrate the camp. They had no room for error. Lena and Rocco spent every second she wasn't at camp together.

The sparks they had when they first met escalated.

Rocco woke early. He had a lot to do if they were going to attack an army with four people. Four people if they counted David, who wasn't much help, considering he was the one behind bars. Rocco drove to the ammo store and got everything from pistols to bazookas. The war ahead was one he wasn't willing to lose.

Lena gasped as Rocco loaded the back of the Lambo with the huge gun. "Where on Earth did you find whatever that thing is?"

"It's a Bazooka. I'm going to use it to get those sick, twisted demon-infested mother-"

Lena held up her hand. "No need to finish. I get the gist. Did you forget we aren't going in Rambo style?"

Rocco didn't respond to Lena, nor did he make eye contact with her. He wasn't taking any chances. This was their only shot. Failure wasn't an option. "Is there anything I can do?" Lena leaned against the car.

"Yeah, how about be quiet already," Rocco turned and grinned at her. He looked into her eyes; he could get lost in them forever. He shook his head, he needed to stay focused. There would be plenty of time for him and Lena after they accomplished numbers one and two on his list. Freeing David and killing the monsters.

"Did you finish the map of the base or whatever you call their hell hole?"

"Let me get this straight." She followed him into the house. "I need to quit talking and finish the hell hole map." Her eyes narrowed as she sat at the table and crossed her arms in front of her.

"Yes, it better be one hell of a map." Rocco gave her a quick hug. "I'm not trying to be a jerk; I just don't want to fail. We can't fail."

"You're forgiven." Lena returned his hug.

Rocco walked back and forth carrying supplies to the car. Lena continued working on the map. She was happy and felt a strong connection to Rocco. Lena couldn't help herself. She was falling in love. Rocco wasn't the troubling monster David said he might be. He was gentle and kind. She knew he had a temper, but he would never hurt her. She hadn't felt so safe in a long time.

After the death of her mother and her father, loneliness threatened to overwhelm her.

She shuttered at the thought of the monsters. There were things they had done to her she never shared with anyone. The closer they were to this battle the stronger her memories grew. She couldn't stop them from flooding her mind. It happened years ago when she was out looking for food. It was the reason she carried her gun everywhere she went.

The monsters trapped her in a store. They told her she was the most beautiful woman ever made. They wanted her beauty and tried to cut off her skin to put it on themselves. They beat her and tried to rape her. Somehow, she'd escaped.

Lena pushed those thoughts out of her mind. She had her prince, her knight in shining armor. He would protect her and Hue. In her heart, she believed he would. She wanted to be happy and would think only happy thoughts.

"Are you alright?" Rocco slid his arms around her. "You don't have to be afraid. I'm here to take care of you."

She looked over at him. Tears rolled covered her cheeks. He dropped to one knee and wiped them from her eyes.

"I'm here to listen if you want to talk," he said softly. "I'm here, even if you don't want to talk." He smiled and hugged her close.

"I'm scared." She whispered. She fell into his comforting arms.

"You don't need to be. I'll protect you from the monsters."

"I know you will." She paused again looking into his eyes. "Don't worry I'll protect you, too."

"What is it?"

"Please don't die," she blurted out. "Who's going to take care of you?"

"I'm not going to die. I tried a few times already. I think God has a sick plan to keep me alive in this miserable life."

"I don't know what I would do without you. I know we have to fight to get David back and it scares me."

"What scares you? Us fighting or getting David back?" Rocco asked with a grin.

She smiled back. "Thank you."

"I need to finish loading the car. When I'm done, how about dinner on the beach? I'll cook."

"I'm almost done. I'll start the veggies."

Lena returned to her map. She needed to make sure everything was correct. The slightest error could cost someone their life. When she finished, she made her way to the kitchen and started preparing dinner. Rocco joined her.

After dinner, they waded in the water and wrote their names in the sand. Life almost felt normal. Like the sunset, they headed into the house.

With the doors and windows barred and locked, they sat on the couch looking over the map, making sure they knew exactly where to go and what they were doing. Rocco leaned back and gazed at her A few weeks ago, he was sure he would go through the rest of his life, sad and alone, now he had Lena, and soon David would be with him.

"What?"

"I'm still trying to convince myself you're real. A few weeks ago I was convinced I'd live the rest of my days alone."

She reached out and laid her hand on his arm. "I'm glad we finally connected, too."

He held her gaze for several seconds.

She blinked, needing to break the spell of the moment. "Do you remember back when the world had television?"

"Yes."

"Do you miss it?"

"Sometimes, but right now no." He smiled. "I like sitting here talking to you. We have gotten to know so much about each other in such a short time. I don't think we would have if we would have had television or the internet."

Lena didn't respond. She agreed, but knew saying so, wasn't necessary. She sunk back into his arms and closed her eyes. The exhaustion from the day's work pulled at her.

"No, you can't leave me" Lena screamed.

Rocco gently shook her until she opened her eyes. "You're okay, I'm here."

She threw her arms around him and held him tight. "I'm sorry."

"There isn't anything to be sorry about. We all have our fears." He hugged her a little tighter. "Do you want to talk about it?"

After a long pause, she decided to share her dream.

"My nightmare has always been about my parents," Lena fought back the lump forming in her throat as she told him about the night, she lost her parents. "My mom was beautiful," she continued with her story. "I believe it's why they took her. She missed her parents and was afraid Rocco would leave her just as they did.

"I'm here for you. I don't know what else to say."

"You being here is enough."

The corners of her lips curved. She wished he could promise her he would always be there for her. After a long pause, Lena continued.

"There was a loud thump on the top of the hatch. I'll never forget, it was the first time I heard my dad cry. His voice was weak and

I knew he was dying. There's nothing I could do. I wanted to help him, but I didn't move. It wasn't long before I saw the red drops coming through the cracks in the hatch. My father's blood-covered me. He died and I couldn't do anything.

"One of the monsters yelled to leave him. They had what they wanted. They had my mom. I can only imagine the things they did to her. She will never be beautiful again. This is the night my life ended." She brushed the tears off her cheeks. "Promise me you'll kill me before you will let them take me."

Lena put her hands to her face.

"I don't think I can."

"Rocco you need to promise me." She sat. "I'm not kidding. You can't let them take me alive. They do horrid things to women if they have them alive. Please," she begged. "You have to promise. Rocco, promise me."

"I promise you I'll not let them take you. As long as I'm breathing, they won't get you." His words were not the comfort she was looking for. "We have all lost family. I'll promise you I'll get you David and the kid out of there safe. We will start anew the four of us. I'll never let them get you."

After a long silence, Rocco started telling Lena about the day he lost his family. He paused after he told her about Kyle and how much he missed his brother. He explained it wasn't he missed him more than he did his parents, but he regretted not paying enough attention to him

"Everyone has regrets. Things we would do differently," Lena said. "I think I would have liked your family. I wish I would have gotten the chance to know them."

She paused, debating whether or not to share her next thought. She plunged in. "David told me you were pretty wild."

"I was after my family died. David knew how to calm me. I thought I was cured until they took him. I went on a drunken suicidal mission and failed at every attempt. I wanted to die. I wanted to be with David and the rest of my family. No matter how hard I tried, I could not die. I couldn't succeed at anything."

"I'm glad you failed." She smiled again and rested her head on his chest. "I think you failed because someone up there knew I would need you. I do need you, Rocco."

"I'm right here." He held her close.

Lena said nothing.

There were so many things she wanted Rocco to tell her, but she knew he couldn't tell her what she wanted to hear. He would be there and protect her, but just like her father, he would protect her with his life if he had to.

She took comfort in knowing he was here with her.

Chapter 36

Morning finally came. The day they were going to rescue David had arrived. Breakfast was awkward, neither Lena nor Rocco knew what to say. Lena broke the silence.

"The kid with me, Hue, he lost his parents too. I need him to be safe. I need you and David to be safe. Rocco, I'm scared."

What could he say? He wasn't going to lie to her. Things might not turn out the way he wanted them to.

"I can promise you I'll do everything in my power to keep the kid, myself and David safe, and most of all you. I'll keep you safe." Her eyes clouded over. He imagined she was thinking about her parents again. "Listen, Lena. I didn't know your parents, but I can tell you if they died to protect you, they thought you were worth it. I'll have to agree with them. You are worth it."

Lena let her tears fall. "Thank you."

"I'm just being real." Rocco kissed her cheek. "You are more than worth it."

She gave him a quick hug and went into the kitchen.

He took the map from the table, and looked it over, studying everything Lena had written on it. They had known exactly what to do and when to do it.

Rocco had never met Hue, he wasn't taking any chances, David's life depended on their success.

Lena made lunch for the road. Everything was set they were ready to rescue David. A day Rocco thought would never come.

Once they were in the Lambo and heading to camp fear gripped his soul. His emotions were pumping through his veins; he was ready for the battle. All the weapons they needed were stashed in the back and Lena sat by his side. He was ready to take on the world, yet he was scared.

"Can you handle it?" Rocco asked Lena, who held the bazooka.

"Yes," she said, her voice steady and firm.

"Well," he chuckled, trying not to hurt her feelings. He had to pause, he was afraid he would laugh. "Whatever you do, please don't shoot the car. It took me forever to find gas and this baby." Rocco said as he tapped the steering wheel. "I like this car." He laughed.

"What? Why would I hurt your car?"

"You're holding it backward. If you fired it, you would blow us both to bits." He couldn't contain it any longer. "Just thought you might like to know."

"I thought it felt weird." Lena giggled as she struggled to turn the weapon around in the car.

"No, it's you who's weird."

"Not fair. It's not like I go around shooting Be-Zoakas all day."

"You're right you don't, because it's a BaZooka," Rocco said, drawing out the word trying to sound it out for her.

"Whatever. When the time comes for me to shoot this thing, I'll blow it to pieces."

"You're going to blow the bazooka to pieces or the target?" He couldn't stop laughing as tears streamed down his cheeks. He had found his soul mate in Lena.

How had he made it this far without her?

Lena punched him in the arm. "Stop laughing at me."

Once they quit laughing, they went over all the code words again. They went over the plans where they were to meet. They even had a plan as to what they would do if one of them faced anything they couldn't handle alone. Rocco wanted to make sure Lena was ready. Soon the car fell silent. The battle ahead sat heavily on them. It was time to focus if they were going to make it out alive.

Rocco had camped in his sites. The sky grew dark. Thunder sounded in the distance and far away lightning pierced the sky, but the rain hadn't started to fall yet.

"Why is it every time I fight these monsters it has to rain? My life's like a bad movie." He shook his head and turned to Lena. "Are you ready?"

"As ready as I'll ever be. Let's blow them to kingdom come

"Remember, I turn the car around, duck, and you fire."

"I got it."

"You'll do just fine." Rocco leaned over and kissed her forehead. "This is it, are you ready?"

She looked at him and smiled. "Ready."

Rocco turned the car so fast it started to tail whip. Lena closed her eyes tight.

Rocco ducked in the driver's seat.

"God help me," she whispered and pulled the trigger.

Complete success. Lena had done it.

There was a huge gaping hole in the wall. They didn't have much time before the monsters came to see what happened. Rocco stopped the car and handed Lena the weapons she would need. This was it. He would either come out with David and Hue or die trying to save them.

There was no turning back.

Monsters covered the wall shooting at them. Bullets were ricocheting off the car.

"We have a battle on our hands, Rocco," Lena said, as she took the M-16 and shot at the monsters on the wall.

"Yes, we do. Remember the plan and stick to it no matter what. Let's get David out of here."

Rocco fired at the dead who were trying to escape through the hole. He couldn't take his eyes off Lena or stop thinking how beautiful she looked holding the M-16. She must be sent from heaven just for him.

He had to get his head out of the clouds and back in the battle, but he didn't know if he could. *How could he stop thinking about her?* He needed to keep her safe. He leaned over and kissed her again. Bullets zoomed past them, and he stopped to kiss her. She was worth it.

"I'm coming back." Again, another kiss. He wasn't sure he would be back, but he was going to make every effort to.

"You better." She returned his kiss with one a little more passionate. "I'll be waiting." Another short kiss. "Are you sure you don't want me to go in with you? I can help."

"Yes!" He didn't want Lena anywhere near the dead. It was bad enough she was at their camp. She should be home waiting for him to come back with David. "Promise me you will stick to the plan. We have to. Lena, if we are going to get David out, we have to stick to the plan."

Rocco shouted as he ran to the hole in the wall shooting anything moving.

"I promise," Lena shouted after him.

Rocco was on the run shooting ducking and hiding in cover. He threw grenades, and jumped over crates and ran into buildings. He felt as if he were a character in one of the video games he used to play.

Finally, he got to an empty room. He had cover to look for the red circle made with lipstick. The circle was where they imprisoned David. Once he spotted the room, he crept to the window to get his bearings straight.

The window shattered and sent glass shards piercing his face.

Rocco cursed as He dropped his gun and ducked. Blood dripped into his eyes. He wiped his eyes with his shirt. He couldn't let this stop him. He was so close to David, too close to quit. He needed to stick to the plan, get David and rejoin Lena. He had promised Lena he would come back to her and it was one promise he intended on keeping.

"You're all dead. You have messed with the wrong guy." With a gun in hand, he started running again.

Chapter 37

David stood in his cell praying someone would unlock his door. He wanted to help his friend. His door should have been unlocked. He'd had an unexpected visitor the night before, and the monster locked the door behind him. From the sounds of things, Rocco was rushing in like Rambo to rescue him. He smiled at the thought. Rocco always did like to put on a show. He waited and listened for the cue from Rocco telling him he was near.

His heart raced. Was he going to get out of there? He had heard Rocco's war cry. It was the sign he was near.

Tears came to David's eyes. "Rocco I'm over here," he yelled.

He didn't expect to be this emotional. Why did he yell? He was the one not sticking to the plan. Hue would lead Rocco to David. He needed to do his part and let Hue do his. David took a few deep breaths to calm his spirit he had to stay focused. Today he would be with his family.

"Shut up," the guard hissed.

"Make me," David said taunting him. It was his job to keep the guard distracted. He tried to get him close enough to snatch his keys or maybe even make him mad enough to get him to unlock the cell.

The monster growled, stormed over to David, and spat at him. "You like it?"

"Loved it, but your aim sucks. Maybe try and hit me next time."

David moved toward the cell door. If he could get the monster close enough, maybe he could grab his keys. He put his face against the door. He needed to keep the guard's attention. He wasn't supposed to be here. They hadn't planned for him.

Aeyden had assigned extra guards last night as if he knew they were planning something. Hue should have been the only one guarding David, now the locked cell door trapped him. Things were not going according to plan. They were going to have to improvise. He held onto faith Rocco would find a way to get him out.

"I said shut up." The monster stepped closer to the cell door. David slid his arms through the bars and grabbed the guard's head. He smashed his face into the bars over and over again, until the guard fell to the ground.

"How do you like it?" David spat on him. "Rocco I'm in here," David yelled, once again forgetting to be quiet and not draw attention to himself.

Chapter 38

Guns fired and bullets flew.

Rocco ran toward David's voice. His heartbeat in a frenzy. He hadn't heard David's voice in a long time. Emotions played with him. He was almost there, when a baseball bat hit his shin, and stopped him in his tracks.

"You think you can run into my place and start shooting my people. Who do you think you are?"

He stood to his feet, surrounded by monsters. He didn't want them to know how scared he was. He had to stay cool. They thrived on other people's fear. He needed to buy time to figure out what he was going to do. It was time to wing it. Nothing they mapped out and planned, was working.

The one with the baseball bat yelled. "This is for my dad." He swung the bat again.

What was the kid talking about? Rocco focused on the bat. This was the same bat, which had hit his hand during one of his drunken rages.

"Look, kid, I'm sorry about your dad. In my defense, he attacked me."

"Yeah, he did," Hue said. "You're the one who kicked our door in." He paused. "You entered my house and you killed him. You killed my dad."

Hue narrowed his eyes and his face reddened.

Rocco stopped in his tracks. He remembered the night, it was the night he'd wanted to die. He'd lost his brother and wanted to join him. He hung his head, ashamed, and embarrassed by his actions.

"I'm sorry," he said again. "So sorry."

He had nothing else to offer the kid. He knew how the boy felt. The rage was the same he'd had when he watched his family die.

"I'm not making any excuse for this crazy world we live in. I was wrong in entering your house as I did, but he was infected like you guys are."

He paused.

The kid was talking to him. He looked infected but wasn't acting like it. Something was different about him.

"It's not an excuse, just the facts. I was drunk and your kind had taken my brother away. I wanted revenge, I wanted to die, I'm sorry kid. I wish I had more I could offer you, but I don't. My apology is all I have."

"I'm not infected," Hue yelled. "I need your help." The boy lowered his bat. His eyes met Rocco's. "I'm Hue. I'm sure Lena told you about me."

"Yes, she did," Rocco felt worse. He was not only killed the kid's dad, but he was the one Lena loved. He feared after all this was over, he would lose her. He wouldn't blame her. He couldn't think about it now. Getting Hue and David out of the camp alive was her only concern. They would sort out the rest of the mess later.

"Kill them both," another monster yelled. "We don't need none of them alive."

Rocco grabbed his pistol and started shooting. He ducked, turned, and got a hold of the kid, knocking him to the ground with his body. More bullets pierced the air over their heads. He reloaded and continued shooting.

"Kid, there's nothing I can do to bring your father back. If there was a way, trust me, I would. I would bring my family back too. I would bring everyone back. I can't. I'm sorry this world isn't what it used to be. We don't have any more time; we need to get David and get out of here. You can hate me later when we are all safe and away from this hellhole. Heck, you can kill me when we get out if you want to. Right now, I need to get you to Lena, and get David out of here."

"David's in a cell around the corner," Hue said.

"Thanks, kid."

"Stop calling me *kid*. My name is Hue."

205

"Sorry, Hue, the name's Rocco. If you go toward the big hole in the wall, you'll find Lena. You two need to get out of here. Tell her I said go to safety I'll meet her back at the house. Hue," Rocco yelled as he continued to turn the corner, "you'll need this." He tossed him a pistol. "Take care of her for me."

"The pistol?" Hue smirked.

"No." Rocco stopped. Smiled. He could like this kid. "Yes, it and Lena."

They ran in opposite directions, seeking cover and dodging killers. Rocco hurled boxes and fences in his path. This was a battle he determined to win but was losing ground quickly.

"I thought you were dead," Rocco said. His hands trembled and his knees weakened. He bit his lip and tightened his fingers around his gun. He inhaled a shallow breath and struggled for another. He blinked over and over trying to stop the tears.

"I thought I lost you like I lost Kyle." He gave in and let his tears flow. "You left me and again I'd left things unsaid."

"I'm here brother. Pull yourself together. We aren't out of the woods yet." He glanced behind Rocco. "Look out, behind you," David yelled.

Rocco took a deep breath in, turned, and fired. The attacker fell to his death.

"How do we get you out of there?"

The locked cell presented another unexpected challenge. He took another deep breath, trying to calm the fear rising inside of him. He wasn't leaving without David.

"The guard has the key, big guy over there." David pointed in the giant's direction. "He's the one who locked the cell after Hue left." The giant was starting to stir. They missed their chance to get the keys while the giant was knocked out.

"What? He has the key." Rocco said, thinking things couldn't get much worse. "Why not? What's this, real-life Resident Evil?" He rolled his eyes in dismay. "How do they find these guys?" They had to think fast. He needed to get the keys and get David out of his cell. Once David was out, he could help Rocco fight their way to safety.

Rocco hated he was now the brains of the operation, it was David's job. He couldn't wait until David would take his place back as the brains. He jumped to his feet and turned toward the giant. His heart raced as he took out his knife. This would be his one chance to take him by surprise.

The giant was about nine feet tall, bald with one good eye. His bad eye bulged out, making him seem even scarier. He had on overalls with no shirt. His chest hair curled over the straps and his belly pushed the overalls out. Rocco hesitated and the monster turned towards him. The giant rushed for him.

Rocco did the one thing he could think to do, he ran. He headed left toward the giant's bad side. With a knife in hand, the bible story of David and Goliath flashed through his mind. "I just need a sling and a stone." Rocco laughed to himself trying to calm his nerves. "If David can kill the giant with one stone just think what I can do with a knife."

He sprinted towards the giant. He jumped onto a crate and leaped into the air; he had reached the point of no return. "Please let me get high enough," he said as he swung the knife with all his might. He hoped to submerge the knife into the back of the giant-killing him, but it's not what happened. The giant turned; the knife pierced only his arm.

The creature shrieked and swung its arms hitting Rocco and knocking him to the ground.

Rocco tasted the iron from the blood running into his mouth. He needed to keep it together. He needed those keys to get David out of his cell and bring him home. Looking at the dirt floor below him. He formulated a plan. Acting fast, he grabbed a handful of dirt and threw it into the good eye of the giant.

Rocco rolled behind him and jumped to his feet.

The giant howled as he swiped at the dirt. Rocco capitalized on the opportunity. He threw his shoulder into the back of the giant's knees, bringing the giant to the ground, but didn't move fast enough. The giant fell on Rocco. Nothing seemed to work the way he had envisioned. He ripped the knife out of the giant's arm. He had one last opportunity to get out alive. The giant reached backward, grabbing Rocco, and putting him in a headlock. He could feel his bones breaking. The giant shifted, lifting his body off Rocco a little. It appeared he was going to try to slam Rocco back on the ground and crush him.

Rocco tried to roll out, but before he was able, the giant's weight came crushing on him again. Out of the corner of his eye, he spotted the knife. He inched closer until he was able to grab it, and thrust it into the giant. The knife plunged deep into the giant's thigh, causing him to fall forward, freeing Rocco. He sprung to his feet, snatched the keys and dashed to David's cell.

He heard the giant moving behind him but kept going. Seconds later a knife sailed by Rocco, missing him by mere inches.

"A little too close for comfort." Rocco tried to calm himself. He feared not so much of dying, but of failing his mission. He didn't want to fail David or Lena.

"Crate in-coming," David yelled as Rocco reached his cell.

David leaped deeper into his cell, and Rocco jumped to the side. The crate hit the cell door, spraying wood chips everywhere. Rocco sprung to his feet slipped a key in the lock. It didn't turn. He tried two more before he found the right key.

"Don't worry," he said. "I'm not leaving without you."

"Boulder!" David yelled.

The boulder crashed against the cell door with such force it popped open.

"Thanks," Rocco shouted at the giant. He handed his knife to David. "It's not much, but it will help."

There was no time for a reunion; they took off toward the exit. The giant was clumsy and didn't run fast. It appeared they might have a slim chance of getting out alive.

"Why can't any of you stop the two of them?" The man in the tower shouted. "Give me your rifle." He grabbed the rifle, from the monster's right side.

"God protects us," David said. No sooner had he spoken the words than a bullet hit his arm. "Nope, not what I had in mind." He winced.

"I don't think he heard you." Rocco snorted, happy to have David back with him.

"I think he heard me. The way I see it, I'm escaping my prison and I'm with you. I have been praying I would see you again, and here you are. Besides, I would rather get shot in the arm than in my head."

"You're right, maybe your guardian angel was on a bathroom break. I guess he got back just in time to push the bullet away from your head." Rocco missed being able to tease David.

"Does it matter? I can still run. I have my legs."

Another shot sounded but didn't come close. Yelling followed their trail. Rocco glanced back. The angry monster shot the cowering one next to him. He shook his head. Good. Let them kill each other.

"Lena? Hue?"

He shouted as he closed in on the hole in the wall. He'd told Hue to get out of there, but he was hoping Lena had stayed. It was a long walk back to the house. He was sore, tired and didn't want to make the trip on foot.

"Where's Hue?" David stopped in mid-thought. "You have a Lamborghini?" He couldn't hide his excitement.

"The kid who helped me find you? I sent him out with Lena."

"You have a Lamborghini?" David repeated himself.

Lena was smart. She left the car so Rocco and David could get away quickly. He told her to go back to the house.

She'd listened. She was safe.

Bullets flew by him as he jumped into the driver's seat. David dove in the passenger's seat. If they were going to make it home, they needed to get out of there fast.

"Where did you get the car?" David asked. "What have you been doing while I've been gone?"

"Joyriding with a hot chick in a cool ride," Rocco teased. "I've been living the dream while you were on the inside."

He smiled.

"Wow, you got it financed and you pushed it all the way to my rescue."

"Yeah, took me some time to find a co-signer." Rocco cranked the engine and the car roared to life.

David looked upward. "Thank you, God."

Rocco stepped on the gas turned donuts in the field and sprayed bullets out of the window towards the complex. It did no good. He didn't hit anything, but it made him feel better.

Rocco had to tell David about him and Hue, it needed to be out in the open. He didn't know how close David was to the kid, he hoped it didn't change things between him and David It might not be the right time, but he blurted it out anyway.

"I'm the one who killed Hue's dad."

David didn't respond.

A rocket exploded by the car. The hood crumpled and glass showered the ground, as it landed upside down.

Rocco's airbag deployed taking his breath away upon impact. David didn't deploy sending him crashing into the dashboard.

"Are you okay?" Rocco pushed the airbag out of his face. He glanced over at David. His face was covered in blood.

"I think so."

"You don't look good."

"I've been shot, and almost killed in a car accident," he smiled. "It's still better than being in the cell." He moved his legs. "Can you move?"

"Yes." Rocco looked at the roof of the car and touched the top of the seats. "We are trapped. How are we going to get out of here?"

David laid his back on the seat and kicked out the passenger window. "We can get out my side." They escaped from the vehicle and ran for cover just before it exploded.

"Way too close for comfort," David said, as they took cover from the smoke and fire. They dove into the woods out of the sight of the monsters.

"No," Rocco stopped in his tracks. "Not my car."

"It was a sweet one, but we need to keep moving."

Rocco didn't budge.

"I think we should go now," David insisted, trying to drag Rocco with him. "It was a great car, but our lives are worth more. We need to get out of here. Rocco, we need to go now."

Chapter 39

They needed to go while the thick of the smoke gave them cover. The car helped them escape. It's not the way Rocco had planned the rescue but was thankful for the smoke which allowed them to get away without the monsters seeing them.

They ran as hard and as fast as their feet would carry them.

"Rocco," David gasped. "I can't go on. I need to rest."

"We have to keep moving. They aren't going to stop until they kill us both."

"I can't."

Rocco slowed to a fast walk. "We'll slow down, but we aren't stopping. We need to get to a place where we can get more weapons."

They had one pistol and a knife for protection. All their guns and supplies were lost in the car. They would be safe at the gun shop. Rocco wrestled with what to do. They wouldn't survive without weapons.

What about Lena?

Lena and Hue were meeting them at the house, he wanted to go there and make sure they were all right. He knew Lena would make sure the kid was safe. It was his job to keep him and David safe.

As much as he tried Rocco couldn't stop thinking about Lena.

How could someone he just met consume his mind and distract him as much as she did? Did she make it out? Why hadn't they taken the car? Were they at the house?

These questions flooded his mind. No, there would be no stopping. He needed to get to Lena first. He and David would have to make the weapons they had last. They would get to Lena, then figure out what to do next.

He couldn't help worrying about her and the kid. Even though the rescue was a success, it didn't go as he planned. They were all supposed to make it out together. Apart from him wanted to turn around and see if she was still at camp. Maybe the monsters had captured them. He knew this wasn't an option.

The last thing he said to the boy was to tell Lena to go to the house. It's where they had to be. He continued walking and thinking, while David talked nonstop. Rocco tuned him out.

His thoughts were of Lena.

"There's a bag of supplies stashed near here. I have things in there to take care of your arm." Rocco said, trying to push the thoughts of Lena out of his head. He looked over at David's arm. It was dirty and swollen. He didn't want an infection to set in. They needed to get it cleaned and dressing on it. "I was out looking for supplies one day, and came across what I like to call my safehouse."

"Safehouse?" David questioned. "Isn't our house safe?"

"It's safe." Rocco pushed David. "This is a safehouse away from home. It's an old gun shop. It looks abandoned from the front. The way in is a hatch on the top. Inside was everything you would need for surviving. It has every weapon and ammo you can think of. It's where I found the gas. I have six different locations where I've hidden supply bags. We're close to one of them."

Chapter 40

"Lead the way, brother." David motioned for him to take the lead. Thankful Rocco had a plan. Right now he couldn't think about anything except for being free. He couldn't wait until he was home safe and in his bed, not sleeping on the concrete floor of his prison cell. He was glad to be free even if it meant he was on the run, at least he was on the run with Rocco.

He'd missed him. David had to confess he hadn't thought he was ever going to see him again. He had almost lost all hope when Hue came. He prayed God would keep Hue and Lena safe until they were reunited.

He thought about what Rocco said. Why did Hue never mention Rocco had killed his dad? They would have to deal with this right away. David didn't know how they would get past this one, but he knew they would. In his spirit, he knew Hue and Lena belonged with him and Rocco. It wasn't by accident they had met. God placed them in each other's paths for a reason. David had to believe everything was going to work out.

Darkness surrounded them when they finally made it to the bag. Cold tired and hungry David longed to be home.

"Stop," David whispered into Rocco's ear as he grabbed the back of his shirt and pulled him to the ground.

He thought he heard someone or something ahead. Rocco crouched and pull out his pistol.

He heard the sound again. Voices. Thanks to his instincts, they didn't walk blindly into a group of the living dead. They exchanged glances not saying a word. They would have to fight. These monsters were not going to stop David from going home and sleeping in his bed.

Armed with a knife and a gun, would have to work. Rocco took the knife from David and gave him the gun. David didn't protest. With his arm, he would be no good with a knife. He took the magazine out of the gun. There were four bullets left. Not much, but it would have to do.

They watched through the thick grass and David counted five monsters in a barn. They lit torches. The barn door opened; the monsters stood gathered around a chair. Hay stacked in bundles lay against the wall. The barn was old, begging to fall apart. The rotting and cracking wood would crumble with a few well-placed kicks.

David crept around some stray bales of hay and gasped. A woman sat in a chair surrounded by monsters. She had long dark hair. Her skin bruised. She struggled to try to getaway. The monsters had her strapped to the chair. In his heart, he knew what they had done to her. The blood trickling down her cheek confirmed what he already knew.

She wasn't a monster.

A heavyset monster kicked her in the chest. Rage swept over David. He started to stand and run to her aid. Rocco pulled him back before he ran off and got himself killed.

"Help," she begged someone to hear her.

Her cries cut short with a backhand from her right.

"I'm going to kill them," David whispered. "Rocco, we have to help her."

"I know." Rocco's brow creased. "We need to hurry before she gets diseased or killed. I cannot have you running in getting yourself killed too."

"When did you become the smart guy?"

"The day you left," Rocco waved his hand as if to dismiss the comment. "I'll backtrack to the rear of the barn. Once I'm in a position you jump out and distract them. When you have their attention, you need to shoot the four at the end farthest away from me. There are four rounds left, no room for error. You can't miss."

"Way to put the pressure on me," David laughed.

215

He could do it. He remembered the times when they were young and he would go hunting but not kill. Times had changed turning David into a killer.

"I'll take the other one out." Rocco walked around to the other side of the barn.

"Help," her scream echoed in the core of David's soul.

"Awe, help me," one of the diseased creatures mocked her.

"We're trying," David whispered.

Rocco slipped through the barn door opposite the one closest to their hiding spot. He signaled to David. Time to get the rescue underway. David jumped up and down, yelling at the top of his lungs.

"Look what we have here," a monster mocked David. "Prince charming coming to the rescue."

David crept closer. "Take me instead of her."

"We will take her and add you to the..." The bullet from David's gun hit him in the head. The other monsters gaped, eyes and mouths wide. David fired the second round

"Two down, one to go," David said.

Another monster grabbed a torch instantly the chair was engulfed in flames. He threw a bottle of what looked like alcohol on her. Her cries pierced David's heart. He couldn't get to her.

Rocco grabbed his knife and charged one of the monsters, killing him. He desperately tried to put the fire out, slapping the flames. He was no match for the flames.

He knocked the chair over and grabbed hold of the legs to roll it over. David spotted a monster behind Rocco a split second before he tumbled to the ground. He landed on the ground next to the burning girl, then struggled to his feet. One of the monsters grabbed Rocco's knife and stabbed him.

He collapsed.

David fought off monster after monster, but they kept coming. He looked over at the girl and lost hope of rescuing her.

Her screams turned to pleas for death. "Please end my pain. Show me mercy."

David used his last bullet as her escape, then slumped in anguish. He couldn't rescue her.

The fire continued to roar, as it moved through the barn as the hay fueled its flames.

Rocco wrestled his knife away from the monster and ended its life.

David had the last monster pinned to the ground, but couldn't do much else. Rocco grabbed the knife, rolled to his back, jumped to his feet, and lunged toward the monster jabbing his knife deep inside him.

The monsters were all dead, but they failed their mission.

David leaped to his feet and ran out of the barn, Rocco followed. The barn burned to the ground.

Chapter 41

Somberly, they continued on their journey to the bag. This time they walked in silence. They had failed the girl. Even though they had done everything they could for her, their best wasn't good enough.

She died because they couldn't help her.

Did Rocco fail Lena? Was she safe?

He shuddered as he thought of what the monsters would do to her. He had to hurry home. He needed to know she was safe.

Only a handful of minutes later, they reached the backpack. Right, where Rocco had hidden it, untouched.

He unzipped the bag, and took out a flashlight and turned it on so they could see. He grabbed two water bottles and handed one to David. They drained the containers.

David rummaged through the bag and removed two magazines and a pistol. He handed one to Rocco.

"I wish we would have had this bag before we found the girl," he whispered. "We could have saved her."

"I'm sorry, David."

Rocco knew he was having a hard time. David believed in everyone and tried to save the world, believing it was his job.

"I know we did all we could do, but it still wasn't enough. Look at your hands. We did this for what? She died. We didn't save her."

"We did all we could," Rocco tried to comfort him. "We did more than most would have. We could have walked away, but we didn't. We tried to help her and in the end, we brought justice to those who hurt her."

David set the bag on the ground.

"My head knows we did all we could, it's my heart having the issues." He paused. "My heart tells me we didn't do enough. My heart says we should have saved her."

"I always said your heart would get us killed."

Rocco grabbed a headlamp light turned the flashlight off and handed David one too. He wanted them to free their hands. His hands were killing him, but he was more worried about the bullet in David's arm. If the bullet was still there, they had to get it out. *How could he get it out when he couldn't move his fingers much?* He had to do something. It was his job to take care of David. He didn't rescue him to lose him.

David took out a bottle of brandy and smelled it. "This is, strong." He put the lid back on it.

"Good. It's just what the doctor ordered." Rocco took the bottle and drank some then he handed it back to David. He held out his burnt hands. "Do your worst."

"Are you sure? Bro, this is going to hurt more than you think."

"Enjoy yourself." He held his hands steady. "You have to do it." David opened the brandy again.

Rocco took the bottle, gulped more than handed it back. "Okay."

David poured the liquor onto Rocco's hands before he could take the bottle away from him again. He laughed as Rocco yelled and danced around shaking his hands. When he stopped dancing, David grabbed bandages and wrapped Rocco's hands, leaving his fingers out so he could hold a gun.

David took a deep breath. Rocco examined his arm. The bullet hit his forearm on the edge so there wasn't a hole and the bullet hadn't lodged his arm. The wound was a quarter-inch graze. Rocco grinned as he took the brandy and poured it in the wound, not giving David any warning.

David bit down on his teeth and groaned.

"You're lucky the bullet merely grazed you."

"This was no graze; it's a groove. No, it's a trench."

"Okay. All I'm saying is you're lucky it didn't stick in you. If it would have I would be using tweezers to dig in your arm for a bullet."

"And you don't believe in God," David said as Rocco finished bandaging him.

"What a great God you have." Rocco couldn't help questioning God. "He saved the bullet from sticking in you and then he let you watched a girl burn." Rocco dropped the bandages and walked into the abandoned gas station. David followed.

There was a desk in the back of the gas station. Rocco sat in a chair. He buried his head in his hands. He couldn't shut his mind off. A fire started to burn in him as he thought of Lena and Hue, wondering if they made it home safe. He let his mind wander to places he knew he shouldn't, but was too tired to stop it.

What if it had been Lena in the chair? Would he have fought harder to save her? Did he do everything he could for the girl?

He hoped he did. He couldn't bear thinking he might have given up too soon. He looked at his hands. *No*, he knew he had done everything he could to help. It didn't matter who she was, he'd put every effort into saving her.

He had no place for his anger to go. He flipped the desk over and slammed the chair against the door. David said nothing. He slid the desk in front of the door. Rocco took a deep breath, trying to get his rage under control. He couldn't say anything.

"We need sleep," David said.

They pulled out sleeping bags from the book bag and lay in them where the desk used to be. The ground was hard and cold. They tossed and turned trying to get comfortable. Rocco thought of Lena and wondered where she was.

"God, please be with Rocco and me," David whispered. "God, it's so hard in this world. I never thought life would come to this. I don't know how it happened or why it happened, but God, this is out of my control. I need you to take control of my life. I don't know what I'm supposed to do. Is there a cure for this disease? I don't even know if it is a disease. I'm lost. I try to lead Rocco to you. With everything going on it's making it hard to show him you're still here, and you're looking after us. God, I need help." He paused. "I guess I'm wondering how this ends. Does it end? I know you have your hands in this world still, you haven't forsaken us. The bible tells us you have a plan and a purpose for everything, even for Rocco and me. Thank you for leading him to me. Thank you for letting him save me. He would die for me if you asked him to. God, continue to lead him as I follow him. Help me. Help us. In Jesus's name, Amen."

Rocco listened to the whispering prayers from his friend, fighting back the lump forming in his throat.

"God, if you're still out there, I need you to lead me back to Lena and Hue. Help me lead us to safety." He said no more.

Chapter 42

A loud banging sound outside jolted Rocco. "Not again. Why can't we catch a break?" Rocco sat and listened more intently to the banging.

"I hope those creatures didn't find us," David said as another bang came from the door.

"I hate life." Rocco stood to his feet rolled the sleeping bag and stuffed it into the backpack. David did the same. Rocco placed a gun for David on a file cabinet and handed him the bag.

"Funny how life makes us appreciate the things we once complained about," David said as he finished stuffing the backpack with his sleeping bag.

"I wonder what life has in store for us next to appreciate."

Rocco and David flipped the desk over and slid it away from the office door. Rocco felt vulnerable without his weapons. With two pistols and no extra bullets, they would have to shoot with precision and accuracy.

The banging outside slowed. The morning fog cooled the air. A breeze sent chills down Rocco's spine, as he opened the door. He raced to the pumps for cover, David following, while listening for the enemy.

At the back of the building, the banging started again. They headed around back, creeping against the wall. Rocco took point while David watched their backs. This is how they did things. Rocco was thankful to have David by his side again.

They stopped and listened, at the edge of the building. Rocco poked his head around the corner. Two large animals grazed next to the tree line. He looked for a minute, then, went back against the wall.

"How many are there?" David asked.

"Um, you wouldn't believe me if I told you."

"Rocco, a few years ago I didn't believe in monsters. I think I would believe anything at this point."

"Okay, here goes. There are two rhino's smacking into each other."

"Funny, Rocco, what is it?"

"I told you, you wouldn't believe me."

Pushing Rocco out of the way, David glanced around the corner.

"Amazing. We didn't even have to pay to go to the zoo."

"Way to be twelve, David."

"Whatever, this is cool. Let's get closer and get a better view."

"Don't be crazy. What are we going to do when we get closer?"

"I don't know yet."

"Great plan. What if they want to use you as a battering ram?" Rocco looked over to the two rhinos, then back at David. "I don't think you would come out a winner." He paused again before he spoke. "Do you want to tell me when our roles changed? I don't like being the rational one. I want to be reckless and carefree. I want my old job back."

"I'm sorry," David apologized. "I think being in the cell so long, changed me. I'll try harder to think smart. Rushing rhinos wouldn't be smart."

They turned to go back to the gas station. David's foot slipped, the twigs under him cracked and spooked one of the animals. David stopped. The Rhinos spotted them and charged in their direction.

"We are going to die, and it is my fault. Run," David yelled.

"I wish we had our rifles."

Rocco ran behind David. The heavy footsteps of eight giant's legs pounding echoed in his ears. They were charging closer and closer. They were not going to be able to outrun these beasts.

David said nothing.

They ran.

Rocco needed David to be the smart one and get them out of the mess he had gotten them into. Out of the corner of his eye, he saw

David jump onto the dumpster and then to the awning on the side of the gas station. From there he climbed to the roof. Rocco stood still on the ground and glanced towards the beasts.

"Jump!" David shouted. "Jump."

Looking back almost cost Rocco his life. He rolled out of the way, as the first Rhino crumbled the dumpster. Rocco flipped to his feet and ran faster with the seconded rhino close behind. In full panic mode, Rocco's mind raced.

Was David going to have to watch him trampled to death by two rhinos?

Rocco chuckled. At least the dead wouldn't kill him. He never wanted to give them the satisfaction of killing him.

"Life is never dull. We escape the monsters only to get killed by rhinos. Some fairy tale this is."

Rocco turned to his left as a rhino smashed into the wall. They continued to follow him. He entered the gas station, ran to the back, and crouched behind the desk. The rhinos charged into the glass and headed toward Rocco.

Shelves and counters crashed in around him. He wasn't safe. He jumped to his feet and leaped to the right. One of the rhinos got his leg. Rocco winced at the crushing blow. It was broke, but he didn't have time to dwell on the pain. He needed to run. Adrenaline surged through his veins, as he darted toward the open door.

He needed to move fast, but his leg wouldn't let him. He fought to block out his pain. He had to stay alive and get to David. Rocco reached the dumpster, put all his weight on his good leg and leaped into the air. His injured leg gave out as he collapsed to the ground.

David slid down the ladder, landed on the smashed dumpster and leaped to the ground. He shot at the rhinos. David helped Rocco to his feet. He flipped Rocco over his shoulder and pushed him in the dumpster, then jumped in himself.

Metal flew through the air as the rhinos hit the dumpster, sending it flipping and flopping before coming to a stop. They lay still, waiting for the rhinos to make their next move. Rocco's leg was more contorted than before.

"Sorry for getting us into this mess," David whispered. "I'll start thinking before I act."

There was no response from Rocco. He wasn't moving.

"Rocco. Come on, you can't die on me." David shook Rocco's arm. "Please wake up. I cannot carry you. Wake up."

The two giants pounded the cement gaining speed as they moved. David tossed things out of the backpack Rocco had. Grasping the flashlight, he turned it on.

"We are in an upside-down dumpster, on top of a manhole. Rocco, I need your help." He sighed. "We need to get the lid off." David shook Rocco again. "Wake up! We need to get the lid off."

"What lid?" Rocco opened his eyes. He shook his head rubbing his eyes. Every part of his body hurt, he wanted to sleep.

"This one." David tugged at the cover. With Rocco's help, they slid it enough to fit through. "The rhinos are coming for round two. You first," he pushed Rocco through the crack. He hit the ground, landing on the better of his two legs. The sewer was dry, and the stench of death filled his nostrils.

David grabbed the backpack and threw it into the manhole. Seconds later, he jumped in himself. Light flashed through the manhole and the dumpster sailed into the sky.

"David?" Rocco's voice trembled. Pain overtook him; he didn't know how much longer he could stay on his feet.

"Yeah."

"I got a great idea. Why don't we get closer to the rhinos?" He crackled. He no longer had to be the brains David was back.

"You had to go there, didn't you?" David laughed too. "It couldn't have been me, I'm the cautious one. I don't take chances."

"I think you did today." There was a short pause. "Did you get a close enough look at them or do we need to take a trip to the zoo?" Rocco continued to tease David.

"I don't ever need to go to the zoo."

"I'm glad to hear it."

Rocco sat on the ground and looked at his leg. It was going to have to be set and it would be a pain he didn't know if he could bear. He couldn't walk or even move it until it was at least straightened.

David searched but found nothing to help him with Rocco's leg.

"It looks bad." David put a little pressure on it. "Does this hurt?"

"I'll show you how much." Rocco took a swing at him. David dodged the punch.

"We need to find a splint and crutches. Your leg's broken."

"Tell me something I didn't already know." Rocco's breaths, came heavy and uneven.

"I pray the bones not shattered." The sarcasm left his voice. "I have to try and pop it back into place. It can't heal like it is right now."

"I figured as much."

"I'm not going to lie to you, it's gonna hurt."

"David, a rhino landed on me, it already hurts."

"We don't have anything for a splint, but we have to get it straight." David handed Rocco the bottle of whiskey. "You might want this."

"It will take more than this. You're going to have to listen to me yell." Rocco looked at his twisted leg again. "Make it quick and..."

"Don't hate me." David grabbed Rocco's leg and jerked it.

The yelling began. Rocco cursed at David. He knew he shouldn't, but it didn't stop him. It wasn't David's fault, well it kind of was. He thought he would get some time to brace himself to prepare for the pain. He didn't care about the lump in his throat or the tears on his face. His pain was real.

"I was going to ask you to say a prayer for me, but I'm glad I didn't." His colorful language continued.

"This isn't fair." David sulked in the corner. "I wouldn't have done it if I didn't need to." He bowed his head. "Just so you know, I did pray for you."

It didn't take long for his pain to ease. "Thanks," Rocco said. "I mean for everything, even the prayers."

226

"You would've done the same for me." There was a short awkward silence. "You did the same for me. You didn't have to risk your life to rescue me, but you did."

"Stop right there!" Rocco sighed. "I did have to come and get you. Apparently, you didn't know how to get home by yourself. I was going crazy without you."

"Can you stand?" David asked. "I know it will be hard, but we need to keep moving."

"I'll give it my best." He struggled to move. The adrenaline was gone leaving pain in its place.

"Don't try and walk." David helped him to his feet. "Lean on me."

Rocco was on his feet. He slung his arm around David for support. This was how it should be; he and his brother together against the world. He would never make it without David. They were meant to be together.

"This is going to be the hard part. Take your time. Put as little pressure on your leg as you can."

"Wait, you thought this was easy until now?" Rocco had to keep his sense of humor going so he wouldn't lose his mind in pain.

"It hasn't been hard for me. It's getting harder now because I have to support your sorry butt."

"I could make it hard." Rocco laughed. "I have missed you."

"I've missed you too." David put his arm under Rocco's and lifted him almost off both feet. "Do not put weight on your leg. Hop! Put all your weight on me. Let me carry you for once."

The two of them walked through the narrow path of the sewer not knowing where it would lead them. It didn't matter because they were together.

The stench almost knocked Rocco off his feet. Decaying corpses lay on the ground around them. During the first breakout when the gas prices started skyrocketing, people killed each other for a few gallons of gas. People stopped digging graves to bury the dead. Instead, they threw them into the sewers to keep the streets clear.

227

Flies buzzed and maggots were having a hay day on the corpses. David propped Rocco against the wall and started moving the bodies clearing a path for them to walk through. He took a deep breath and held it as he closed the gap between him and the bodies. They were merely bones and clothes.

David started dry heaving.

"I wish we were home, or anywhere but in a stinking sewer moving corpses."

He closed his eyes and breathed hard. Something jumped out, and ran across his hand. David pulled his pistol from the back of his pants and shot with great speed precision and accuracy. The whole thing took about four seconds.

"We have dinner," Rocco laughed at David's instinct to kill.

"I'm not eating a rat."

"Maybe, I will."

David gently put the headless rat, in a cloth tied it and tossed it to Rocco, who tied the other end to his belt loop.

"Look you cleared the path, and you managed not to hurl."

"I didn't see you doing anything but sitting there." David smiled

"Don't hate." Rocco returned his smile. "We will count them both as wins."

David again lifted Rocco to his feed and they continued deeper into the sewer.

They needed to find a way out. The longer they stayed the more likely infection would set in. The ladders at every manhole were gone.

They weren't getting home anytime soon.

Chapter 43

"Where are we going?" Hue asked as he followed a few steps behind Lena.

"Home," Lena answered.

"Really?" Hue knew where Lena was taking him and he wasn't sure he wanted to go. "This isn't the way to our house. I don't know what happened between you and Rocco, but I need to know what we're doing. If we are going home, I think you're heading in the wrong direction."

"This could be your home." Lena glanced back at him. "I mean if you want it to be." Lena stopped and sat on a rock.

The sun was high in the sky. They had been walking all day. Hue was grateful for the rest. They'd made good progress and deserved a break.

"You still didn't say where we're going." Hue plopped next to her.

"I told you where we are going."

"Home, okay. Do you mind telling me where home is? This doesn't look like the way home to me. Are we going to Rocco's?" Lena nodded her head.

Hue didn't want to talk to her anymore. How could she just move in with Rocco? Did she expect him to go with her? He didn't want to go. Did she know Rocco killed his dad? Why would he go there, or have anything to do with him? He hated even helping him at all. No, he had helped David, not Rocco.

"I quit," Lena said. "What's wrong? Yes, we are going to meet Rocco and David at their house. There we will figure out what we are going to do."

She paused. After a long silence, Lena started in again.

"Hue, you knew this was our plan, why are you acting so weird about Rocco? I'm not saying we are going to live there, but it is an option. Hue, you have to talk to me. Tell me what's going on and why the sudden mood swing?"

"Don't worry about it." He stood and walked away. He didn't know where he was going. He just needed to go.

"I'm worried about you." She sounded like she was about to cry. "You're the most important thing in the world to me. Sit and start talking."

"No," He knew they would never agree.

He would have to get used to being alone. It was nice having Lena around while he had her. There was no way he could live with the man who killed his father and left him behind.

"I see he has sucked you into his world." Hue stopped himself.

He thought about Rocco. Why was he so upset with him? Yes, he killed his father, but Hue was going to do it anyway. Rocco had apologized to him. Killers didn't say they're sorry. What was he doing? He couldn't let his dad ruin his last chance at happiness. If it hadn't been for Rocco killing him, Hue might be dead himself. His dad's anger was escalating and it wasn't long before he would be the dead one.

Then, there was Lena. If it weren't for Rocco, he might not have met Lena. She saved him from himself and cared about Rocco. Maybe Hue needed to give him a chance too. He couldn't risk losing her.

"Come on, Hue." She raised her eyebrows. "What's going on? Why don't you want to go to Rocco's? Did something happen I need to know about? We can fix this."

He hesitated, but only for a second, and sat back next to Lena.

"Rocco killed my dad."

There, Hue said it. It was out in the open. He didn't want to hurt Lena, but he needed to tell her how he felt.

"Oh," Lena exhaled. "I know how you felt about your dad. I also know you wanted to be the one who killed him." She paused again. "Listen, we do not have to go back to their house." She spoke slow.

Hue could see tears forming in her eyes. "You say the word, and we'll go home. We'll go home, and never see Rocco and David again. Hue, you're the most important thing in the world to me. I would give my life if it meant you would be safe and happy. I will not abandon you for anyone, *or anything*."

She brushed a tear off her cheek and turned away from Hue.

How could he make Lena sad?

It wasn't often you find other humans in this world, especially someone to fall in love with. He couldn't take this away from her, not when he didn't care Rocco killed his dad. He was angrier Rocco left him behind.

How could he be angry about it since Rocco had thought Hue was a zombie?

Hue was a ball of intense emotions. He didn't want to make Lena sacrifice her happiness, because of his anger, and he wasn't sure why he was angry. He wasn't sure if he liked the thought of sharing Lena with Rocco.

Would she fight with Rocco and leave him as his mother did?

No, Lena would never leave.

She would take him with her if she were going to leave. She would always take care of him.

"Lena." He touched her shoulder. She turned back towards him. "I'm sorry."

Hue hated how he acted. He wiped the tears from her cheek.

"I don't know what to feel. I know David and Rocco are humans, and they will fight and protect us. We will be better off if the four of us stay together. I don't hate them. I hate thinking I might lose you to them."

"You listen to me, Hue." Lena sat straight and narrowed her eyes. "I will never leave you. You are stuck with me forever. If things don't work out with David and Rocco, we will leave, you and me. Do you understand?"

He shook his head yes, as he smirked. "I understand and promise not to be a spoiled brat anymore."

"You're allowed to act like a twelve-year-old once in a while." Lena returned his smile. "But not too often." She glanced around them. "Hue, I think we are lost." Her tears fell again. "I know I am supposed to be strong, but I can't. Somehow in the rush to get away from the camp I have gotten turned around and lost."

"What?" Hue jumped to his feet. Looked to the left. Looked to the right. Hue tried to find any sign of the ocean, or water anywhere.

"Yep," Lena looked around. "I'm sorry." She sighed and looked to the ground. "I'm so sorry."

"How are we lost?"

"Not funny Hue. I said I was sorry. I got turned around, and I don't know where we are."

"You told me his house was by the beach?" Hue smiled. "Why don't we just head to the beach?"

"If I knew what way the beach was, we would." Lena sighed. "I'm sorry, but I don't."

"I do. It's this way," Hue said, pointing to the right. "Wait, I mean this way." He turned to the left then to the ground. "Dang it, we're lost." He wanted to remember his way to the beach. He hated seeing Lena sad. She was trying hard to be strong for him. He slumped back on the rock.

"I guess we backtracked and circled a few too many times. We did a good job throwing them off our tracks, though." Lena hung her head.

"I wasn't paying attention to where we were going. I'm sorry." Hue wanted to be sympathetic, but he was finding it too hard. "So, we could be heading right back to the camp?"

"No," Lena answered. "I don't think we are. Nothing looks familiar. If we were heading back to camp, I would know."

"It doesn't make me feel any better, and I'm hungry."

He was doing it again, whining. He hated when he did, but for some reason he kept doing it, he would have to work on being strong. Hue wanted to be home in his bed not lost hungry and scared.

"Me too," Lena tried to make things right with Hue. "Are you good with a rifle?" She took the rifle from her shoulder and handed it to him.

"Yeah, but I'm still hungry, and I can't eat the rifle."

"Then, let's see how good you're. We need food."

"We're going hunting?"

"Yep." Lena stood and headed toward the trees.

"What do you think we will find?" Hue followed.

"Zombies."

"I'm not eating one."

"Ewww, gross." She laughed.

"I hope we find a big fat juicy burger." Hue's stomach rumbled in agreement.

"There's a burger joint over there." Lena pointed to a fallen building sign on top of a car. "Should I go to the drive-through?"

"I think someone already did, and we forgot to bring the car."

They walked for hours, without any sign of life. No Zombies. No animals. Not even wind to move the trees. The sun was leaving. There was no moon to take its place. The clouds covered most the sky so no stars could be seen either. Hunting diminished as an option. They didn't find shelter. It would be a night under the open skies. They had a rifle a pistol and empty stomachs. Thunder boomed through the sky as a way to introduce by the rain.

"This is nice." Hue threw himself in the wet grass.

"I agree it is lovely." Lena sneered. "This isn't what we need." She looked to the heavens. "Why," she prayed. "Why can't you help us?"

"Why did we leave the woods," Hue grumbled. "We had shelter there."

"This grassy field isn't enough shelter for you?" Lena sat next to him.

"It's perfect. Look, we even have light when the lightning flashes."

"Yes, it's pleasing to see there's nothing around you," Lena said with all the sarcasm she could muster. Every strike of the lightning made it easy to see the faces of the dead, off in the distance.

"Looks like we found those Zombies you were talking about." Hue inched closer to Lena.

"This is no time to joke." Lena jumped to her feet.

"I'm still not eating them."

"Would you shut up? We could die."

"If we die, do we get to come back as one of them? We could eat other people and at least have food in our stomachs," Hue rambled as he followed close behind Lena. They used the lightning as a guide to get away without the Zombies following.

The rain fell in sheets, making visibility almost impossible. They trembled with every step they took. The wind howled and blew and the icy rain pelted their faces. Lena held tight to his shirt. Hue had the rifle on his shoulder. Lena had the pistol out ready to shoot if she needed to. With five bullets left, they would need to make them count.

They walked until there were no more flashes of lightning to lead them. Darkness surrounded them. The wind howled. Making it impossible to hear anything. Thunder rolled. A bolt of lightning struck a barn and it caught on fire.

Hue turned toward the fire and was face to face with a Zombie. The light from the fire flickered across his face and the face of the monster. Hue took a deep breath and held it. He couldn't show the monster his fear. He kept eye contact with the creature, kicked the creature and knocked him to the ground. Lightning flashed. They took off toward the fire. If they could catch the wood on fire, they would be able to light the monsters on fire. They needed to save their bullets. If they did nothing, they would die. Dying wasn't something Hue wanted to do. He knew Lena didn't either.

They sprinted toward the fire. Lena tripped and landed on top of Hue in a hole.

"Looks like this might be a shelter," Lena said.

The light from the fire wasn't tall enough to light inside the hole. Hue felt around trying to find a handle on the door. It wasn't until the lightning flashed across the sky; he saw it.

"The hatch had a padlock on it." He twisted, kicked, and cursed it trying to get it to open. Nothing worked. Lena took out the pistol, pushed Hue out of the way, and shot the lock.

The barrier to their safety shattered.

Chapter 44

Heavy breathing echoed around them. They weren't in the hole alone.

"Dee nnera," a monster howled. With the rain and a heavy Russian accent, it sounded like the monster was calling Lena's name.

"Oh, God." Lena dropped to her knees burying her face in her hands. "This can't be happening."

Lena tried to shake off her fear. They had found shelter from the rain and cold, but now with the monsters in the way they couldn't get into it.

"What is it, Lena? You're scaring me." Hue reached for the gun and pointed it toward the voice.

"Dinner." The monster sounded closer.

Hue shook his head. He grabbed the bullets from his pocket and loaded the gun.

"Lena." He whispered. "I need you to tell me what to do."

He shot in the direction of the voice. And missed, by a good three feet. The flash from the gun gave them a little light. Hue closed his eyes, took a deep breath, and pulled the trigger four times. Two bullets shot out. One skimmed the zombie's arm.

He was no marksman.

Hue charged the monster wrapped his hands around its neck, and proceeded to choke the life out of him.

The monster flung Hue to the ground.

Lena opened the hatch. Lightning hit the sky, illuminating the hole long enough for her to grab Hue and jump inside.

She noticed three things. One it stunk. Two, Hue's leg was injured. Three, the rifle was still loaded.

An explosion of lights lit the place again. Hue turned and fired a direct shot ended the monster.

"Are you okay Hue?" Lena rushed to his side.

"I think the thing broke my leg."

"Can you walk?" She shut the hatch, no monsters could get in, and they couldn't get out.

"I don't think so, not without a crutch or something. We aren't going to find any here in the dark."

"We can't go back out there. They will kill us."

"How can they stand the cold? They act as if it doesn't faze them, but a bullet to the chest does. There has to be more than one strand of the disease. I have seen zombies who can talk and think. Then there are the ones who can't even stand alone. I don't understand any of it. How are we supposed to know what kind of zombies we are fighting?"

"Those are good questions, but I'm afraid I have no answers. I know we're safe. We need to rest and at daylight, I'll get us home."

"Where is home again?" Hue smiled. "I'm kidding."

He paused for a brief moment.

"Lena, what happened to you out there? Why did you freak out?"

"It's a long story." She sat leaning against the cold cement wall. Hue slumped beside her.

"It looks like we aren't going anywhere." Hue looked at her. "We have the time and I am a good listener."

"The sound brought back memories of my childhood friend, Karen." Lena leaned her head against the wall.

"Did something happen to her?"

"Yep."

Did she want to tell the kid about Karen?

She was his age when it happened. Karen had always been kind and a good friend, Lena couldn't remember her as Karen, but only as a monster.

"If you don't want me to know it's okay. I understand."

239

"It's not that." Lena bit her lip to try and stop her tears. "Karen and I had been friends since I can remember. I don't remember a time she wasn't in my life. We were about your age when it happened."

She made eye contact with Hue.

"I don't want to scare you; I am only telling you this to help protect you. You can't joke around about being infected."

"Do you mean I can't play dead?"

"No." She reached out and touched his cheek. "I'll just tell you what happened and then I think you will understand. I knocked on Karen's door like I did every day. I heard a response which sounded like the monster today only it said 'Lena, Laa-eee-nn-a.'

"I answered and when I walked in, Karen lunged at me and knocked me to the ground. We had played as monsters when we were little so I thought she was joking. 'Laaa-eee-nn-aaa.' Karen said again as she reached out digging at my face."

She paused and looked away.

"I'm sorry I pushed you to talk." Hue took a deep breath.

"No, don't be," she looked back at him through her tears. "There is nothing of my past I want to hide from you. "I remember scanning the room for anything to defend myself. I finally found a knife and stabbed her over and over until she stopped moving. She was my first encounter with a monster, and the first one I ever killed."

Her heart felt numb remembering her friend.

"I'm sorry you had to kill her."

"Look at you." Lena smiled with pride. "All grown protecting me."

"I only wish I was a better shot."

"Me too," she laughed. "I want you to know I will never joke about the infection, and I want you to promise me you won't either. I don't want to accidentally shoot you or you shoot me. I know we have had to play dead but this is different."

"I promise." There was the smile Leana loved to see. "Did you happen to notice where we are?" Hue changed the subject.

"I can smell where we are."

"We're in a sewer, aren't we?"

"Yes, we are. I'm thankful it's dry." She put her arm around him. "We are going to be okay, I promise." Yet, in her mind, she thought they were going to die, and nothing she could do would prevent it. She needed Rocco and David.

They needed to get out of the sewer.

Chapter 45

Rocco yelled.

David jumped to his feet, ready to fight. "What's wrong?" It took a second for him to remember he was in the sewer and Rocco was the one yelling. "What's wrong?" He asked calmer. He scanned the room for any possible danger and found none.

"My leg, I think I'm going to be a cripple." Rocco sat with his back to the wall. "You'll have to take care of me for the rest of my life."

David looked at the hatch. Why did it have to be so high? Where had all the ladders gone? He needed to get Rocco out of here, but how? Even if he could scale the wall, which he couldn't, it was too smooth, he would have no way of getting Rocco out. He had to find a different exit at ground level or a ladder.

"I have a good feeling we'll out of here today." He ignored Rocco's comment.

"Is that so? Who are you going to call for help? Let me guess, you're going to call an ambulance."

"Good idea, can I borrow your phone?" David rolled his eyes and the sleeping bag.

They needed to get started if they were going to find a way out. He didn't want to take any chances of the dead finding them. He gave Rocco a gun and the headlamp.

"You to stay here. I'll find a way out of here. There is no sense of me carrying you around. I can move faster alone." He paused. He hated the thought of leaving Rocco for even a second. He took his rolled sleeping bag and let Rocco use it for a pillow.

"Do you need me to help you do anything before I go?"

"No, I'm just going to sit here." He closed his eyes and leaned his head against the wall. "I'll be fine."

242

"I'll find something to fix your leg. It needs to be in a splint."

"Don't do anything stupid like run out and get a tree branch." Rocco didn't even smile. "I just got you back. Don't make me come get you again."

"I'm not going to let them get me." He looked at Rocco. "I'm coming back for you. We are both getting out of here today."

"If you find Leonardo and the rest of the turtles, see if you can get some pizza. I'm starving." Rocco smiled.

"I will. Don't forget you have the rat you can eat."

"Really? You want me to eat Master Splinter? Now they're not going to give us any pizza. I hope you're happy."

"Get some rest." David laughed. "I'll be back as soon as I can."

"Fine, but I'm not eating Master Splinter." Rocco tossed the rat to David. He rolled on his back with his head on the sleeping bag and closed his eyes.

David didn't know why but he stuck the rat in his pocket and walked away.

He hadn't envisioned his rescue quite like it has turned out. Rocco saved him last night and today they were separated again. He wanted a simpler life. He liked the life they had at the house, planting and locking the house tight at night. He wanted to get back home where he was free. Rocco didn't feel the same way. He always said freedom didn't mean roaming hell freely. In a way it made sense, but David relied on God. He believed God was still here and was in control.

God would never leave him nor forsake him.

His dad taught him no matter how lonely he was, God was there with his arms around him. David had seen God move at a youth camp. He felt his power on a mission trip to Ecuador. Rocco told David he felt God move too. David wouldn't quit on his brother. He would continue to pray for him as long as he breathed.

"God, I need you to guide me. I know you're here with your arms around me. I need you more than ever, more than yesterday." He didn't try to stop his tears. He prayed and walked, searching for a

243

way home. "I'm in the shadow of death, and I'm afraid Lord, I'm more afraid than I have ever been. I don't fear the dark, but I fear this. I fear where my life is right now. I fear for Rocco's life. God, please guide me. Help me to follow you. Give me wisdom and understanding to adapt to this world. Every day something new and more evil comes against me. I feel Satan lurking in every doorway, and around every corner. I need you. I know you heard me the first time, but I need you, I need you, Lord."

David continued to talk to God and walk. He worried about Rocco, Hue, and Lena.

How would he get Rocco out to safety? Where were Hue and Lena? Were they safe? How could he fix Rocco's leg, even if they got out of the sewer?

"How am I going to do this? God, it's not like there are any doctors around. I don't know what to do, I need help. I'm scared."

Around the next corner, he saw, yet another pile of bodies blocking the tunnel.

"This is nasty," he yelled to no one.

He bent, lifting one body at a time. He pulled on one of the bodies and a leg came loose in his hand.

"Gross." He threw it to the ground.

"This was once a person. It was someone. They were long dead now and reduced to bones and clothes." He took a deep breath and continued to move the bodies from his path. He knelt and grabbed hold of the leg bone, and took a closer look at it. "You're the femur. I remember something from school, a lot of good it does me now." A smile crossed his face. He could use it as a splint for Rocco's leg.

"This is kinda sick," David said aloud. "People donate blood, to blood drives. They donated bone marrow too, so why not use the bone itself?"

He took some of the easier to tear clothes to tie to the bone to Rocco's leg for the splint. He gathered another femur to use as a blunt object in case he ran out of bullets. The femur was light. It weighed less than one-pound David guessed. It would work great for a splint not too heavy, but strong and sturdy.

244

The idea as a blunt object wouldn't be very effective to kill, but to keep someone at bay it would do the trick. He put his gun in his back belt, put one bone in his bag, and held on to the other one like a baseball bat, and continued walking. There had to be a way out he needed to find it. They couldn't stay in the sewer much longer.

After a few more turns he came across some forks in the road. He decided to keep to the right, hoping to make it easier to remember his way back. He had to get back to Rocco. He found a few exits, which had ladders. The ladders were either too broken to climb, which he tried, or they were so far off the ground, they were unreachable.

Famished and needing to rest, David sank to the floor. He found no way out. There had to be one he'd missed. He drank the last bit of water he had.

"I'll find a way home," he told himself. David closed his eyes.

A hand touched David's shoulder. A surge of power shot through his body. David knew this power. It came from something spiritual, not from this world. He looked but couldn't see a face. The man was blurry. He rubbed his eyes trying to get them to focus.

David wasn't afraid, although he thought he should be. He struggled to get as close as he could, he longed to be with him. This man was no ordinary man. He was from heaven, an angel maybe. He wore a bright robe, yet not white, but colorless. David hadn't seen anything like it before, but it didn't matter, it was merely a robe. Nothing mattered except being with this man.

He must be God. David prayed and the man reached out.

"I'm with you." The man took his hand off David's shoulder. "Stand," his voice was soft to David's ear, and yet it thundered through his soul. "Open your eyes and I'll leave you a guide."

As fast as he came, the man disappeared. David opened his eyes. He no longer felt famished or tired but rejuvenated. He had a new life flowing through his bones, and happiness where he felt despair before.

"Thank you, God." David prayed. "Thank you for caring enough for me, to comfort me. Thank you for your touch, your strength, and your love."

It had been years since he had felt something supernatural. He thought it would only happen in a church service, not a sewer. If God wanted to touch him and give him strength, in a sewer, David welcomed it.

He looked around. Nothing had changed.

The stench of death filled his nose and he found no way out, yet he was happy. Rocco would call him crazy, but deep in David's soul, he was happy. He had a new outlook on life and was glad to be alive.

David longed for paper and something to write with. He didn't want to forget the moment. The man said he would send him a guide.

"Did I wake too early?" David started to let fear creep its way back in his soul. "He never got to show me the way."

The man told him to stand, and he did. His heart raced with excitement. Had it been a vision, part dream, and happen in real life too? He looked at his shoulder. He could still feel the hand resting on it, yet there was no hand.

"God. lead me and I'll follow."

He continued walking. He needed to hurry to find the way out and get back to Rocco. In his head, he questioned his decision to leave Rocco behind. Maybe they should have stayed together. David pushed these thoughts out of his head and kept taking right turns. He stopped at the next intersection.

There were three tunnels.

"Keep to the right," he told himself. "Keep to the right."

He looked left. Something flew into the left tunnel.

"A bat." He ducked.

Was there a swarm of them waiting to attack around the corner?

As dumb as it was, David didn't run. He did the opposite. He walked a little closer to the flying creature. He didn't see a bat he saw a blue and yellow bird perched on a pipe. Its colors were vivid and bright. Even in the dark tunnel, David could see it. The bird flew into the left tunnel and out of sight. He wanted to follow it but didn't want to get lost.

He looked. The bird waited at the entrance of the left tunnel. The bird looked at David and then continued for the second time in the left tunnel. David had to follow the bird. He had to go left.

"Is this my guide?" David questioned. "You have used a talking donkey before, why not a chirping bird?"

A little while in the left tunnel and the bird disappeared. David walked for what seemed like a mile. He tried manhole after manhole, but they wouldn't budge. He knew there were cars parked over them. He could never lift them, not even Rocco was strong enough to lift cars and he was the strong one.

Nothing he did worked. He found no way out of the sewer. He would have to head back to Rocco and figure out what they were going to do next. They were hungry and out of water. They wouldn't be able to survive much longer. It was his job to find a way out. David wanted to stop. He wanted to sleep and dream of the man. He longed to feel his power. He didn't stop and rest. He continued.

"Two more turns," David said to himself. "If I don't find any way out, then I'll go back. Tomorrow Rocco will come with me." He walked faster his foot slipped on something wet. "Ouch."

His arm scrapped across the rough wall. He moaned rubbing his arm. His bandage had come off and he could feel a thick sticky paste on his hand confirming he had reopened the bullet hole.

"What am I doing?" He ran his fingers through his hair leaving a trail of blood across his face into his hairline. "I need to get back to Rocco."

It was getting late. Fear creeped into his soul.

Chapter 46

Pains of hunger woke Lena and Hue. They had nothing to eat. The sounds of the dead outside moaning and scratching at the hatch to get in filled their ears.

In the corner there was a pile of dead bodies, only bones and clothes were left. Lena took the clothes from the dead to keep her and Hue warm. This helped some, but a chill set in deep within their bones. Lena needed to search the sewer to find a way out but knew Hue couldn't make the trip. She wouldn't leave him alone. He might look grown, but he was a frightened twelve-year-old boy.

"Are we going to die in here?" Hue asked, voicing her thoughts. "There was a time in my life I would have welcomed death, today isn't one of those times."

"I don't plan on it."

Lena didn't want to give him any false hope. He was a smart kid and she didn't hide her fear well.

"I can't walk, and you're just a girl," Hue grinned at her.

"I think this girl kept you warm last night." She punched his shoulder. "You should be thankful for the extra clothes."

"I know it's the end of the world and all but did you have to shop at the thrift store? Oh wait, it was more like you stole them from dead people. On second thought, I wish you had gone to the thrift store. Not only are they dead people's clothes, but they were still in them. Do you think they will be collectibles one day," He laughed. "I have an original zombie shirt."

"Maybe you can sell it on one of those internet sites which were popular before all this happened."

"I would try and sell it, but I don't know what you're talking about."

"I don't doubt it for a second." She didn't bother to try and explain the internet.

"Do you think there are more people out there?" Hue leaned back against the wall.

"Yep, I can hear them now."

"No, not the zombies, real people. People like you and me, not the dead."

"You do know they aren't zombies, don't you?"

"Yeah. They might as well be, and I'm going to keep calling them zombies. They're zombies with a heartbeat."

"I think there are lots of people out there like us, but no one has phones or internet, so we can't tell each other we're alive."

Before she found Hue, she thought a lot about other humans. She knew they were out there, but she didn't know how she could reach them.

"It's kind of like we traveled back in time. We don't have access to other people around the world in seconds like we used to. She sat next to Hue. "There was a time if you wanted to go from one side of the world to the other all you did was get on a plane. When the fuel ran out, so did travel. It set us back in the 1800s where your world consisted of the land you were living on.

"When I was your age we could travel to the other side of the world in a day, now we would have to use a sailboat and take months. Without TV and radio, we don't hear of others like we used to. This is why we think we are alone. I bet there are millions of people around the world who think they are the only humans left. We found each other, you Rocco David and me. It's safe to say there are more people in the world. When we get out of here we'll find them and restore the human race."

"You might be right." Hue leaned back against the wall. "Thanks for caring about me."

"Thank you for letting me."

Moaning from the tunnels filled their ears.

"I heard something." Hue huddled closer to Lena.

"Hush," she whispered. "We don't want it to find us."
She paused.
"Do you have the rifle?"
"Yes."
"Aim it down the tunnel."

Chapter 47

David couldn't help moaning. His arm hurt; exhaustion took over his tired body. He lost his footing and fell on the cement.

"No."

He scraped the left side of his body on the jagged edges of the sewer floor. He let out another yelp. He should turn around. Yes, he needed to go back to Rocco. He shouldn't have left him in the first place.

With a loud boom and a flash of light, David tumbled to the ground.

******

"Stop, don't shoot," Lena yelled too late.

Hue had already pulled the trigger. David lay on the ground in a pool of his blood.

"What? Why?" Hue rolled on the ground grabbing his leg.

"It's David," she whispered.

He wasn't moving. For the first time, Hue had hit his target.

"Why would he be in the sewer? Why couldn't I have missed it? I didn't want to kill him." Hue couldn't think of David lying on the ground. He liked him, now he killed him.

"Why are we in the sewer?"

"The zombies chased us." Hue dropped the gun to the ground. "The zombies could have chased him too."

Hue hobbled toward the fallen man.

"I think I killed him." His voice was strained. "No, please tell me I didn't. I was only trying to protect us."

Lena clung to David trying to wake him. He didn't respond. She laid his head in her lap and tore his shirt away from the bullet hole.

"We need to get the bullet out. He isn't dead yet. He won't live long if we don't get him help."

"Where do we get help? We are in a sewer? Trapped by zombies, with no way out. We have no help."

"Rocco," David didn't open his eyes. "You need to get Rocco. We were chased by Rhinos, Hue play dead."

His breathing slowed, and he fell silent.

"Where is he?" Lena panicked. "Why would you leave Rocco behind?"

David grabbed Lena's arm.

"One right and then all lefts. Find him." His head hit the cold pavement.

"You need to fight," Lena begged. "I'll find Rocco."

She grabbed his backpack and rummaged through it hoping to find some supplies to help. The things in the pack impressed her. "Hue I'm going to need your help." Lena moved to David so he was lying flat on his back.

"What are we doing?" Hue wiggled to the ground and sat next to David. Lena handed him a pair of scissors.

"You need to cut more of his shirt off, then hold this gauze to his wound."

"I have never killed anyone before, not even a zombie." He brushed the tears out of his eyes.

"You won't be killing anyone today. We are going to save David and get Rocco." She braced herself as she poured the liquor in David's wound. She knew it would hurt.

"No, you're killing me," David's screams haunted Hue.

"Did you kill him? He isn't moving. Lena, what did you do?"

"I used the vodka as a cleanser. I have to sterilize the wound before I try and get the bullet out." Lena took the tweezers and tried to find the bullet. "He's not dead. He's in shock, but he's still alive."

"Were you a doctor?"

"No, but I watched a lot of TV."

"You used to watch the TV?"

"I don't have time to explain TV."

Lena found the bullet, but couldn't get it out. If she didn't get the bullet out David would die. She wasn't about to let him die. They needed him.

"Why didn't the bullet go all the way through?" Hue rambled.

"I got it." Lena held the bullet with her tweezers and examined it.

"Do you think this is going to paralyze him?" Hue helped Lena wipe the blood from around the wound.

"No, he isn't going to be paralyzed."

"How do you know, you're not a doctor?"

"The bullet was nowhere near his spine. Why all the questions?" Hue said nothing.

Lena dug through David's bag and found a needle and thread. They were in a sewer, surrounded by germs. The wound had to be closed. Their situation was far from normal. Because of the risk of infection, she needed to stitch David's stomach. She poured a little more of the vodka on the needle after she threaded it, and stitched David back together. She knew a stomach wound should be open and packed, she couldn't leave it open here. When they got to the house, she would open and pack it.

"We need to keep him warm and his dressing clean. Grab his jacket, and help me put it on him."

The jacket was on the ground next to Hue.

"Look at this," he pulled something out of David's pocket.

"What is it?" Lena wasn't looking at Hue.

She was trying to figure out what she was going to do with both Hue and David while she went to go get Rocco. She couldn't get Rocco out of her mind. There had to be a reason David left him behind.

What happened to him? She wished David was awake and could tell her what happened.

"I don't know, it's where I shot him."

254

"Let me see." Lena took out the object. "Hue, how nasty," She screamed and threw the rat on the ground.

"I don't even know what it is."

"A rat." Lena glared at him.

"I wouldn't have given it to you if I knew." He couldn't help a little smile. "Why did he have a rat in his pocket?"

"Maybe he was going to eat it."

"Gross." Hue was silent a moment. "Can we eat it?"

"No," Lena said, disgusted at the thought of eating a rat. "Well, we can't eat it now. This rat has a bullet through the meat, and we have no fire."

"Do you think it's why the bullet didn't go all the way through?"

"Yes. The rat possibly saved his life."

"He looks dead Lena. I think the rat poisoned him?"

"No, Hue."

"Why? The rat's blood could have got into the hole in his belly."

"True, but when I poured the vodka on the wound it cleansed it."

"Vodka kills rat poison?"

"You're funny. Vodka kills germs. Rat poison is a pest control chemical it kills rats, and it was made by humans. It doesn't come from rats."

"If you say so. I guess there is a lot about the old ways I don't understand."

"I do."

Lena took the bullets for the pistol and rifle out of the backpack and turned the headlamps on for light. She turned the light off almost as fast as she turned it on. They were in a tomb, blood and bodies covered the grounds. Lena chose to use the light later, and let the shadows hide the evil lurking in them.

"Hue." Lena broke the silence.

"Yeah,"

"Did David tell you to play dead?"

"Yes."

255

"He wanted to tell you something. I know what playing dead means, but why would he tell you to play dead? It had to mean something. This might be our way out." She gave an encouraging smile. She would get them out of here, all four of them. "If we play dead, the monsters won't bother us. We can get out of here. The monsters will think we are one of them. I have never seen them attack one of their own. I have to get you out of here, and fix your leg."

Lena leaned over and felt David's head. His skin was on fire. "I need to get him medicine."

"Speaking of legs, why did David have them with him?"
"I don't know." Lena examined the two femurs. "They seem to be from the same person."

"Why does he have them?"

"I still don't know. When he comes to you can ask him. Right now we need to make me look diseased. I need to get out of here."

"You said to get you out of here," Hue looked away, his tears covered his face. "Are you planning on leaving us here?" He refused to look at her.

"I'll be back for you both," Lena leaned over and rustled his hair. "I wouldn't leave you guys. You're all I have in this world."

"Get clothes from the dead pile. You will need to have the same odor they have and you need to look diseased. This is the nasty part."

"I have a feeling I know what you're going to tell me to do."

"You have to have skin peeling off your face. If you don't, they will see right away you're not sick." Hue flashed a big grin.

"Knock the smile off your face, or your leg won't be the only thing hurting."

"It's funny in a sick way," Hue's smile grew. "This was easier when we had makeup wasn't it."

"No, you don't mean, take the skin from the dead."

"Yes, exactly." He flashed her a grin again.

"It's too gross." Lena cringed. "I'm not doing it. Why didn't we bring the makeup?"

"We might as well join the pile of bodies."

"I'll smell like them," Lena could live with the smell. "I won't let them see my face or my eyes. Hue I can't do it."

"I don't know what else to tell you. I'm scared. Don't take any chances. You can't do anything to get yourself killed."

Lena had to think of another way.

"I'll use the dead's clothes. I cannot put their skin on. I'll use a hoodie to cover my face."

"Where are you going?"

"I'm going to get help." She knelt looking Hue in the eyes. "Don't worry, I'm coming back."

"Who are you going to get? There are no other humans out there. Lena, we need you here."

"I'm not going to get anyone." She smiled. "I'm going to get supplies. I'm going to see if there's somewhere else, safe enough to move you guys too. We need medicine. David is going to need antibiotics if I can find them. Remember him, the guy you shot, he needs help."

"David was the one grunting and stumbling around like a zombie. He's lucky I didn't shoot him in the head." Hue turned away. "I thought I was protecting us from a zombie attack. I didn't set out to kill our friend."

"You're right."

Her heart went out to him. He was merely a scared little boy, and she wasn't making things better.

"I'm sorry." She sat next to him and slid her arm around him. "I know you didn't mean to shoot him. I know you were protecting us, and I should never have said what I did. I'm sorry."

"It's true. I shot him. I didn't mean it, but I was holding the gun. Please don't let him die. I'm sorry."

Chapter 48

Lena said her goodbyes. She couldn't waste any time. If David didn't get the help he would die. She needed to find medicine and get back to the sewer as fast as she could. Her mind raced to Rocco.

Was he okay? Would she get to him before the monsters did? Why did David leave him? Was he hurt?

She couldn't let her mind go there. She would get to him before dark.

David had to be her main focus. If he didn't get help, well, she couldn't think about the what if's. Her heart told her she needed to go to Rocco, but her head told her if she went to Rocco, David would die. She couldn't let David die; Hue would never forgive himself. Rocco could take care of himself. In a few hours, they would all be together. She had to protect Hue and help David.

"Please be safe," Lena whispered to Rocco. "Hold on. I'm coming for you."

Seconds after she shut the hatch to the sewer, she encountered three monsters.

Don't freak out, she told herself. *Stay in control. There will be plenty of time to freak out later after the guys are safe.*

Lowering her head, she spoke slowly with a deep-hoarse voice. She did her best to sound like they did.

"They are dead and never coming back."

She let out a cracking laugh and continued on the path. She did it. They walked passed her not even giving her a second glance. Their rage blocked their judgment. Lena moved through the monsters with ease, out of the clearing, and into the woods unnoticed.

Where could she find medicine?

She tried but couldn't shake the feeling in the pit of her stomach she should have gotten Rocco before leaving the sewer.

Every three or four trees she walked past Lena dug an x so she could find her way back. Her step quickened as her thoughts raced to Rocco. Despite everything David told her about him, she fell for him. In the short time, she had known him; she couldn't imagine what her life would be like without him. She remembered the time he tackled her outside his house. He is everything she wanted in a man.

He was strong and handsome, the kind of man who would lay down his life for his family and friends.

How could she have left him? He was hurt and needed her. How could David leave him?

Hue and David were hurt too and she was leaving them. Nothing felt right. They should be together.

She couldn't turn her mind off. Rocco needed her, and she didn't run to him. They needed food and supplies, or they would die. It was her responsibility to get supplies and hurry back to Rocco. She trusted David left Rocco in a safe place. She couldn't think of him anymore. Her priority was finding medical supplies for David. She had to save him for Hue.

Too many 'what' doubts occupied her mind.

The shadows kept her out of sight.

"You will be back soon," she tried to convince herself.

David needed medication and she was the only one who could get it. After hours of walking, Lena came to a road she recognized. From here, she knew her way to a hospital. It would be a long walk, but one she had to make. *What choice did she have?* People were counting on her. The sooner she got the supplies the sooner she would get to Rocco.

"No, no, no," she cried.

The hospital was right in front of her yet she couldn't get to it. Water surrounded it. The only bridge to it was no longer standing. Lena looked up and down the banks of the river, but she could see no crossing. The river's waters were calm and she knew how to swim. The other side of the river was a football field away.

Taking in long deep breaths calmed her and cleared her head. She had to get to the hospital. This was her only chance to get the medication which would save David's life. The only way across would be to swim. Lena didn't want to get sick or freeze to death. She needed to stay healthy to take care of Hue and David. They needed her.

She couldn't give herself time to think, she knew what had to be done. She gathered branches and wood scattered around the ground and used the shoelaces to tie the wood together making a small raft. The raft wasn't for her, she didn't have enough laces. The raft was the only way to get her backpack across dry. Her clothes would also need to stay dry. Looking left and right assuring herself she was alone, she slid off her pants then her shirt until she was completely naked. The clothes also went on the makeshift raft.

"Lord please don't let me freeze to death. I need to get back to Hue."

She sank into the icy water. Her hands trembled as she carefully swam to the other side of the water. Lena was careful not to get the backpack wet. She could no longer feel her hands and feet. She wanted nothing more than a raging fire to warm herself by. Shaking violently, she fumbled with the backpack to get a shirt to dry off with.

In minutes, she was back into dry clothes with the hoodie covering her wet hair. Still freezing, she hurried to the hospital door. She sped her pace hoping the movement would warn her. She continued to look to her left and right. There were still no monsters in sight even though she could feel their eyes watching her from the shadows. Only time would tell, but unfortunately, time was the one thing she didn't have.

Most of the doors and windows were nailed shut with boards. Lena pushed and pulled on every door, none of them budged.

Why was she alone? Did she hate it?

She had nothing to pry the doors open with or break the windows. There had to be away in. Why couldn't she find one?

"I'm going to need a warm bath after this."

Her teeth chattered and her body shook. Talking to herself made being alone more bearable. She was starting to shiver uncontrollably.

"I'm never going to get in. We are all going to die."

There wasn't time for a pity party. They weren't going to die; she wouldn't let them. The guys were counting on her.

She pushed through the cold knowing the longer she took here, the colder the water would be on her swim back. Her frantic search continued. She needed to get in.

"I wonder if there's anyone in here?" She tried to calm her nerves. "If there is anyone, I hope they are not diseased."

What if the hospital was their hideout?

Maybe she should be quiet. *No*, she didn't like the idea. If this were a zombie home, they would already know she was there. In silence, she persisted in her search for an entrance.

On the back of the building, she could see one window, which had no bars or boards on it. Finally, a way in. All she needed to do was get to it. She found a ladder close to the window. It was a built-in ladder; she couldn't move it. She tightened the pack to her shoulders and climbed the ladder. She couldn't give herself time to think about what she was doing. Heights freaked her out.

At the top of the ladder, she scaled the side of the ledge to get to the window, which was about five feet away. She pulled herself to the ledge and pushed on the window.

"Locked. I have to get in," she cried out. "I need to save my friends."

Lena hated guns but couldn't let her fear stop her. She took the pistol from her side, turned her head, and pulled the trigger. Shards of glass sprayed through the air, clearing her way in.

Lena took a much-needed breath. Getting to the hospital was harder than she anticipated and she was proud of herself for everything she had done. She'd taken a bullet out and stitched David's wound closed.

The job wasn't perfect but the bullet was out and the hole stitched. She'd overcome her fear of heights, scaled a building, and broke a window to get in. Her fears were fading as she reminded herself of all the things she had conquered. People depended on her. She needed to be their hero.

Growing up Lena stayed in the background letting other people take charge. Today, forced her to take charge proving to herself she could.

"You need to hurry," she chastised herself. "You don't want to be a hero to a group of dead guys."

The stench of rotting flesh filled her nostrils knocking Lena to the ground. She fought hard to keep from vomiting. She grabbed a surgical mask put it on to block some of the odor, and continued her search for supplies. The hospital shelves were stocked full.

Lena found the items she came for. She loaded her pack with everything she thought they might need, taking cold medicine for herself, antibiotics for David, and pain pills for both guys. She gathered warmer clothes from lockers and drawers. The hospital had a well-stocked kitchen. She couldn't carry all of it, but she got enough food and water for the four of them to last several days. She gathered everything they would need to make it out of the sewer alive.

St. James Hospital was her haven. She filled her stomach and continued. One of the rooms had inflatable mattresses and bedding. She would give anything to snuggle under the covers and take a nap. Pushing the thought out of her mind, she continued her search for crutches. She followed the directions on the walls for the ER. They would have splints and crutches.

The feeling of eyes peering at her hit her again.

A crash resounded from another room. In an instant, she dropped to the ground, reached for her pistol. She thought she was alone and had been careless. The gun wasn't there. She emptied the bag on the floor. Still no sign of the gun. She couldn't defend herself without a weapon.

Her breathing grew heavy, her hands clammy and her body trembled.

Who was in here with her? How could she be stupid enough to lose her gun?

264

She had to find it. She retraced her steps. Without the gun, she wouldn't make it back to the guys. The light from the tops of the uncovered windows disappeared with the sun. Her hand rested on a flashlight, she knew she couldn't turn on.

How could she get back?

"Play dead," the words of David echoed in her mind.

If she played dead, she could turn the flashlight on. *What if the noise didn't come from a monster, but from a hungry animal?*

It could be a human-like her. However, just because someone wasn't diseased didn't mean they were a good person. Not every human was good. Her pace quickened.

Where did her gun go?

She had to get it and the crutches then leave. Her friends were depending on her.

The darkness caused her mind to race back to a place she didn't want to go. She could see her father dying to get her to safety. His blood was running into the cracks of the door and dripping on her face. She hated these memories.

She wanted to remember happy times with her dad. He used to take her for ice cream, and ice-skating. Again, her happy memories were interrupted by memories of his death. She hated how her brain chose horrifying memories and haunted her with them. The memory of her dad's death came naturally to her. She didn't want to see it, but it had been burned into her mind as if it had happened yesterday.

Her pace quickened with every memory. She wanted her gun. Nothing stopped her as she tumbled to the ground and landed face-first into the rotting belly of the dead. She jumped to her feet wiping the contents of the stomach off her face. She fought hard to keep the food she had just eaten from coming up.

"What a bloody mess," the monster standing in front of her said.

"It's sick," Lena tried to act diseased.

"What brings you here?" The man could talk well for being diseased. Lena couldn't wrap her mind around how the disease worked.

Why could some people talk and others could only grunt?

"I need my yearly checkup." She knew she failed at fooling this beast. He wasn't zombie-like.

"This will be your last checkup." His breath alone caused Lena to step back.

Playing dead wouldn't help her with this monster. She did the only thing she could think to do, play the part of a seductress. The desire for sex and to kill drove the diseased men. Lena used this knowledge to her advantage.

Not giving him the chance to rape or kill her, but allowing her to kill him. Her immediate goals were to, stay alive, and to kill the beast before her. She promised Hue she was coming back for him and she intended on keeping the promise.

"I can see you're a powerful man." She edged her way closer to the monster letting her coat slip to the floor.

Stay calm, she silently reminded herself.

He could see fear. Her insides twisted in knots as she tried to control her shaking body. Deep breaths in and out, she needed to stay focused and get out of here alive. Too many people counted on her, and she wasn't going to fail them. Lena reached her hand out to the monster. She shuttered as she touched his shoulder.

"You're what every woman wants," she whispered in his ear. "I know you're what I want." Lena fought hard not to vomit. The smell of the monster repulsed her. She slid her shirt off exposing her shoulder. "Do you like what you see?"

He stammered and stepped backward. The monster cocked his head and looked at Lena. This was her chance to getaway. With all her might she kicked him between the legs. Howling, the monster crumbled to the ground. She rushed away, not looking back to see if he were chasing her, hiding under the cover of darkness. She needed a weapon, specifically, she needed the gun.

How could she have been so careless?

Losing the gun could cost her not only her life but the lives of her three friends. She found herself in an operating room. There were plenty of sharp objects she could use as weapons. The only problem with them was she would have to get close enough to the monster to kill him. Guns were so much easier. She hated herself for losing hers. Frantically, she searched for something sharp to kill the monster. Pain shot through her fingers. She had found a knife, and the blood oozing from her hand was proof it was sharp.

Darkness covered her body. Both inside and out. It hid her from the monster. She stood silent behind the door letting evil take a hold of her. There only was one way she knew she could kill the beast. She silently cried for help. Praying the simple one word would be enough to get her out of this hospital alive and back to her friends.

"Where are you, whore?" the diseased proceeded to curse at her.

He tipped over anything standing between him and her. He stumbled over boxes and furniture. His proclamation was proceeded and followed by crashed and bangs. The noise helped Lena know where he was. She had no time to think, he would be at the door soon. She needed to be ready for him.

Jumping out at him, she jabbed her knife into him over and over again. She was sure she stabbed him in the chest, only to find she had missed her mark. How could she have blown her one chance to rid herself of the monster. Her knife rested in his arm.

"What are you doing?" He threw Lena to the ground. She scrambled to getaway. She couldn't let him get to her.

"You're not going anywhere. When I'm done with you, you will be begging me to take your life." He grabbed her hair and flung her on a gurney. He came at her with such force the gurney fell over and he fell with it.

"Oh, God."

She gave in to the fear she was going to die. The three men she would leave behind would be fated the same. Lena had promised Hue she would come back for him. He feared she wouldn't come back. She could not die. She had to somehow make it out of here and back to the scared little boy she left behind.

"See how far praying gets you." The monster continued to drag her.

Lena screamed and kicked, fighting with all her might. She held tight to his hand, as he dragged her through the hallway. She managed to turn her headlamp on with one hand. She needed to see if she could use anything as a weapon to kill the beast.

"Are you afraid of the dark? I'm still here. The light won't make me go away," his voice was as liquid fear pouring into her soul. The hatred followed was fearsome.

Searching between tears for anything she could use, she scanned the area for a weapon. She wanted a second chance to end this monster's life. This was her fault, if she hadn't lost the gun, she wouldn't be in this situation.

She had to fight.

She had to live, not only for herself but also for Hue. He needed her. She couldn't stop her thoughts from racing through her mind. Did the hate she felt make her a monster too or was it justified by his actions.

Her mind played with the idea of Jesus as he was crucified, not fighting back. Then to the scriptures where he said to not resist evil people and to turn the other cheek. Then, her mind went to the story of Peter. He was the one in the garden who cut the priest's ear off.

He had been defending Jesus. *Did this mean self-defense was okay?* She stopped her thoughts there, as she knew Jesus healed the ear. She didn't want to remember how it ended.

She wanted her killing of the monster to be justified. It helped to ease her mind a bit, knowing she needed to kill the beast.

He came to a stop at the top of the stairs. Lena feared what would happen next. Knowing her fate didn't make it any easier. With one shove, the monster watched her body bounce off one-step to the next.

His laughter echoed through the empty stairwell. The steps hit her hard. Lena gasped for air as her ribcage crushed in around her lungs.

Was this the end?

How much more could she bear?

If her end had come, she prayed it wouldn't take long. Lying face down on the floor, she opened her bloody eyes. She wasn't going to give the monster the satisfaction of seeing her cry. If he was going to kill her, she would look him in the eye and smile. What was lost now was found. Her 9mm lay a few feet from her hand. The gun must have fallen out of her holster when she filled the sack with the medicine. She turned her head to see where the beast was. A fist full of power smashed against her cheek. She flew backward, smiling because the gun was now underneath her. Lena needed to take the gun off safety, point, aim and shoot. The only signal her brain sent to her hand was to block the foot coming at her head.

Adrenaline raced through her veins. She rolled to the left grabbed the gun from under her, and flipped the safety off with her thumb. The only thing left to do was shoot. She pulled the trigger and the diseased man landed on top of her.

"Thank you," she prayed, pushing the monster off. "I know you have done enough for me already. If it's not too much to ask could you please let me get back before it is too late to save the guys."

With her gun in hand, she made her way to the emergency room to finish getting the supplies she needed. She found crutches and a splint for Hue. She was ready to head back. On her way out, she grabbed one of the inflatable mattresses to use as a raft.

Not being in the mood to scale any walls, she exited by a side door. Lena left the door unlocked, but covered it with pallets and other debris she found around the grounds. The building had more supplies than she could carry. She would bring the guys here when they were well enough to travel.

Lena used the light of the moon to make her way to the water while she hid in its shadows out of the sight of danger. She had no strength left within her to fight off another monster. She wanted to get back to the sewer and find Rocco.

"Please let me get back with no more confrontations," she prayed.

Chapter 49

Lena crossed the water quickly and was on the road heading into the woods, glad to be out of the hospital and on her way to her friends. The marks she left on the trees made it easy to navigate her way through the woods and allowed her to focus on the sounds around her. There was nothing out of the ordinary, yet the sounds scared her.

Her body ached and her eyes grew heavy. If she didn't need to get back to the sewer right away she would sleep here. Hue and David might not make it another day without medicine. Then, there was Rocco? She didn't even know where he was, or if he was safe. She couldn't obsess over whether they were okay. Staying positive and walking were the things she needed to concentrate on.

The colder she got the faster she moved, fighting her way back to the guys. In her speed, she remembered to stay quiet and not draw attention to herself. The pain of the bruises and scrapes from her last encounter with the dead slowed her enough, she couldn't risk anymore. A little further and she would be safe back with Hue and David.

The last set of markings was in her sight. It wouldn't be long before she would be safe with her friends. Something hard and cold hit her. She fell to the forest floor. Her head pounding, darkness screamed at her to let it in, and with no strength left, she gave in to it.

The warm sunlight shown on Lena nudging her until she opened her eyes. Her body wrenched with pain. The earth's floor wasn't kind to her. Her head hurt. She felt around for her bag, it was gone. Panic-struck. They needed medicine for David. Why had someone taken it? Turning, she looked behind her.

To her surprise, the bag was on the ground untouched. She searched the pack for some medicine for her headache and took four. She had no time to waste. She should have been back with the supplies the night before. She couldn't dwell on what happened to her or how she landed on the ground.

She needed to get to the guys.

The hatch to the sewer was in her site. She stopped at the edge of the tree line, there were diseased in the clearing. How would she get to the sewer without being noticed? These dead were not like the ones in front of the sewer when she left. They were roaming around bumping into each other, a trait of the diseased she had never seen before. The creatures were more like zombies, as Hue called them.

Most of the diseased she had encountered could think and talk. These didn't appear to be able to do either. They roamed around as one would see in a bad zombie film.

Why, after all this time, were they still here?

She counted fifteen infected people standing between her and her friends.

Why did everything have to be a fight? Couldn't one thing work out?

She was so close to getting Hue and David the help they needed. Now, one more obstacle stood in her way. There was no way those monsters were going to stop her. Nothing would keep her from getting to her friends.

Playing dead wouldn't work this time. She didn't have the clothes the smell or even the skin falling off. She would have to find another way past them.

"Come on," she begged herself. "Think. The guys are counting on you."

Her friends were a few feet away from her. They were in desperate need of food and water. She had everything they needed but didn't know how to get it to them.

"Oh God," Lena cried out. "Are they going to starve to death while I sit out here with food?"

Why were the dead still there? Did they need to eat? Did they have a camp nearby? Were they on patrol? Was this another strand of the disease she had never encountered? Could they be dumb like zombies?

It would make sense if any of it could make sense. A disease which turned people into killers could also eat at their brain and turn them into a zombie.

Is this the same disease just the after-effects of time?

Maybe the ones before her were some of the first infected. Lena tried to think of how she could get past them. She had to try something. She couldn't sit here and do nothing. The guys were counting on her. She needed to get back alive.

"Think, Lena, think." She begged herself again. "You can't let the guys die."

Lena buried her things under the leaves. She took a pistol. Her plan wasn't well thought out, but it was the only one she could think of. She ran to the other side of the field. She would create a distraction by making noise, then sneak back around to her bag and the crutches and race to the sewer before the monsters caught her.

Lena reached the other side where she wanted to make the diversion. She jumped, a woman walked toward her, no, not a woman, but a monster.

"Did you see where they went?" Lena asked trying to play dead.

The monster didn't say anything. She kept walking toward her. Lena pointed the pistol aimed and shot. The diseased fell with a thud to the earth with.

"I think I got the diversion I wanted."

The monsters started walking toward the sound of the gunshot. Lena raced to the other side of the clearing through the cover of the trees. It didn't take long to gather her supplies and head towards the sewer.

The monsters were turning in circles and running into one another. For once, something went the way she planned. She prayed Hue and David were still alive.

She stood motionless at the hatch making sure none of the monsters followed her. Once she knew it was safe, she knocked on the hatch and spoke the password.

"Hue is king." The hatch opened and she dropped safely inside.

"I think he's dead." Hue closed and locked the hatch. "I didn't think you were coming back."

"I told you I would be back. I'm sorry it took longer than I thought. I brought the supplies we need." What Hue said sank in. "What do you mean you think he's dead?"

"I haven't seen him move in hours, and his body is cold." Hue had been crying. The poor kid thought he would be alone again.

"Please God, don't let me be too late," She leaned over David to check for a pulse. "He's alive. Thank you, God." Lena redressed his wound after covering it with antibiotic ointments. "David," Lena shook him. "I need you to wake up. I brought food and water." She shook him again, a little harder this time. "David, open your eyes and talk to me."

"I'm awake." David didn't open his eyes. "I'm cold."

"I have medicine for you. I got pain meds and antibiotics." She handed David the pills.

David said nothing. He sat a little and swallowed the pills with a bottle of water.

"I'm hungry," Hue said. "Did you find food?"

"Yes." Lena helped Hue sit next to David and gave them both food and more water.

"I know you just got back, but you need to get Rocco." Hue implored. "I would go myself if I could. Lena, he can't be alone any longer. I want to thank him for saving me by killing my dad. I have been thinking a lot about it, I know I wouldn't be able to kill the man. If Rocco hadn't come when he did, I would be the one dead right now. Lena, you are the only one who can walk, you need to go get Rocco. He should be here with us. It is my fault he is out there alone."

"David," Lena said grabbing a headlamp and water from the backpack. "How do I get to Rocco? Hue's right we can't leave him out there alone any longer.

"Take your first right, then it's all lefts until you get to Rocco. Lena, he's in bad shape, you need to hurry."

"Hue, I got you crutches," Lena said handing them to the boy. "You will be able to move around if you need to. I'll splint your leg when I get back."

"Rocco will need them." David opened his eyes. "Rhino crushed his leg."

"Sorry, Hue." Lena took the crutches back. "It looks like I might need them." She was thankful to be back safe and, on her way, to get Rocco.

"Gun," David mumbled. "Don't forget a gun."

Lena grabbed a backpack and filled it with food and water. Whatever else Rocco needed would have to wait until they returned. She strapped the crutches to the pack and slung it over her shoulders. With a loaded gun in hand, she was ready to get Rocco and bring him back.

"I'll be back as soon as I can. You two make sure you stay safe. Hue, look after him." She scanned the room making sure she didn't forget anything. "I'm not sure how long it's going to take me. If I'm gone overnight you will need to change David's bandage, and put cream on his wound."

"Okay." Hue's voice was shaky. "I don't want you to go, but Rocco needs you. I'll take care of David," he assured her. "You need to hurry this time. We need to get out of here."

"I'll hurry." Lena kissed his forehead. "I'll be back soon."

Lena let the light of her headlamp lead her. She didn't waste time looking at her surroundings. She needed to get Rocco and return to Hue and David as fast as she could. Her mind drifted to thoughts of Rocco. Thoughts of him kept her feet moving swiftly, not giving her time to think about how sore and exhausted she was. She wondered if she and Rocco could ever be a couple. They'd never had a real talk about dating.

Then again, *what would a date be like in the world they lived in? Would he come to her house for her on his bike? Then they eat a picnic in the park?* They both would be carrying guns ready for battle. Some date it would be. *Would they have to stop in the middle of a kiss and kill a few monsters? And then what?* With blood splattered on his face, he would lean in to caress her again. She grinned at her thoughts. *Yep,* this was what a date in the world would they lived in would be, and she didn't hate it.

Quite the opposite, she liked it.

Her mind went to Hue. She promised him they didn't have to see Rocco and David when they were safe at home. *How could she not see Rocco again?* It would kill her. She would do it if it's what Hue wanted. Even though she didn't give birth to Hue, he'd become her son. His needs would come before hers. If it meant giving up her happiness for his, she would gladly do it.

Something was different about Hue. He was the one who pushed her to get Rocco. He feared she would be too late. Maybe he was warming up to the idea of the four of them being together.

Hope sprung within her.

In the past, there were plenty of so-called fish in the sea. Not now, in the world with the dead running it, there weren't many fish left. Most were rotten ones, the ones mama always told her to stay away from. Rocco and David were different. She was determined to make their new family work.

She was lucky to have found the three best men in the world. They may be the only ones left.

She walked for about an hour, and thought, she would be to Rocco soon. David had done all the hard work when he came to them, moving boulders and bodies out of the way, clearing the paths for her to walk through.

Lena's legs moved fast through the tunnels. She wanted Rocco. A body laid in a sleeping bag right where David said Rocco would be. Yes, it had to be Rocco. *Was he sleeping or dead?* Lena rushed to him. The cold body made her heartache.

Was he dead? His arm which hung out of the sleeping bag had already started turning blue. She laid her head on his chest desperate to hear a beating heart, but there was nothing. There was no breath in his chest.

"No," Lena wailed, unable to stop her tears.

277

If she had come here first, he would still be alive. She knew CPR. She had to try to get his heart pumping again. Maybe she wasn't too late. Lena pulled the sleeping bag from over his head, she needed to try and save him.

"No, this can't be." Her body shook, she jumped back. "No."

She couldn't bring herself to look at the headless body of her love. She didn't get there in time. If she would have gotten Rocco before she went to the hospital, he might still be alive. Lena pulled the sleeping bag back over the body and sunk to the floor.

"This can't be happening. I need you," she cried out to God. "You know I needed him. Why would you take him from me? Why? I was helping David and Hue and you took him."

Lena flung herself over Rocco's dead body.

"Why did you die? I planned on us spending the rest of our lives together, have children and grow old with each other." Her chest hurt. The thought of living without Rocco was more than she could fathom. "I loved you."

She soaked the sleeping bag with her tears. She had failed him. She had found love in this desolate world, and let it die. This was the world she lived in whatever someone loved would be taken from them.

This couldn't be happening. A cloud of depression blanketed her body. Her heart filled by guilt. She had failed everyone. She let David get shot, Hue break his leg, and now her love had been beheaded.

A hole grew in her heart no one but Rocco would ever fill. She let her tears cover her love's hard, cold body. The sewer was his tomb. Lena longed to make it hers too. *How could she live without him?* She didn't want to. She would stay here with him until she died and could reunite once again with him in death. Hue had David; they would be okay. Rocco was alone. She couldn't leave him alone.

"You're not dead. You can't be dead. Please, Rocco, don't be dead." Lena whispered. "Yet, here you lay." She sobbed over her love. She lifted the sleeping bag again, needing to see his shirt. Hoping it wasn't him. She knew it was, but she had to check one more time.

There was no mistaking it, this was the shirt she had seen him put on when they went to rescue David. All hope left her.

Anger and hatred infiltrated her soul.

She could have saved him if she were quicker. If she hadn't lost the gun in the hospital she could have gotten back to Rocco yesterday. Would she have been in time to save him? Something inside of her yesterday told her to go to Rocco first. Why had she ignored her inner voice?

Why didn't she listen to her gut and get him when she had the chance? Why didn't she go to him first? Why was going to the hospital more important than going to Rocco? David and Hue would have lived, and now Rocco was dead.

Hours passed and Lena didn't move. She wanted to hold on to Rocco as long as she could. Taking a deep breath, she stood and looked around for anything she could put on him as a grave marker. She wanted something like a cross on the side of the road letting others know someone died there.

There was a box of matches on the ground.

"I'll give you the funeral you deserve." She brushed the tears off her cheeks. "I'll make sure the dead will never mess with your body again."

Her mind raced as to what to say. It had been years since she had attended a funeral. Her parents didn't have funerals.

"Rocco, I know we would have been good together." It took a long time for her to control her emotions enough to talk. "Rocco, I'll love you forever. This world is no different from the past. People died in both worlds. I've seen parents lose babies, and others witness their kids die at age twenty-five. Now, here you're one more, gone too soon, and for what? There's no reason, just death. I know you're with your family. You and Kyle are throwing the football. You're getting to be the big brother you have always wanted to be. I want you to know we will miss you. Keep watch over me my, angel."

She closed her eyes and thought of the first time Rocco kissed her. A slight smile crossed her lips. The kiss had been one of true love.

She felt like Snow White when Prince Charming kissed her and wake her.

She leaned over and kissed the sleeping bag, where her love would forever rest. In some small way, she hopped her kiss would wake him, but it didn't. She needed him, yet she knew would never see him again.

Her tears flowed in steady streams. Her heartfelt lost and broken. She took the bottle of alcohol from her pack and dumped it onto the sleeping bag. She prayed for Rocco's happiness and her sorrow. The time had come for her to say her final goodbyes.

"Until we meet again my love. Save a place for me next to you."

She lit a match, tossed it on the sleeping bag, and watched as her love's remains turned to ash. There wasn't anything more she could do for Rocco. She'd failed him. It was time to go back to David and Hue. She would bring news of a hero coming to save his best friend, to save his brother from the monsters, dead. He lost his life because she failed to get there in time.

She couldn't save him.

Chapter 50

"Hue."

David didn't open his eyes. The pain had left, thanks to the medication Lena had given.

"I'm here." He didn't move.

"What did you do with the bones I had with me? They were for Rocco. After making the journey here with Lena, he'll be hurting and will need them."

"They're with the dead bodies. Why will he need them?"

"I'm going to use them as a brace for Rocco's leg." He opened his eyes and looked at Hue. "He hurt it real bad."

"A leg helping a leg," Hue smiled. "Good thinking."

"Yes, it's like a helping hand."

Hue let out a laugh. "I got a kick out of it." Hue laughed more. "Did you get it I said a 'kick' out of it."

David chuckled. He forgot Hue was twelve. He had been through so much in his young life, to David he seemed older.

"This is the most fun I have had in a long time."

"Me too." He stopped laughing.

"What is it, Hue?" David turned and looked at the kid. "You can talk to me about anything."

"It's my dad. I was thinking about him." He paused. "You know Rocco was the one who killed him."

"You told me what happened to your dad, but I didn't know Rocco killed him." David didn't let him know Rocco had told him. This was something they were going to have to get past. David knew Rocco was drunk when he killed Hue's dad, which was no excuse for his actions. No, it was the facts. He also knew how much Hue hated his dad. He didn't know for sure how Hue was going to react to seeing Rocco.

"Your dad wasn't your dad, he was..." David said starting to defend Rocco.

"I know. He was a zombie," Hue interrupted. "I'm not even mad at Rocco for killing him. A part of me is thankful. When it comes to my dad, I have no feelings. I thought I would cry and feel bad, but I don't."

David said nothing.

He wanted to comfort Hue, but he didn't know what to say. When his dad died, he was an emotional wreck. He couldn't imagine not loving his dad.

"I don't know how Rocco is going to react to me being here." Hue continued. "I don't think he likes me. I need him to forgive me."

"Forgive you for what?"

"The night he came to my house I beat him with a hockey stick. He didn't do anything. I wanted him to kill me and he did nothing. He stood motionless mumbling something about someone named Kyle."

"Kyle was Rocco's little brother."

"What happened to him? Maybe if you tell me about Kyle, it will help me understand a little more about Rocco. Lena's in love with him, so I need to give him a chance."

David didn't like to talk about it, but he didn't want Hue asking Rocco. They would have enough to talk about when he and Lena got here. He hesitated at first but decided to tell Hue the story of Rocco's family.

"It is a long story. The short version is, Rocco watched as a monster shot his mom, dad, and little brother Kyle. Rocco lost all faith in humanity, his life changed right before his eyes. Turning him into a different man with a hardened heart. He used to be loving and carefree. If he saw someone in need he would be the first one there to help them.

"He trusted everyone. After this, his life ended, and this new Rocco was born. The new Rocco, the man you know, hates the world. He trusts no one. He would just kill you. He was determined to never let anyone he loves die again, so he chooses not to love.

"I know Rocco killed your dad. I'm not trying to make any excuses for him. I need to know if you're okay with Lena bringing him back here. I mean, do you want him dead? We don't have to stay with you and Lena."

"No, I don't want him dead or you guys to leave. I used to want him dead, but not anymore. The night he killed my dad. I took a hockey stick and started hitting him with it and he never moved. He didn't do anything. I wanted to be the one to kill my dad. I had a hockey stick was in my hand ready to kill him when Rocco came. My dad wasn't a nice man, even before he became a zombie." Hue looked over at David. "I don't know why Rocco didn't kill me. He looked at me with tear-filled eyes and left. To him I looked like a zombie, I was playing dead and he let me live. Did he know I wasn't a Zombie? Could he see through my disguise? I was angry then because he let me live, now I'm glad he did."

"I don't know."

David thought back to the younger Rocco. He would do anything to save a kid. He would take a bullet for anyone he thought was in danger. Things changed the night the monster took his family.

"I thought you were one of them. You had me fooled."

"He could have killed me twice, but he never even attempted once."

"Twice?"

"When I was acting as a guard in the prison, he let me live then too. I thought he should have killed me. I tried to kill him for killing my dad, but it wasn't worth it. I mean my dad wasn't worth it, so I didn't kill him. I helped him instead."

"How did your dad get infected?" David wanted to keep Hue talking. The boy had a lot of things bottled inside; it was best he got them off his chest before Rocco got there.

"My mom." Hue paused, took a deep breath, and continued. "There was a time I loved her more than life itself. She was the one who protected me from my dad. One day she had enough of the abuse and left. She left me behind." He brushed his tears from his eyes. "She didn't care about me, or what dad would do to me when she left. Mom walked out on me and my dad. When she came back, she was diseased. I guess it's what she got for being a cheater. My dad was happy she came back to him. I think he let his guard down and then she infected him. Then, they both left me. A few weeks later, my dad came back. He said they'd killed my mom. I had to play zombie so he wouldn't try to infect me, too. It worked, my dad never tried, in fact, he never showed any affection for me. He treated me like a stranger.

"He would make sure I had food and water, but nothing else. The beatings were getting worse, to the point I thought for sure he would kill me. I knew I would have to kill him or be killed. I had a choice to make. I would let my dad end my life or I would have to end his, but then Rocco made the choice for me. He came in the house drunk, pulled his trigger and ended my dad. He did what I didn't have the strength to do."

"I'm sorry Hue. You should never have had to go through what you did." David struggled but put his arm around the kid. He wasn't an adult; he was a scared kid. "How did you end up with the dead?"

"I was trying to find Rocco. I wasn't sure if I was going to thank him or kill him. I wanted to kill him for leaving me. How could I blame him, for all he knew I was one of the dead, a zombie? I was at the camp because of my dad. He worked for Aeyden, the leader of the dead. Aeyden took me in and let me guard you because he thought I was one of them." Hue leaned his head on David's shoulder. "Lena was the one who saved me. She found me the night I lost my dad."

"Kid you deserve an Oscar."

"What's an Oscar?"

"It was an award for movies. You'd win the best actor award for playing dead."

"If you say so."

They laughed and talked until it was time for David's medicine. Hue scooted across the floor and gave David the pills Lena had left for him. David took a look at Hue's injury. It was his foot.

285

"The good news is I don't think it's broken. It looks like you might have some torn ligaments. If you stay off it for a few weeks it should heal with no complications." David looked through the bag of medication Lena brought back with her. He found some Motrin and gave it to Hue.

"This should help with the swelling and pain."

"Thanks, Dr. Dave."

The cool night air settled in around them. David and Hue huddled close and waited for Lena.

A noise awoke David. Lena stumbled in and fell to the ground next to him.

"What's wrong?"

David sat. Rocco wasn't with her. She wouldn't have come back without him by choice.

"He's dead. I was too late." Tears raced over her cheeks. "I should have gone to him first. They killed him in his sleep and they cut his head off." Her cries turned into sobs. "I'm sorry I failed you. I didn't get there in time."

"He can't be gone." Hue said.

"I'm sorry." She reached out to touch his face, he jerked away.

"You were supposed to bring him back." Hue buried his face in the sleeping bag and cried.

David didn't know what to say or do. The muscles in his stomach tightened shooting pain through his body. His head spun.

Why had he left Rocco behind?

They should have stayed together. It was his fault Rocco got attacked by the Rhino. Then he left him alone, and now he was dead. He closed his eyes thinking of his brother. He wanted to say something to comfort Lena and Hue, but nothing came to his mind. He needed to comfort them.

No, Rocco was his brother, and he was the one who needed comfort. *What was he going to do without him? Why did he leave him behind?*

David knew the rules. You never leave your battle buddy. Yet he'd left Rocco. He left him because it was easier to travel the sewer alone, and now Rocco was dead, leaving David alone.

It was David's job to tell Lena and Hue everything was going to be okay, and they were going to make it out alive. He should tell them they had to have faith, but when he opened his mouth, the words wouldn't come.

How could they? He didn't believe them himself. No, with Rocco gone, things were not going to be okay. They would never be okay again.

Hue sat up and brushed the tears from his eyes.

"David." He reached over and took his hand. "I'm sorry Rocco is gone. You are not alone. Lena and I are here for you. Please don't give up on life. We are going to continue our mission."

"I don't think so, kid."

"There is a reason the three of us found each other. We need to heal and get ready for a battle. We are going to take down the zombies for Rocco."

Lena joined hands with the two of them. "For Rocco."

David smiled. "For Rocco."

....to be continued in Book 2

Definitions

Tzaraath - a Hebrew word used to describe a sickness that disfigures the skin. In the Bible, Tzaraath is uses to describe leprosy and Ancient Rabbis taught that it was the wrath of God brought on by sin. The disease is manifested through decaying skin and was seen as spiritual separation from God. It is used as a form of supernatural spiritual discipline.

 **Author Ric Lee Steinert,** lives in Southern California with his wife and four children. Ric is a Bishop in the Church of God and an associate pastor at his local church and also has completed his Bachelors in Theology at Lee University.

 **Author Linda Steinert** lives in Southern Texas with her husband, and two of her seven children. Linda is a teacher with a Bachelor's degree in Early Childhood Education and has worked as a children's church teacher for over 30 years.

Please check out Ric Lee and Linda Steinert's website:

ricandlindasteinert.com

CPSIA information can be obtained
at www.ICGtesting.com
Printed in the USA
LVHW050847271120
672645LV00003B/232